In Search of Solace

Also by Emily Mackie

And This Is True

Emily Mackie

In Search of Solace

SCEPTRE

First published in Great Britain in 2014 by Sceptre
An imprint of Hodder & Stoughton
An Hachette UK company

1

Copyright © Emily Mackie 2014

A CIP catalogue record for this title is
available from the British Library

ISBN 978 0 340 99252 4

Typeset in Sabon by Palimpsest Book Production Limited,
Falkirk, Stirlingshire

Printed and bound by Clays Ltd, St Ives plc

Hodder & Stoughton policy is to use papers that are natural, renewable
and recyclable products and made from wood grown in sustainable
forests. The logging and manufacturing processes are expected to
conform to the environmental regulations of the country of origin.

'Do I contradict myself?
Very well then I contradict myself,
(I am large, I contain multitudes.)'

Walt Whitman, 'Song of Myself'

THE BEGINNING

There it is.

The blurred image of a man.

Standing. Stock still.

For one minute and

thirty-

three

seconds.

On the roof of a derelict Office Shop
warehouse.

In Bristol.

There it is.

That wicked footage. Downloadable. YouTubeable. Twitter.
Email. Facebook. A voice, 'I think he's going to jump.'
Followed by another, 'Poor bastard wants to end it all.' Both
female. Both young. And the blurred playback from their
mobile phone. There he is. That man standing stock still,
the material of his trouser legs ruffling in the slight breeze,
his trench coat undone as though trying to catch what little
wind there is, like a sail, as though nature might push him
back, stop him from falling. But that long jacket – ha! – it
looks more like a cape with its loose hems flapping. His
body is dark against the grey sky, his hair unkempt and
tousled; he certainly has the appearance of a man about to
take flight. And then. His foot. Slowly stepping out. Hovering
for that split second.

It begins.

Elohim, Jehovah, Allah, Yahweh, the strong creator, the self-existing, the Lord, the Master. God has many guises. Many names. Many faces. Krishna, Buddha, Abba, Shiva, Vishnu, Bhagavan, Satnam, Christ. Shiftshapes, moulds, stretches, dissipates. Olódùmarè, Yazata, Ishvara, Parvardigar. And God's greatest power? To be all-seeing, all-knowing. Paramatma, El Shaddai, Brahman, Hu. But I am no spirit. I am not God, yet I have this power. Thus spoke Zarathustra. 'On earth there is nothing greater than I.' And I am no more and no less, none other. I am 'I', the all-seeing, all-knowing.

Let me show you.

One cannot fly into flying, they say.
Although one can fly when with I.

God speed.

Across fields, across forests, over mountains, through gorges.
Don't linger.
Don't lag.
Over rivers, through valleys.
Feel the gust, the thrust, the rush of wind.
Grip tight and ride, glide, swoop and slide.

Ha!

I will ground you, dear reader, don't fear, never fear. You are in safe hands. Of sorts. It is true that with me as your guide you will see the awkward uncomfortable, the gruesome grotesque, the rancid bilious retching of life. But with all the earth's sores there is a light and bright side. You must trust me, dear reader. Don't be afraid.

Come, let's perch on this man's shoulder as he walks. The city reaches out before us, streets and roads twisting, turning, interweaving through the manmade tissue of concrete walls and bricks and mortar. This man we are hitching a ride with is walking at a brisk businessman's pace. From his neck creep the subtle undertones of sweat amid the musky scent of an expensive cologne and the crisp fresh of his pressed shirt collar and dry-cleaned suit. He raises his arm to look at his wristwatch, but the precise time is of no interest to us. It is still daylight, it is summer, it is hot. What more do you need to know?

Would you like to see a nifty trick? Let's slip into this man's ear, fight through the wax, coast through the looping canal, past the wafer-thin, vibrating skin of the drum. *Shit. Fuck. I'm late. C'mon c'mon, turn green, you bastard.*

And out again, through the other ear.

Can you see now, dear reader, the real power I have? I can be everywhere. I can see everything, inside and out. I do not even have to travel from one place to the next in the normal fashion. As quick as a click I can teleport. From standing on the city street next to a pedestrian crossing to *click* squatting up a dark alley watching rats scuttle around the wheels of skips to *click* inside a packet of crisps with the large fat fingers of a man looming towards us to *click click click click*, in and out of the minds of others, backwards and forwards in time.

*

There is a boy I want you to meet. Look, see, he is walking, feet-scuffing, home from school. His hands are plunged into pockets, his shoulders are hunched, his toes point inwards. This is our protagonist. He is ten years old. He keeps his head down as he walks, peering out from behind a floppy fringe as the other school children swarm homewards around him. The humdrum of laughter, gossip, the clapping of feet against pavement, whistles and cries, the purr of bicycle wheels; these sounds spill out from the school gates and surround the young boy. The depth of his silence draws them in.

He arrives home at 23 Gunney Drive and notices, as he pushes open the gate, the blinds of the living-room window are closed. He slows and does not let the gate swing and clack shut behind him as he might normally do. He glances into his neighbour's front garden, mowed lawn and potted plants and bright pansies in the flowerbeds; from an upstairs window a lace curtain drops and a shadow moves behind it. The boy bows his head. He is careful as he walks not to step on the black slugs on the paving stones with the weeds pushing through the cracks.

The neighbour's front door opens and a young woman steps out onto the welcome mat. She holds an arm over her heavily pregnant belly and lifts one corner of her thin mouth into a sort of smile. The boy does not respond. At the front door he bends his face close to the letterbox and looks through. 'Mum?' He can see a slice of the hallway and the first four steps of the stairs. From the living room he can hear the soft ticking of the clock.

'I don't think your mother's very well today,' says the woman.

The boy rattles the door against its bolt.

'I think,' says the woman, 'that there may have been some bad news.'

The neighbour is standing by the fence now, still holding and stroking her belly. We can see the black of her bra beneath the thin white of her vest top and the shape of her belly and breasts pressing against the material. This mother-to-be turns her face towards the sun as though basking. Her hair is halo gold in this light. With a slim hand and long fingers she scoops some loose strands behind one ear. 'Listen,' she says, turning back to the young boy standing in the shade of the doorway, 'if things are difficult at home, you can come round any time, do you know that?'

The boy moves back further into the shade.

'Did you hear me?'

He spies on the blonde hair, the belly and the breasts. He bites down onto his bottom lip. 'It's OK,' he calls to the woman. 'I have a key to the back door.' And he steps out into the late afternoon sun and into the gaze of his neighbour, who is shading her eyes with her hand. 'I have a key,' he says again. He digs his thumbs under the straps of his rucksack to relieve the weight from his shoulders. 'I'd better go in.' He turns his back to the woman and walks the length of the house, glancing once more to make sure, before slipping down the side passage, that his neighbour is still shielding her eyes and watching him.

We will let the boy push through the weeds and long grass of the back garden and kick over the plastic pots in search of his key. We can just slide through the letterbox into the hallway and drop onto the gathering junk mail on the doormat. Take a moment, dear reader. Look around.

There is the threadbare royal red of the carpet, the off-white wallpaper, a broken mirror, a chest of drawers, an empty vase, a large stone lion garden ornament, an overflowing ashtray. Take it all in. Make your judgements as to who might live here. Smell it. Every house has its own unique smell. This one has a scent not dissimilar to peeled potato skins mixed with old fag ash and dusty rugs.

'Mum?' The boy is in. We can hear him moving in the kitchen beyond. We can hear also the tick, tick of the clock from the living room and from somewhere a trapped fly buzzing and butting itself against a closed window. But beneath these sounds is another; a keen ear would be able to pick it up, the short, sharp intakes of wet breath, sobbing. As we creep towards the open living-room door the sound becomes clearer and, peering round, we see her: a small grey woman on a faded floral armchair. Her hands are covering her mouth, her eyes are puffy. She rocks. A floorboard creaks as the boy steps into the room beside us.

'You're crying,' he says and thrusts his hands into his pockets. His eyes glance at the clock on the mantelpiece. Four thirty-five. 'I suppose this means he's dead now?' He is talking about his father. The grey woman's mouth widens as though wounded by the words. Her fingers grip at the torn tissue in her hand. She strikes her weak fist against her chest, three dull thuds against her breastbone, as a long low moan aches out. Her hand strikes her chest again – *see, this? It's hollow* – but the boy, her son, is no longer there. He has already left the room. He *will* return, but not until much later, when his mother has exhausted herself with grief and sleeps restlessly with her head back and wounded mouth still gaping open. He will tiptoe into the living room, to the mantelpiece where the carriage clock *tick, tick, tick*, ticks and quietly, he will turn back its hands until they point at four and thirty. At that time, he would have just been opening the gate. He would have just seen the lace curtains in his neighbour's upstairs window drop. 'I think that there may have been some bad news,' she'd said.

It is time to fast forward to the present, dear reader, or at least what the present is for the purpose of telling this story. It is June 2011 and another hot summer's day. Our protagonist is no longer a boy, he is a thirty-three-year-old man. Look, see, there he is, walking, feet-scuffing, from the train station. One hand is plunged into the pocket of a long grey coat, the other tows a small cart piled with four boxes and a red and blue holdall. His shoulders are hunched, his toes point inwards. The sounds of the city surround him, traffic lights and car horns and engines and exhausts, wheels on hot sticky tarmac, the squawk of urban gulls. A siren screams past, blue lights flashing. The man keeps his head down. He peers out from behind his floppy fringe and sweats.

Perhaps you might take one look at him and see clearly the boy from twenty-three years before, but you would be wrong, or at least not quite right. He has changed. He is taller, more gaunt, his skin is pastier. He smells of old cigarettes. His teeth and nails are stained nicotine yellow. His chin is patchy with rough bristles. In the green cart he is tugging along behind him he carries his life experiences; the wheels clack over every join in the pavement slabs.

These boxes look heavy and the green cart too small, too weak, to contain them.

A beggar sits by a cashpoint and calls out for spare change. 'Mate, I need just a couple o' quid for the shelter, mate, will you spare us a couple o' quid?' Our man in the grey coat, our protagonist, stops. He roots deep in his trouser pocket. 'Aw mate, you're a ledge, you have a good day, mate, nice one.' But our man wants to speak. He hunkers down by the beggar sitting on the square of cardboard and hands him something. 'I'm looking for this woman,' he says, as nearby a man in a hardhat and high-vis jacket starts drilling at his cordoned-off stretch of road. *Rack-it-it-it-it-it-it*. The beggar flinches at the noise. He raises his voice: 'What's this? Another missin', is it?' He studies the face in the picture. 'How come she's got no clothes on?' He asks this question loudly, just in time for the drilling to stop. Two passing women glance at each other and giggle.

'Never mind that,' says the man. 'Do you recognise her?'

The beggar shrugs. 'Naw mate, sorry mate.' He fans his hot face with the picture before handing it back. 'I aint never seen 'er.' The drilling begins again.

Let's push off, dear reader, leave the land where it is and soar above these hot city streets with their skyline of church spires and clock towers. The sea dazzles in the sunlight and laps at the city's contours; a river curves through its centre. We can see, from up here, where the city stops and the hills begin. The heathered moors and the marshes, the valleys and the glens. The green of the pine, the yellow of the gorse, the blue-grey of a tucked away lochan. We are in the Highlands of Scotland, dear reader, but we are not to stray too far. I am taking you only to another part of town, to a pub called Pauper's Inn, an old granite building on a street of billboards, greasy spoons and estate agents. An A-frame is propped near the door of the pub with GET YER STOVIES HERE written in chalk, and in one of the bay windows a handwritten note has been taped: 'Room to rent'. One corner is curling back, the sticky peeling in the heat.

Inside, there is a fat woman behind the bar. Let's watch her for a while. She is sitting in a kind of crouch on a tall barstool; her bare feet – her heels – digging into the topmost rung; her black legginged knees up and pressed together. The small electric fan she points towards her face whirrs out a limp breath of air. She glances around the pub at her customers, at a balding man with big glasses in the corner booth supping at his pint and two regulars sitting over by a painting.

'Oi, Dougie.'

'Whit's that?'

'Fix 'im for me, would ye?' She nods at the painting that has gone askew above them. The old boys look up from their card game to the lighthouse.

'Squint, eh?' Dougie gets to his feet and stretches for the corner of the frame, tipping it slightly. 'Say when,' he calls.

'That'll do.' The fat woman takes out a handkerchief and presses it to her forehead. 'Cheers, Doug.'

'Hot the day, eh?'

'Aye.' She swigs at the pint of water she's poured for herself. Some liquid misses her mouth and dribbles across her cheek and under her earlobe. She wipes it away with her wrist. 'Aye, it's hot.'

This is Big Sal. She is the proprietor of this place. I have described her as fat and perched on a barstool, now I want you to imagine her fatter. Skin folds around her waist, her thick thighs are always touching, her breasts are heavy swells that hang low even when supported. The fat on her upper arms sways whenever she moves, or ripples along with the rattle of the window when a lorry stops outside with its engine running. She sweats even in mild temperatures. On hot days like this the wet on her forehead is visible and sticks her thin fringe to her temples. She has damp patches underneath both arms and in between her legs.

Big Sal closes her eyes and listens to the sounds all around her. The hum and whir of the battery-powered fan, the soft slap of Dougie's cards being set on the table, the urinal in the men's toilets gurgling and splurting with its autoclean system and then a faint *clack, clack, clack, clack,* the sound of wheels rolling over a dirty pavement. She looks up to see a man stopping outside the window. A tall, thin, ill-looking man with dark hair cut into curtains. He is reading the handwritten note, 'Room to rent'.

Big Sal turns to the old boys playing their cards. 'Did ye hear them say it on the radio this mornin'? Tiz the hottest day o' the year, they said.'

'Aye,' comes the reply, 'there will be a storm yet on its way,' just as the door opens and there stands our man in the long grey coat.

'Good afternoon,' he says. 'I was wondering if I might enquire about the room?'

I

A short forewarning, if I may. This story does not have any chapters as such; it is divided instead by conversations between our protagonist and a lover, a girl curled under his arm. Think of these moments, if you will, as the end of a chapter. The perfect place to pop in a bookmark, a piece of scrap paper, an old receipt from your pocket. For example, here:

> The girl moves sleepily, her feet pawing at the
> mattress. She opens one eye to see that he has
> both his eyes open. 'You're still awake,' she says.
> 'I can't sleep,' he says.
> 'Is something wrong?' she says.
> 'No.'

Have a breather, dear reader.
Rest awhile.

Time is of the essence. Time is money. Time is fleeting. Time travels. Time warp. Time delay. The End Times. Hard times. Real time. Imaginary time. Set in time. Step in time. A stitch in time saves nine. Time is relative. Time is slipping. Times are changing. The time is now. We are still at Pauper's Inn and Big Sal is still perched on her barstool, but now she is writing a postcard. So far it says, 'Oi, Bev, you'll be pleased to know I found someone for the room.' The ballpoint pen she is using keeps running out of ink. Sal has to suck on the nib, shake it in the air, and slowly go back over the words that have left only indentations on the card. She sighs and looks up, rolling one shoulder and then the other. Her two regulars have gone, but the balding man with large black-rimmed glasses is still sitting in the corner booth sipping at the last of his pint.

Sal shifts a little on her stool. She is looking again at the painting, at the tall white lighthouse beaming out over the waves that slam against the cliff and send sea spray into the air. She is remembering the day she bought it, a hot day like this, at a car-boot sale. The painting had reminded her of her husband. He wasn't a seaman, he was a rigger, but that was all the same to Big Sal. In those early years when she was young and in love and missed her man terribly she used to scour the charity shops and garage sales and local church fetes for anything that related to the sea. Bottled ships, compasses, toy boats, a collection of chipped ceramic naval officers saluting, a stuffed cuddly duck wearing a sailor's hat. All this bric-a-brac, all this

14

junk, to fill the hole Beverley left when he went to work offshore for weeks.

She picks up the postcard to reread the note: '. . . I found someone for the room.' She is wondering if there is anything else to put down and toys with the idea of describing the new lodger in more detail.

An odd wee manny, like, comin' in 'ere wi' 'is winter coat on. An' all skeletal like a sacka bones. As skinny as I am fat. Musta bin fair hot under that jacket mind. I canna understand it. Tis what? Twenty-six degrees outside the day. Aye, an odd wee manny. Shame he's English, right plumb an' proper. Shame. But beggars canna be choosers. Aye, an' I'll say as much t' Bev when he brings it up. Beggars canna be choosers.

But something is troubling her. She chews on the end of her pen as though chewing over whether to admit her unease on the postcard.

The thing of it is, Bev, the man didna know who he was. At least, not at first. I asked him his name and he says he didna know . . . 'I'm not sure,' is what he said. Not sure? How can ye not be sure of your own name?

But she doesn't write anything more. She simply signs her name. Eight years ago she was writing her husband long letters and now she sends half-filled postcards with naff pictures of lochs and hills or amusing Scottish-themed cartoons on the front.

'Och, what's it to me?' she mutters and taps her pen against her lower lip. 'As long as he pays his rent on time.'

The balding man in the corner booth is fidgeting. He is beating at the table with his finger, we can hear it, *bap bap bap*. There is perhaps only one mouthful left of his pint and yet he lingers. Every so often he allows himself a glance out of the window and then looks away again, his leg jittering nervously. Sal calls out to him. 'You all right over there? Need another?' and she nods at the almost empty glass. The man shakes his head. He pushes his spectacles up the bridge of his nose. 'No. Thank you.' His cheeks flush a little red. 'I think that really,' he says, 'really I must be off. Shortly.'

Outside the pub, just across the road, there is a group of four girls. They are young, perhaps fourteen or so, still dressed in school uniforms; short grey skirts and knee-high socks. It is these girls our man in the corner booth keeps glancing at; quick, quiet, discreet peeks. One in particular, the one holding an ice cream, the green of the mint chocolate-chip melting and dripping over her knuckles which she absentmindedly lifts to her lips and licks. She is beautiful. Even when he turns back to the pub and looks at his almost empty glass, he has the smooth pale skin of her legs in his mind, that titillating flash of flesh above the knee and the bumps of her developing breasts underneath her school shirt.

A loud girlish guffawing startles him. He turns again, another glance at the teenagers laughing, smiling, touching in that overly demonstrative way girls do. The cause of all the amusement is the ice cream. There had been the initial hugs and greetings and squeals of excitement as a friend had run to meet them, followed by an exclamation: 'Oh, an ice cream! Where'd you get that? I want one.' And the girl had mischievously licked her mint chocolate-chip a little too exuberantly, poking her tongue in deep to tease, and the whole head had toppled off, plopping onto the

16

pavement with a splat. The girl is acting out her mock-annoyance. She throws her cone onto the ground in an exaggerated huff.

'Och, ye daft bint,' another girl quickly says, 'I wouldae had that!' And they giggle all the more.

People walk past them – two women pushing a pram, chatting about where to stop for lunch; a short stocky man taking a large bite from a sandwich; a woman clutching at the bottom of her suit jacket and holding a briefcase, her heels striking out sharp clicks on the pavement.

'Here, I'm no' bein' funny, right, but look over there.'

'Where?'

'Over there, in Pauper's. See that man in the window? He's fair gawkin' at us.'

'He is an' all.'

'Flash 'im yir tits, Mand.'

'What tits?'

The girls laugh and jostle one another playfully.

'I'll flash 'im ma finger, mind,' says Mandy, the very same girl who'd dropped the ice cream, and she thrusts her middle finger into the air at the man, whose bulbous eyes widen at the sight and his face quickly ducks from view.

'Pervert!'

Forget these girls now; the person who interests us is the new lodger at Pauper's Inn, the man who apparently doesn't know who he is. We can see him now if we look up above the sign of the pub – there, at the sash window. We cannot see him well from this position; the pane is dirty and the sunlight gleams off the glass. But we can distinguish the outline of his lanky figure and movement as the man fumbles with the latch.

17

We should take ourselves closer, ogle from a better angle, and though it would be easy for me to finger-thumb *click* and take you into that room up there, I know there is little to see right now other than a skinny man in a long coat struggling with the latch on a window. Better to go back once more to the moment he arrived. But not with a *click*. No, not with a *click*. Please, reader, allow me some time to play. After all, narration can be such a dry business at times, full of old rules and expectations. Such lack of personality! It sits like trapped wind in the gut. Better to shake things up, don't you agree? Inject some fizz into omniscience.

Look down the street. Do you remember the two women pushing a pram and the short stocky man eating his sandwich? Yes? No? It doesn't matter. The man is now sitting on a bench sucking the ends of his fingers and crumpling the sandwich packaging with one hand. The two women, they are studying a menu in a cafe window. Now, reader, watch closely as we take one finger and wind backwards the clock hands of Time.

The man is uncurling his fist and as he does so the packaging unscrews and reforms in his palm. He pulls his fingers from his mouth and there is mayonnaise on his nails. See his Adam's apple move? The chewed food travels back up his throat into his mouth where he masticates for a while and then pulls out with his messy fingers the corner of his sandwich.

The two women are walking backwards, winding their way around an A-frame advertising a £5 meal deal at Piccalitos, their feet walking toe-heel, toe-heel, pulling the pram. The man stands up, still chewing and regurgitating fully formed pieces of chicken and lettuce between two slices of malted loaf. They are all walking backwards now. Back the way they came. And see, across the road, there is the woman in her suit jacket, backward scurrying from an estate agent's door and jog-skipping on toes in between reversing cars.

'Trevrep!'

'Dnim, regnif am mi' hsalf ll'i.'

The warped cackle of laughter splits the air and the teenage girls smile with open mouths, jostle-jerking. They seem to inhale the noise. Ahah ahah! They suck in devilish words from the sky, their mouths moving as though the sounds make their lips smack. From the grey pavement the ice-cream cone whips up into one girl's hand and the mint chocolate-chip unsplats itself, travels through the air as though lifted by a freak wind and perches perfectly on the cone just as the girl retracts her tongue.

Stop.

Look at their smiling faces freeze-frame. Their eyes are bright and glassy with laughter. Their cheeks rosy. Noses freckled by the sun. One girl has a red spot forming on her temple. Another has a glistening string of saliva stretching from lip to lip that she hasn't noticed.

We shall return to Pauper's Inn. Let's wait in the narrow corridor out the back, away from the ugly bustle of the world in reverse and all its dissonance. Here it is quieter and unmoving to the eye, though things are, of course, still shifting. There is an unsettling sense of microscopic movement. Even the smells are reversing, beginning first, it seems, in our very own brains and then pushed out through the pores of our noses. In this corridor we conjure up the stuffy damp that then seeps out from our bodies into the carpet and walls, the smell of stale beer and cigarettes.

Let us turn back Time's arrow and rejoin its forward familiar motion; familiarity is the key to comfort, after all. Here comes Big Sal. She is walking through from the bar and now makes her way up the narrow staircase, her left hand gripping hold of the banister, her right hand pressing into the wall to help steady the weight of her body. The man, our protagonist, follows directly after her. He peers out from behind his floppy fringe at the painted red fingernails of Big Sal. When she pulls her fingers away from the wall to move up another step, a greasy mark, an indentation even, remains. The walls are soft, the plasterboard damp. He touches his own thumb to it, presses in and watches as the print shows in the yellowish wallpaper. His eyes travel to the black-spotted mould around the cornicing. We can see him breathe in through his nose; he is smelling what we are smelling, the damp and stale beer mixed with Big Sal's syrupy sweet perfume, that saccharin scent and . . . (sniff sniff) . . . what's that? The acrid bite that hits the back of the throat when a woman is menstruating. Sal's fat behind moons out inches from his face in those tight black leggings. Her thighs rub together. Her breathing is a soft pant as she struggles with every step.

At the top of the stairs Sal stops, out of breath. A few hairs have come loose from her tight ponytail and stick flat to the wet on her forehead. She smiles, almost chuckles, as she fishes for the handkerchief tucked into her leggings.

'Aye, well, they don't call me Big Sal for nothing.' She

points down the hallway. 'In there, my love, on you go. First on the left.'

The man walks slowly. The floorboards creak beneath him. Big Sal pulls down the neck of her baggy T-shirt and mops at her cleavage. She watches the strange skinny man creak forward. He pushes at the door of the room, which has been left ajar, and peers in from his spot in the hallway. Big Sal raises an eyebrow.

Aye, he's an odd one, eh? He'll be cooked wearin' that jacket in this blindin' heat. Flasher's jacket. Paedophile. Heroin user. Alcoholic. Bev'll no' like it. Aye, he'll have a word or two to say about it, right enough.

'I'm sorry, my love, but I've clean forgotten your name. What was it again?'

The man hesitates. 'I didn't tell you,' he says.

'Oh, well, that'll explain it,' she says, but her smile soon wanes as the strange man remains silent. He is staring at his shoes. Big Sal can see now that the leather is worn and the soles are broken. 'Well?' she prompts.

'I'm not sure,' he says.

'You're not sure what your name is?' she asks.

'It's complicated,' he says.

Sal frowns. 'Aye, well, complicated or no', love, I'll need a name to call ye. It's difficult to get by in life without a name, ye know?' She forces a laugh.

'I'm looking for someone,' the man says.

'Oh, aye?'

'An old friend.'

'I see.'

'She knows who I am,' he says.

'Right. Good.'

The man nods and Sal slowly mimics him. She wets her lips with her tongue, waiting for more to be said, but nothing comes.

'I'm sorry, my love,' she's decided that the man must be a little simple, 'I canna rent a room out to someone if I don't know their name . . . ?'

These words at last register with the man. He agrees with a sharp nod and says, 'Oh, of course, I understand,' and then, 'perhaps it's best if you call me Jacob.'

'Jacob,' repeats Sal.

'Yes,' says the man. 'Jacob Little.'

Big Sal finds herself nodding again. The nodding seems to help her accept the unusual conversation. 'Right enough,' she says, clapping her hands together. She is nodding now all the more vigorously. 'Well, no use standin' out in the hall, eh? The room is no' goin' to view itself.' And she motions for the man to move inside.

In the bedroom there is a rickety wardrobe and a very worn-down, very stained single mattress pushed against the wall. The light is coming from a bare bulb hanging from the ceiling. Big Sal motions to the pieces of furniture as she walks in behind the man. 'This can all stay if you need it, Mr Little.' She is testing the name, expecting a *please call me Jacob*. 'It was all left by the last occupant.' But Jacob Little says nothing. He stands silently, glancing about him. 'Nice big window,' Sal says. She heaves herself forward, snapping back the curtains to let in the sun. The sudden shaft of light picks out the dust and tiny hairs spiralling in the air.

Big Sal seems pleased with the sash window, single glazed. She informs Jacob it is south facing. It is not. She tells him the street below is always a hubbub of activity, interesting people going about their business. 'Always something to see out of this window.' She does not remark on the way it rattles whenever a large vehicle drives past. Nor does she mention the wood rot on the crumbling windowsill or the white gloss splattering the edges of the glass. Nor does she inform Jacob the frame is loose, so when he goes to unlatch it from its stiff screw-lock in a few moments it will slam down and become firmly wedged. But now, at this moment, he still stands and listens quietly to the fat woman who leans near the rattling window and sweats.

'You'll no' find a cheaper room in the city,' she says. 'One eighty is all I ask. First month up front.'

'One fifty,' says Jacob. He is not looking at the woman, his eyes are moving over the carpet with its fag burns and stains. They rest on the mattress with its darkened spots of dried blood and coffee.

Big Sal is scowling politely. 'You think I canna shift this room at one eighty?'

'I'll pay cash,' says Jacob.

'Well.' Sal stops. 'Right then. Cash it is.'

Her new tenant nods.

The landlady spiel continues as though never interrupted. She expects the rent on the first of every month. Cash in hand. All inclusive. Smoking permitted. Pets allowed. Bring home girls, boys, prostitutes, she won't bat an eye. But if he's late with payment she'll expect him to work in the pub or around the house. And if he refuses, well, she'll have to fetch Bev to visit specially. Understand? 'Do you understand, Mr Little?'

'I understand. Yes. Thank you.'

'The bathroom is further down the hallway.'

'Yes.'

'Kitchen downstairs.'

'I'll show myself around.'

'Oh aye?'

The two are held in the swaying damp heat of the room.

'Well, Mr Little. I'll need some money to secure the room. 'Til the first of the month, like.'

'Of course,' Jacob replies. 'May I . . .' He pauses. 'May I bring it to you later this evening?'

Big Sal nods once. Her lips are straight, her eyes are sharp. In her mind she is scolding herself for not asking for two hundred. Then he would have cut her to one eighty.

'Thank you, Mrs . . .'

'Just call me Sal.'

'Right. Well. Thank you, Sal.'

And now we find ourselves alone in the room with Jacob. Big Sal can be heard creaking her way down the hallway towards the stairs. Jacob is still standing in the same spot, his face turned towards the door. He cocks his head to one side as though listening. His thin lips are parted and we can see the yellow of tiny teeth. An incisor is broken. Jacob's tongue glides over his jagged tooth; for a moment he looks as though he is sucking on a boiled sweet. And then he moves. Not quickly. Out of the room. We can hear him walk away from the stairs, further along the landing. A door is pushed open. A pause. We hear it click shut.

No need to follow, let's wait by the window. Outside we have a good view of the street, although it is murky through the glass and the sun is shining directly above the line of rooftops opposite. Over those roofs, if we squint against the sun, we can see the long point of a church spire.

Looking down you can see the four teenage girls. You can even hear their laughter through the thin slice of glass.

Jacob has re-entered the room. He moves over to the window, shades his eyes against the sun, but sees very little through the grime. He begins to fumble at the latch.

2

Jacob pulls the girl closer to him. 'Come here,' he says. 'I want to hold you.' And the girl smiles as she presses her cheek against his bare chest. 'We should do this again sometime,' he says. 'Tell me you'll come again?'

Time goes by. Only time will tell. In due time. In good time. In no time. To do time. Time is a complicated thing, dear reader; the past, the present, the future, it creates us. Without it what would we be? Perhaps free?

I would like to show you now a certain moment in time that changed our strange protagonist, Jacob Little, significantly; and over the years the memory of this moment would continue to change and shape him. It is the year 2000. We are standing in a steam-filled bathroom. Small. Narrow. Condensation creeps down the pale walls with their peeling paint. The mirrors on the medicine cabinet have misted from the heat of the bath water. There is a frosted-glass window above the toilet that looks out onto a busy roundabout. It is cracked and letting in a bitter draught and the noise and stink from the traffic outside. It is cold. It is February.

The sound of a radio drifts in from the gap under the door. And there in the plastic tub of hot water amidst the warm bubbles is Jacob. He looks younger, early twenties. His skin is less washed out, his teeth not yet stained yellow, his chin free from patchy rough bristles. The young Jacob has just finished shaving. There is a small spot of blood where he has nicked his jawline. Every part of his body has been soaped and scrubbed, his arms and neck almost rubbed raw with such vigorous exfoliation. His dark wet hair is limp and flat against his head. He is not at ease. He sits in a crouch position, his feet pulled in close to his buttocks, hugging his knees. He stares absently at the taps.

In the room next door a young woman is lying on the rumpled duvet of a single bed. She is masturbating. Not with any real attempt to make herself orgasm, but in a gentle, companionable way. Her left hand is pushed underneath her elasticated joggers and is brushing over her trimmed pubic hair. She caresses her clitoris, semi-daydreaming. Not about sex. She is thinking about the milk that has gone off in the fridge and about the essay she has to write for university.

Following Adorno, it can be suggested that in the modern world, the 'aura' of the artwork has been replaced not by a democratised mass culture but by commodity fetishism. Discuss.

This young woman, pale blonde hair, ivory skin, is an unblemished sort of beautiful. She is stretched out on the bed, one arm up, the other arm resting over her pelvis. As the winter sun slants through the window, you would be forgiven for thinking it was the same fair-haired woman as before. Do you remember? The next-door neighbour from Jacob's childhood. The white light picks out the shine in her hair and turns it halo gold.

The hand underneath her joggers is now unmoving. It rests on the warmth and faint throb of her genitalia. She is daydreaming at last of sex, of penetration. Under her breath she says the word 'fuck'. She finds it sexy. 'I want you to fuck me.' She sighs. She is both aroused and bored.

Ten minutes. Fifteen minutes. The young woman lies and listens to the radio. When Abba comes on she groans, reaches her hand out and switches it off. In the new silence, which is not really silence, she can hear the swishing of bath water and the squeaking of Jacob's feet on the bottom of the tub. He is getting out. And it seems by the way the water is moving he is getting out quickly. There is a *thuck* as the bolt of the bathroom door is pulled back. And then there he is, in the doorway. He looks odd. He wears only a brightly coloured stripy towel around his waist, which he is holding up by the hip. The rest of his body and his dark hair is still dripping wet with bath water. His feet have made damp footmarks on the carpet of the living room. His face is full of manic excitement. The young woman raises her eyebrows in anticipation.

'I've had an epiphany,' he says.

'Sounds great,' she says. 'Do you wanna have sex?'

What the young woman hasn't noticed is the slither of red that is dribbling from Jacob's wrist into the palm of his hand. She will notice it soon enough, but right now she is digging both her thumbs under the elasticated waist of her joggers to pull them down over her buttocks.

'Wait. What are you doing?'

The young woman raises an eyebrow. 'I'm taking off my joggers.'

'No. You have to leave.'

She stares at Jacob blankly. She is frozen halfway in the act of pulling down her trousers.

'You have to leave,' he repeats.

'Are you being serious?'

'Deadly. I've had an epiphany. Things need to change. Starting right here, right now. With you.'

The young woman blinks. 'That sounds very rehearsed.' She takes a moment to look at Jacob still standing in the doorway. A hint of peevishness has entered his manic excitement. 'Have you been practising that? In the bath? Is that why you were in there so long?'

'No,' Jacob tells her plainly. 'Actually I was going to kill myself.'

It is then she notices the red from Jacob's wrist and palm; it has dribbled down his middle finger and now drips from its tip. Once. Twice. Onto the pale dirty carpet. 'Oh,' she says. She can see the bead of blood bubble again just under the nail, waiting for enough weight to . . . drip . . . a third time onto the carpet. 'But you didn't.'

'No.' Jacob can see she is looking at his hand. He presses it into the side of his leg and the towel.

'No.' The young woman seems more bored now than she did before. She sighs and rolls onto her side. 'Well, why not, Jacob?'

Jacob is silent.

'I mean,' the young woman clarifies, 'what stopped you?'

Further silence.

'Well?'

'Are you actually asking me *why* I didn't kill myself?'

'Yes.'

Jacob makes a flurrying movement with his blood-smeared hand. The gesture suggests both familiarity and annoyance. It silently says the words, *This is so typical of you, how could I expect anything else?* 'You sound *disappointed*,' he says.

The young woman shrugs.

'Well,' he says, 'isn't it obvious?'

'No,' she says.

'The epiphany!'

'Oh, right. The epiphany. Of course.'

This young woman's name is Solace. She is twenty years of age. She met Jacob two years previously in a nightclub called *Synergy*. He'd been drinking alone at the bar when she approached. Her opening line was this:

'You look depressed.'

Due to the loud music in the venue and its general busyness, the young woman had to almost shout this at Jacob to make herself heard. 'YOU LOOK DEPRESSED.' A few other heads in the very close vicinity turned to take a look at the pair before switching their attention back to waving notes at the barmen.

'My name's Solace,' she'd said.

It was the name that had made him look up from his drink and properly take notice of her, though only because (she found out later) he'd misheard it. Soul-less instead of Solace.

'I'm here alone,' she said. 'What about you?'

'I'm here alone,' he told her.

The two of them drank together. They exchanged a few words. Mostly they just sat and looked at their hands and into their drinks. After leaving the club, they fucked in an alleyway next to some dirty-looking skips. She asked Jacob if he'd walk her home. He said he wouldn't. So she asked if she could stay with him for the night. He agreed. It was while they were in bed together she'd corrected his spelling.

'My name's Solace,' she said. 'S-O-L-A-C-E.'

Perhaps it was her accent, she explained. Scottish. Jacob had seemed strangely disappointed. He'd left her lying alone in his bed. In the morning she'd found him asleep on the sofa.

Two years later and Solace is still in Jacob's bed. She supposes she considers him her lover, although not exclusively. There is another boy who lives here at the flat. Bertie or Brian or Benjamin. B— is what they call him. And Solace would occasionally swap Jacob's bed for his. She knew that Jacob could hear them together. Headboard beating against the wall. B— would staccato grunt his way to an orgasm and Solace would join him with varying wails of delight. She often confided in Jacob after such occasions the sheer pleasure she gained from faking an orgasm with B—. They made music together, she said. His repetitive bass-beat grunting keeping perfect time with her wild impromptu howls. She'd tell Jacob how it reminded her of the night she met him at the club. 'What terrible music they were playing,' she'd say. 'It's just like the music B— and I make together. Terrible and yet glorious because it reminds me of you.'

'So, tell me what it was like. This epiphany. I mean, what was it about? What did it feel like?' Solace has no intention of leaving the bedroom. She's rolled onto her stomach and is looking at Jacob with mock enthusiasm. 'I've never had an epiphany before,' she says.

Jacob shakes his head.

'Oh, come on, Jacob, I'm so *bored*. The least you can do is tell me.'

'Why are you here, Solace?'

'Oh, I get it. This is another one of your deeply morose and pessimistic philosophical enquiries about the meaning of life and human existence. Right? Did you discover there was no meaning, Jacob? Is that it? So you attempted suicide only to realise there was no meaning or point in that either? Oh, how very Sartre! How very Camus! How so very, very *absurd* of you.'

'Shut up, Solace. I mean why are you *here*? You're always fucking *here*.'

For a moment Solace stops. Stares. And then she begins to laugh. She rolls onto her back in her own self-contained hilarity and pedals her feet and legs in the air. 'You can't be serious. No, wait, you *are* serious!' And she laughs all the more. 'Oh, Jacob, you are *killing* me. Tell me you're not *seriously* serious?'

'What is wrong with you?'

'*God*, Jacob, you're such a fucking bag of shit.'

'I'm just asking you a question,' he says. 'A simple goddamned question. Why are you here? You're always, *always* here.'

'That's because I *live* here, Jacob. God!' She says this in amazement, not anger. She shakes her head almost admiringly as she looks at Jacob standing framed in the doorway. He seems stumped by her reply, his mouth a little open.

'You don't live here,' he says. 'Since when have you lived here?'

'Since I started paying *your* rent, Jacob.'

'You're paying my rent?'

Solace rolls her eyes and sits up on the bed. She reaches for her cigarettes. 'You want one?' She places the cigarette in between her lips. Jacob stands unmoving in the doorway. His face is turned away from her. He's staring into the corner of the room, miserably. Solace feels almost guilty as she watches him. 'Jesus, Jacob, you look as though I've just burst your balloon.' She lights her cigarette. 'Jacob?' She exhales her first draw of smoke. 'You know, I don't really think you're a great big bag of shit, OK? Not really.' No reaction. 'I mean, you *can* be a bit of a prick sometimes.

But, you know, who isn't, right?' He just stares into that dusty corner of the room. 'Oh God, please, if this is what epiphanies do to people I'd rather never have one.'

And then slowly Jacob begins to move. He is tying the towel more securely around his waist.

'You're not taking me seriously,' he says. 'That's OK. You don't have to take me seriously. I don't *need* you to take me seriously.' The word 'seriously' is forced into the air, a sneering echo from earlier in the conversation. Jacob steps over to a chest of drawers. He begins pulling out clothes and stuffing them into a red and blue holdall.

Solace watches him. She smokes.

'You always think you're so clever, don't you, Solace? So *fucking clever*. You look at me with such *mild fucking amusement*, like I'm a child. Like I . . . like I don't know anything and I'm just coming out with cute ideas and phrases. You look at me . . . like the little old lady who pinches and shakes a kiddie's cheek.' He is pulling on boxers, some socks, he is reaching for a pair of blue denim jeans. 'Well, damn you, Solace. You think you know everything, don't you? You think you know fucking *everything*.'

'*Au contraire*, Jacob,' she knows this will annoy him more but can't resist, 'as the great Socrates once said, I know that I know nothing.'

'Fuck *you,* Solace.'

'Mmm.'

'No, *seriously*, fuck you.'

And with that Jacob leaves; and so begins the slow, eleven-year process of falling in love with the woman he has just left.

3

'I think you're beautiful,' Jacob says as he cups the girl's face with his palms. 'Such smooth, pale, bone china skin, glossy hair and glass marble eyes. You have the delicacy and beauty of a doll. Has anyone told you that before?'

It is raining, a summer storm. The city roads are jet black with the wet. The sky has gathered low and grey and grumbling. Heavy drops of rain smack against the paved surfaces, creating what looks like a wet mist millimetres above the roads and pavements. Traffic pushes through the fast-forming puddles. People rush between shops, linger in doorways, cower beneath awnings. Brollies of all shapes, sizes, colours flourish, like the blossoming of a thousand rain-starved flowers, metal stems with nylon petals. Feet make slapping sounds as they run. And everywhere the patter and pour and drip of the heavens opening and that refreshing smell of a wet sky breaking, the humidity clearing.

But we are not in this city. We are in a car, stationary. It is pulled up overlooking a river. Trees line the opposite embankment. They look dull under the grey sky; their branches whip and rustle with each gust. The rain spatters over the metal roof and fills the small car with its noise.

In the driver's seat there is a boy. Blond. Seventeen. His hands are resting on the steering wheel, his fingers tapping. He is puffing out his left cheek and then his right, then his left, before letting the air quietly explode from between his lips. A soft popping sound that is lost amidst the noise of rain.

In the passenger seat there is a girl. Long dark hair. Sixteen. She is staring out at the rain falling into the river. Unlike the boy, she does not look awkward or uncomfortable or bored, she just stares. After a moment more of silence, she speaks: 'It seems unfair that some raindrops get to fall in the river and others fall on the hard earth.'

The boy's face looks both puzzled and mildly annoyed. He turns away from the girl so that she can't see his frown. 'Yeah,' he says. His warm breath mists the side window. He wipes it without thinking with the end of his sleeve and watches the rain tracing trails and veining out over the glass. He frowns again, but only briefly, before turning to the girl and touching her lightly on the leg. Her thigh. He is smiling now. 'You're so deep, Lucy,' he says.

The girl seems to appreciate this compliment. She smiles and blushes, but only a little. She turns to meet the boy's eyes but cannot bring herself to gaze at him.

'I mean . . .' the boy stammers, 'you're much deeper than any of the girls in my year . . .' but the moment is lost. The girl, Lucy, has turned away from him. She is leaning her elbow on the bottom of the passenger window and covering her mouth with her hand.

'We'd better go,' she says. 'I told Sal I'd be in early tonight.'

The boy returns his attention to the steering wheel.

'Sorry, I forgot to tell you.'

Above the bar at Pauper's Inn is mounted a small flat-screen television. Four men are sitting silently watching a football match from their stools. They sip regularly from their pints and murmur remarks on the game to no one in particular.

A man wearing a suit walks in, shaking a black umbrella. He nods at Big Sal sitting behind the bar. She is eating a bag of crisps, ham and mustard flavour. She nods back at the stranger; her mouth is full. She brushes the crumbs and grease from her fingers onto her leggings.

'What can I get you, love?'

A group of university students sit in a corner booth with books spread over the table. They are deep in discussion, writing notes and interjecting comments and questions. They point at pages crammed with closely printed text. Occasionally they laugh.

'I'll have a pint of lager. Tennent's. Thank you.'

Big Sal pours the man a pint.

'Nasty weather,' the man says.

'Aye.'

'You'd never think it was so hot this morning.'

'No.' Big Sal is matching the stranger's tone. 'They said it was the hottest day on the radio.'

'Aye, well, we needed a good storm,' says the man.

It is a very dull conversation. Both parties know it. They are silent for a moment, neither wanting to continue. Big Sal finishes pulling the pint and sets it on the bar, edging it towards the man with the tips of her fingers. 'Two fifty,' she says.

And then through the door, bursting in as though the wind gusted her forward, comes our girl from the car, Lucy Westbry. Her entrance feels strangely like a missed cue, as though really she should have entered after the words 'we needed a good storm', but for some reason she was waylaid backstage. Big Sal smiles. The man looks relieved. He takes hold of his pint and moves off to a solitary seat in the corner.

'All right, Sal?' Lucy looks around her. 'Christ, it feels like someone's died a death in here.' She is wearing a rain jacket with the hood up. It is speckled with wet. 'I've never seen a happy hour so dreary.' Her fingers are unpopping and unzipping the jacket.

'You're early,' Sal says.

'Uh-huh.' She's moved offstage again, to the corridor out the back. Her voice travels through the open door. 'I told Billy you needed me. If he asks will you back me up?'

'If that's what you want.'

'Thanks, Sal.' Lucy reappears in the doorway, no longer wearing the jacket. 'What's with all the boxes?' she asks.

'New lodger,' Sal says.

'Oh aye?' Lucy glances back into the corridor, presumably at the boxes. 'Male? Female?'

'Male.'

'Is he nice?'

'Bit odd.'

'Oh?'

'A bit English.'

'Ha! Bev'll be pleased.'

'Och, if he pays his rent on time . . .'

'Good looking?'

'Not my type.'

'Skinny, then.'

Big Sal smiles. 'I canna pay you for these extra hours, Lucy. You know that, don't you?'

'I know. I just need somewhere to hang out. Read. You don't mind, Sal?'

'Course not.'

'Thanks.'

The boxes in the corridor are all piled on top of a green cart, the sort young children use to pull their toys around in. The cart has a long matching green handle for tugging it along. The boxes, all four of them, are tied in tight with bungee cords and string. Lucy is running one hand over the topmost box. She glances up at the ceiling to where the new lodger's room is. 'Hey, Sal,' Lucy calls through to the bar. 'Is the new lodger in?' Big Sal calls back that she doesn't know. 'I'm gonna take these boxes up. Introduce myself.' She can hear Big Sal say something more in reply, but her words are lost in amongst the sounds of the television. Lucy is already untying the boxes and releasing the bungee cords. She takes the first one into her arms, testing its weight before pulling it away from the pile.

On the landing upstairs, the door of the lodger's room has been left open. Lucy moves towards it. She calls out a greeting before peering round the door. Her eyes are drawn to movement by the open window. The limp brown curtains are whipping in the wind and the drizzling rain is coming in. Lucy sets the box down and walks over to the flapping material. She attempts to heave up the back sash.

'Damn thing's stuck.' She makes a mental note to tell Big Sal. On the mattress there is a small red and blue holdall. Next to it there is a green jotter. Lucy leaves the room. We can hear her making her way down the stairs. She returns less than a minute later with another box. She leaves again. Comes back with a third box. Each time she re-enters, her eyes fall on the holdall and the green jotter. She goes to the bathroom. Not because she needs the toilet, but to check that the new lodger is not in there. He is not. She fetches the fourth box. Heavier than the others. She struggles to get it up the stairs on her own. Books, she thinks. So the new lodger is a reader? She wants to peek inside, but the box has been taped shut. She drops it next to the others and touches her warm forehead with one hand.

The slight wind that is coming in from the window feels good against her skin. She moves across the room to stand close to it, hands on her hips and eyes closed. The wind lifts the ends of her dark hair a little and cools her cheeks. She is thinking about the green jotter on the mattress. She wants to read it. And of course, we know that she is going to, don't we? Why else is the green jotter there if not to be read? Lucy does not even close the door. Within moments she has the jotter in her hands. She flicks through the pages, quickly at first. Fine, neat, careful handwriting with a slight backwards slant fills the book. Pictures are taped to the pages. Postcards and newspaper clippings. There are scrawling sketches and doodles in the margins. She stops flicking on a page that has a painting taped to it. A blonde woman. Naked. She stops at this page in particular because there is an old feather wedged into the spine, acting as a bookmark. It says this.

Dear Solace, it is almost your spitting image, your reflection, don't you think? Look how her hair falls in those thin, wispy ringlets and how her rose lips part slightly into that innocent, virgin pout – that lie, that deception – just like your own wide-eyed gaze. Your tongue would be toying with your teeth, wouldn't it, Solace, when you looked on like that? Feigning your greenness. Look at her soft touch, those long fingers, almost caressing her ashen white skin. Me? she asks, pointing to herself. What, me? Her breasts, Solace, look at her breasts. Are they not the same size and shape as yours, enough to cup in a man's large palm? And her pubic hair, trimmed and tidied, perhaps the only clue to her real experience, for what virgin ever thinks of her hair there as anything other than natural, so would let it grow?

You remember I wrote you a poem. You remember I read it to you one night when we were lying together.

> *We lie back and take in the sky, you and I,*
> *We lie back and you, with your long fingers point*
> *and pinch peel the moon, until there is nothing*
> *but that black blanket pinpricked with stars.*
> *The lunar pickpocket, thief of the pale white glow.*
> *I'll weave you a soul, you say.*
> *Do you believe in miracles?*

You remember, Solace. I know you remember. You were curled under my arm, your head resting on my bare chest. Your hair was streaming over my body. When I finished reading the poem we were silent together. Where you had been stroking your finger over my stomach before, absentmindedly playing with my navel, now your hand was still. You asked me this.

– Do you love me, Jacob?
And I didn't answer.
– I am your muse, you said. You should love your muse.
– Love is tainted, I told you. Love is imperfect. Love is not good enough for you.

Lucy Westbry stands with the green jotter in her hand. When she has finished reading this page she does not turn to another, but reads it again. She mouths the words. She looks at the painting, the 'spitting image' of a woman that this man, Jacob, knows . . . or once knew? A strange feeling comes over her. A shiver. In her mind there is the clumsy voice of her boyfriend, Billy. *You're much deeper than any of the girls in my year.* The comment had annoyed her, though at the time she'd not understood why. Now she did. When Billy looked at her, he didn't just see *her* but all the other possible girlfriends out there. He compared her to them. She was simply another girl standing only slightly apart from everyone else. But this Jacob. When he looked at Solace, nobody else existed. And *love*. It was too much of an everyday word to express how he felt. *Oh, Billy, nobody wants overlooking rivers and fumbling hands on thighs. You don't have a clue, do you?*

They say girls mature faster than boys. Lucy believes this to be true. Billy is a year older than her and yet he still seems so very young. Clumsy. Inexperienced. Impatient. Desperate. He's been pushing for sex ever since Lucy turned sixteen, as though suddenly it's his legal right to do so. 'We've been dating for over six months,' he said once. 'Do you not feel ready yet? I mean . . . I love you.' Even now the words grate on Lucy. *I love you.* Like it was an afterthought.

From the hallway Lucy hears a squeak. A footstep on the topmost stair. The green jotter is dropped back onto the mattress. Lucy moves into the centre of the room. She stands there for a second, maybe two.

Weird. If the new lodger walks in, he'll see me standing in the middle of his room, staring like an idiot. Better to go out there and bump into him. Aye. Just say about the boxes.

Lucy is already moving towards the door.

Better just to go out there and fall over the man, like they do in the movies.

She begins to wish she was carrying something she could drop. Something he could help pick up.

The hallway is empty. This surprises Lucy almost more than bumping into the man would have. She feels both relieved and strangely disappointed. The squeak. She must've been hearing things. She stands listening, holding her breath. The whole building seems to creak when she listens hard enough. She considers going back to the green jotter, to read another page, but doesn't dare. Instead she goes down the stairs to the corridor, lifts the little wooden cart and carries it to the new lodger's bedroom. May as well finish what she began. She places each box back into the cart, in the same order as she found them. She even, though she isn't sure why, ties the pile back up with the bungee cords and string. As she tightens the cord over the topmost box a faint smell of incense escapes from inside. Incense? Perhaps the lodger is a bit of a new-age hippy? She imagines him then as skinny, tall and long-bearded, wearing loose-fitting clothes and sandals . . . with socks. She adds a garland to his head for extra effect.

'Hey, Sal.' Lucy has gone back into the bar. 'I've taken those boxes up for the new guy.'

Sal is holding the little fan up to her face. 'Aye.' The blades of the fan purr through the air, the battery inside hums. 'He asked me to pass on his thanks, like.'

'He was here?'

'Not long left.'

Lucy looks around the bar. The football match has ended and the sound of the television muted. The bar is empty now the rain has stopped and the evening sun is out. Two men sit on the picnic bench outside the door, smoking and sipping at pints.

'Did he see me?'

Sal raises an eyebrow. Lucy looks a little perturbed. Disconcerted. No, wait, Big Sal is not the type of person to use words such as 'perturbed' or 'disconcerted'. She is more likely to think Lucy looks a little 'worried'. But it is not quite the right word to use. Perturbed is much better. It suggests the unsettling feeling of being worried but also ill at ease. Disconcerted adds an element of anxious embarrassment, slight confusion. Altogether much better words to describe what Lucy is feeling at that moment. Ruffled. She has even had that sinking *thu-thud* of a heart palpitation.

'I don't know if he saw you, lass,' Sal says. 'He saw the boxes gone from the corridor. I told him you took 'em up for him and he said to pass on his thanks. Then he left.'

'Oh.'

'Are you all right, Lucy?'

'Aye.' Lucy nods once. 'I'm fine.'

4

Jacob is holding the girl close to him. He spirals his right index finger over her pale skin. He circles the shoulder joint and traces his finger up and down her arm. The girl is stroking the thin line of soft hair that runs from Jacob's navel to his pelvis. She is not ignoring the bulge in the material of his trousers, she is aware of it, her eyes are drawn to it. But still she strokes those soft hairs. She pretends it is not there until at last Jacob takes her hand and guides it down.

Pauper's Inn: gold lettering on a black background. You can imagine it as an impressive theatre set. This two-storied Scottish pub with its granite walls and bay windows; the old-fashioned sign squeaking on its iron bracket, its picture of a bedraggled red-faced man raising a tumbler to the skies. For the stage the building would be made to look more crooked and sunken than it is in real life, an artistic attempt to portray the play's themes of distortion; a symbol of the unfolding misdemeanours that lie therein (or are yet to come). The facade could be hinged to open like two granite French doors, transforming the stage into the pub interior; long-suffering beams exposed in the walls, bending with age and adorned with all things sea and sailor: lighthouse paintings, nautical maps, ship's wheels and compasses. Fishing nets could drape from the ceiling. Oars could be nailed to the wood-panelled bar. Vintage-style fishermen's lanterns attached to the walls. Amidst the glints of light flecking off glass bottles on shelves, there could be the occasional oddity: a plastic toy boat, a wind-up duck, a ship in a bottle.

And by some clever feat of stage engineering the entire set could swivel ninety degrees and allow the audience to see into the dark cobbled courtyard behind (lit by a brash automatic outdoor light). Here is where the bins are kept, where deals are made, where lovers neck and grope in the crude oil of night and the scuttle of sharp rat claws can be heard in the corners and echoing up the drainpipes. Cafe smells could be pumped into the air so all around would linger the scent of stale coffee, greasy food and beer.

Forgive me my playfulness, dear reader. I am only dramatising what is really there.

> *'All the world's a stage,*
> *And all the men and women merely players:*
> *They have their exits and their entrances;*
> *And one man in his time plays many parts.'*

Let's go for a walk. At least it's not raining. We'll go out the back door of Pauper's, into that small cobbled courtyard with its lingering smells. Footsteps echo as we walk under a narrow archway into a skinny alleyway and out onto a street leading off from the 'main' road. I use inverted commas because no streets in this area of the city can be classed as 'main'. We are a good twenty-five minutes' walk from the centre. Around here there is a launderette, an estate agent, some small cafes, an independent butchers and a DVD rental store that has gone out of business. There is a Tesco Express five minutes down the road and a little closer, a small convenience shop. There is a store that sells cast-iron doorknobs and bells. Another store that sells carpets and fine rugs. Predominantly the stores up and down these streets are the kind no locals ever shop at. This is the sort of area you come to if you're a plumber looking for brass taps or a builder who wants a sign printed on the side of your white van. This is the sort of area where people come to live if they want cheap accommodation.

There is a small playground in amidst some houses. The climbing tower and slide is shelter for a group of teenagers who often come here in the evening to drink dirty cider and cough over cigarettes. We can smell the sweet scent of weed in the air as we pass this particular group of youths.

Out onto another small street lined with parked cars. There is a pub, a newsagents, a Chinese takeaway. Further down the street there is a small motorcycle showroom and next door to it is a grubby open doorway with peeling wallpaper in the hall. The heavily curtained window offers 'adult massage', no appointment necessary. I will not take you in there, dear reader, although I admit it is a curious hobby of mine to hang around the brothels, dipping in and out of the minds of punter and prostitute. It amuses me, you see, to observe such a colourful spectrum of emotions under the one roof in the one evening. Guilt, disgust, aggression, boredom, hilarity, relief. And let's not forget euphoria! The sweat and toss and turn of bodies that leads to that orgasmic release.

Enough. We are looking for Jacob and here he is, hands in pockets, staring in at the motorcycles that are on display. He is still wearing the long pale grey coat. He is also wearing a hat, a fedora. Two youths cycle past on their BMXs and one calls out, 'Oi! Inspector Gadget!' The other cackles. They don't stop, they cycle on, laughing and talking. In the distance you can hear them shout, 'Go go Gadget!'

Jacob is walking back the way we came. His eyes glance over the doorway of the brothel and its sign. He walks on. A greasy, square piece of paper that was once wrapped around a portion of chips is pushed towards his feet by a breeze. The polystyrene tray is further up the street in the gutter. A wooden fork is speared through its base. Cold grey chips litter the tarmac around it.

It is beginning to get dark, owing not to the sun setting, but to the grey clouds that have pulled together once more. The air is close. A car creeps along the street looking for a parking space. A young kitten darts across the road and settles underneath a van. We can hear the sound of chatter and laughter from the pub up ahead, The Foreman's Reach. A giant wall banner advertises SKY SPORTS HERE. A man is smoking outside the pub doors. He is watching Jacob approach.

Let me describe him in more detail, this man, for in a few moments Jacob will stop to speak to him. He is middle-aged, well built, medium height. He has a handlebar moustache, the rest of his beard black stubble. He has short dark hair. His weathered skin is a dirty sort of tanned. On first impressions you'd guess this man is a labourer of some kind. A biker. Maybe gay, but not the camp kind. His thick fingers squish the white rolled cigarette he is smoking. He sucks at it through red lips. He is wearing a white T-shirt underneath a leather waistcoat covered in pins, patches and badges. When Jacob has walked a little closer, this man says to him, 'Shit. Are you no' hot, man?'

Jacob slows his pace as he nears the stranger. He is looking at the cigarette in the man's hand. Jacob takes off his hat, revealing his floppy dark hair. 'I don't suppose I could trouble you for a cigarette?' he asks.

The man narrows his eyes. He seems to be chewing on his empty mouth, sizing Jacob up. The red lips pout a little. He juts out his cleaved chin. 'Aye,' he says. From the inside pocket of his leather waistcoat the man pulls out a tin. He opens it and offers Jacob a pre-rolled cigarette.

'Thank you.' Jacob takes one.

'You didn't answer my question,' the man says. 'Are you no' hot?' He holds out a lighter. The tobacco glows. 'You sure as hell look hot in that jacket.'

Jacob steps back as he inhales and then exhales his first lungful of smoke. He looks at the end of the cigarette. The smoke spirals towards him, into his chest. 'I suppose I am,' he tells the man. He places the cigarette in between his thin lips and the fedora underneath his arm. He fishes for something in the deep pocket of his coat. The smoke is pushed by the breeze up his nostrils and into his eyes.

The man thinks Jacob is reaching for a wallet to pay for the cigarette. He shakes his head and is about to say he doesn't want any money, it's just a fag, but Jacob has pulled out a card. On the card is a picture, the same picture we have seen in Jacob's journal of the blonde, wispy-haired woman. Jacob takes another draw from his cigarette as he looks at this picture. He turns to the moustachioed man in the leather waistcoat.

'I'm looking for this person,' Jacob says.

The man takes the card. 'This person?' He draws on his rollie as he studies the picture. 'Fair bonnie, eh?' he says. He takes a moment or two more. 'But this isn't a photo. This looks like . . .' He turns the card over, but the back is blank. 'This looks like a painting.'

'It *is* a painting,' says Jacob. '*Honeymoon Nude*. It's by an artist called John Currin.'

'Ah, right,' says the man. 'Well what? Are you looking for the model or something, is that it?'

'No. I'm looking for a woman who looks like this.'

'Huh, ain't we all, eh?' But the man can see that Jacob

isn't smiling. 'Right,' he says. 'Well, I canna help you, I'm afraid. Unless you have a photo?'

'What difference does it make? She looks like this.'

'Aye, well, no offence, mate, but there's probably about a hundred blonde lassies in the city who look something like this.'

'No. I mean almost *exactly* like this.'

'Oh, right. Aye. OK then.' He hands the card back to Jacob, who immediately returns it to his coat pocket. 'Sorry I canna help.'

Jacob nods. He seems agitated. His hand remains in his pocket, fingers touching the card and drumming against it. He takes a long draw on his cigarette. 'This is her hometown,' he says.

'Oh, right.'

'She went to school here.'

'Aye?' The man pauses. 'Which one?'

'I don't know.'

'Best start calling round then, eh? There's quite a few. Just give them her name and see if she was a pupil there. I guess that's the best place to start.'

But Jacob cringes. He turns his face in the other direction. He looks up and down the street.

'What?' says the man. 'You dinna know her name, like?'

'No, it's not that. It's just . . .' A woman walking a small Jack Russell is approaching. Jacob steps aside to let her pass. He flicks his cigarette into the wet gutter and watches the woman's retreating back and the small dog pulling at the lead to get at the grey chips on the road. Enough time passes for him to recompose himself. He looks squarely at the moustachioed man. 'She told me her name was Solace.'

'Solace, eh? Unusual name, that.'

'Yes, well, I'm not entirely convinced it was her real name.'

'Ah.' The man nods knowingly. 'I see.' He presses his fat red lips together. 'Fake number too, eh? She's not worth it, man. Do yourself a favour, dinna bother yourself with the lassie. You gotta keep some dignity in these situations, you know?'

'No, you've misunderstood. She's an old friend. It's just . . . I only ever knew her as Solace. I mean, maybe it *is* her real name.' He doesn't sound convinced. 'The last time I saw her was eleven years ago.'

'That's a long time.'

'Yes.'

The man turns his face up to the sky. Grey. He feels a speck of rain hit his forehead. The breeze has turned a little cooler. He opens his hot palms and spreads his fingers so the slight wind hits his skin. He does not want to be standing outside talking to this strange floppy-haired man in the long coat. He wants to be inside the pub ordering his next pint. And yet he stays. Because . . . why? Because it would be rude to leave? The man isn't sure he cares. He looks at the stranger standing before him. The guy's unhinged, he tells himself. I have my own problems to deal with. In a split-second flash he thinks of his daughter, his ex-wife, his ill ex-mother-in-law. He thinks of money, bills, debt. He thinks of the house he is trying to sell. He thinks of his job, which he loathes. 'I'm sorry,' he says. He holds his hands up in the air. His gesture says, I have nothing.

'Wait.' Jacob pulls out the card once more. 'Take it,' he says. 'I have lots of them.' And the moustachioed man finds himself looking down at the painting of the nude blonde as it's pushed into his hands. 'I'm staying at Pauper's Inn. Do you know it?'

'I know it.'

'Ask around,' Jacob says. 'Show people the picture.'

The nude blonde points a finger into her left breast. *Me?* she says. *You're looking for me?* There is something unusual about the painting. The hips are too square. The shoulders too slanting.

'My name is Jacob Little.'

Another speck of rain. The puddles on the road are rippling with invisible drops of drizzle. 'All right,' says the man. 'I'll ask around.' He notices then for the first time Jacob's teeth, yellowish in colour, naturally a little gappy. He notices this because Jacob is smiling at him. To the man this smile looks both grateful and desperate. 'Right. Well.' He waves the card in the air. 'Good luck with finding your friend.' He no longer believes the woman exists. The more he looks at the stranger standing in front of him the more he thinks he's a man gone mad. A tramp? A tink? He looks pale and half starved; his shoes are scuffed.

Jacob is looking up at the sky. He blinks into the spitting wet. He places his hat back onto his head just as the sky breaks with a rumble and rain pours in long heavy smacking lines. The shoulders of his pale coat are soaked to a dark grey within seconds. The drops beat on his body and spin off his hat and drip down from the rim. Jacob is looking at the moustachioed man, who has stepped back into the shelter of the doorway. 'Pauper's Inn,' he says.

Jacob nods a farewell, but says nothing more. He has turned from him. He is walking up the street, his hands deep in his pockets, his feet sending up tiny slapping splashes from the wet surface of the pavement. The moustachioed man looks on after him. He thinks of Humphrey Bogart in *The Maltese Falcon*. The man is trying to imitate Sam Spade, he thinks. He looks down at the card in his hand and tells himself that Jacob Little must fancy himself a detective.

Probably just a homeless bum with a screw loose. Hell, I'd play at Bogart if there was nothing else in my life and I had teeth like that. Hell, I'd play at anyone except me.

Spots of rain have struck the card and dribble over the woman's bare body. The man steps back into the dry. He takes up the bottom of his white T-shirt and wipes the wet from her belly and breasts. 'Solace.' He says the name out loud, but for no particular reason.

5

'Don't tell me your name,' Jacob says to the girl curled under his arm. 'I don't want to know your name. Not your *real* name. And shhh, don't tell me one true thing about you. See, you can be anyone with me. Anyone at all. Just make it up. Names can be so binding, don't you think? So limiting. But with me, see, you are limitless.'

A different year, a different, time, a different place. May 2002. The time is 3.17 p.m., and we are at 23 Gunney Drive. A postcard is pushed through a letterbox along with a letter addressed 'To the Home Owner' and another from a bank offering loans. The postcard has a picture of Wells Cathedral on the front and as it drops it somehow flips and lands sunny side down on top of junk mail already pushed through earlier that morning. Convenient for us; we want to read the message on the back. You will recognise the writing. It is the carefully penned back-slanting hand we have already seen in Jacob's green jotter. It says the words, 'Rest assured, Mother, I am in good health and have found a way to live a life somewhat contented. There is no need to search for me any longer.' It is signed with the initials J.L.

And where is he, our Jacob, when this postcard is delivered? I assure you he is not in Wells. He went there only once and that was to purchase and post the abrupt message to his mother. No, when the postcard finally drops through the letterbox of 23 Gunney Drive, Jacob is sitting on a bench beside a canal walkway somewhere in the north of England. He looks a mess. His boots are broken at the seams, there are rags tied around his ankles, he is layered with tattered clothes, most notably a stripy woollen jumper with the hood of a hoodie underneath pulled up over his head. His beard has been left to grow for months, but still it is patchy; areas of pale skin can be seen under the curling, wiry, slightly ginger hair.

One other thing perhaps worthy of note, something you will recognise, is the green cart that is parked next to the bench. The very same green cart that Lucy Westbry nine years in the future will carry up the stairs of Pauper's Inn. Inside there is one box and Jacob's holdall, red and blue. Next to the cart there is a medium-sized artist's canvas facing the pathway. Passing pedestrians will be able to read the words slathered in red paint.

> I AM A HOMELESS ARTIST.
> ALL MONEY GOES TOWARDS
> FOOD, PAINT AND ART SUPPLIES.
> THANK YOU.

Signed in the corner is the name *Wilhelm*.

The May spring sun is high on this day and yet the air is crisp with a coolness. Jacob sits, breaking a poppy-seed bread roll in his hands and pushing pieces between his lips. There are white crumbs in his beard. He chews slowly. At his feet there is a dog, a terrier, mixed breed, almost fox-like in appearance. It sits with its head cocked to one side and its paw raised, begging. Occasionally Jacob will hold out some bread torn from the roll and the dog will gently take it from his fingers.

An elderly couple with arms linked amble in his direction. They fall silent as they approach. Jacob does not look up at them, he keeps his eyes on the jaw-licking canine. The old couple stare at the homeless man – and really, they *do* stare – in a semi trance-like state. They read the words on the canvas, they study the clothes, the dirt, the crumbs in his beard. When a cyclist comes up close behind them, ringing his bell, they both jump. They spin around on their heels and step to one side. Bike, man, helmet, skintight jersey, cycling tights, 100 per cent polyester. Ding ding. He rings his bell again. He calls out, 'Thank you.' He has already passed and is out of sight, under the bridge, around the corner. The bell can be heard in the distance ringing again. The old man grumbles, 'Bloody cyclists,' while the woman presses a hand to her chest. She glances hastily at Jacob, or should I say Wilhelm? They amble on.

2003. A smoky old-man pub, wood-panelled walls, gnarled tables, mismatched furniture. There is a large open fireplace with a small gas fire in its centre burning artificial coals. Jacob is sitting at a rectangular table. A group of five sit with him. They are each drinking pints of locally brewed real ale. Tiddler's Winkle, The Bell-ringing Bear, Pig for Brains. They are talking literature. Why write, is the question at hand? For whom does one write? What *is* writing? And what is literature? But Jacob has drifted from the group discussion, his eyes pulled by the flickering images on the muted television screen above the bar. Scenes from the Iraq War flash up. Frightened faces of civilians, and soldiers carrying guns, and explosions clouding the skies.

'Immortality,' the only woman in the group says. She is mannish in her appearance, with a strong square jaw and deep voice. Her long hair is tied back and fixed with a plain clasp. 'That's what they say, isn't it? If you write, then even after you die, a part of you lives on.'

'I was *born* to write,' says the second in the group. 'It's in my blood. Does that sound silly?'

The third shrugs. 'I write because I have something to say,' he says.

'Real literature,' says the fourth, changing tack, 'is not escapism. Literary fiction is the *real* literature.'

'Why complicate the matter?' says the final fifth. 'I write because I like writing. End of story.'

This group, all talking and no one listening.

'Merton?' The large balding man in a grey, creased, linen blazer leans over the table to tug at Jacob's sleeve. 'Merton, we've lost you there, friend.' His voice is soft with a camp lilt. His face is flushed red with the ever-present embarrassment of self-consciousness. This balding man is the second speaker, who writes because he was *born* to write, it's in his blood; he often feels silly.

The fifth, a young lip-ringed, nose-pierced, goat-bearded man sitting next to Jacob, who writes because he likes writing, end of story, is fiddling restlessly with his beer mat. He follows Jacob's line of sight to the television screen just as footage of the toppling Hussein statue flicks on. 'They say it's about oil,' he says. 'They say this talk of overthrowing dictatorships is a load of bull. It's about oil. It's about money, greed and power. It's about who's got the biggest nuke hidden down their pants.' He taps the edge of his beer mat against the table surface. 'I don't know jack shit about politics, but if the government's involved then when is it not about money and greed and power and big nukes?'

The five faces glance at the television screen. They mutter words like 'so sad', 'awful', and 'what a mess the world is in'. An awkward silence follows. From the next room the clack of a pool cue can be heard striking a white ball, then the clack-clack-clack of yellows and reds ricocheting across the table.

'Merton,' says the mannish woman, 'tell us what you're working on at the moment. You said you had a new project on the go?'

Jacob's attention is finally drawn away from the television. He looks around at the group all sitting at the table, this small band of writers as mismatched as the pub's furniture. '*Expositus vulgaris.*' His voice has the depth that comes after being silent for so long. 'Exposing the everyday.'

'Is that your working title?'

Jacob/Merton does not answer this question. He seems bored by it. He picks up his almost finished pint of ale and turns it in his hand, eyeballing the dark liquid inside. 'Did you know,' he says, 'on my way here this evening I saw a woman on the bus.' He does not look around at his companions as he speaks, his eyes remain on the brown liquid in the glass. 'She was a disabled woman. Fat. Boss-eyed. In an electric wheelchair. Crooked teeth and twisted face. And she was wearing the brightest lime green fleece I've ever seen. She was sitting at the front of the bus – you know, where the seats fold up? So she was travelling backwards, which means she was facing all the other passengers travelling forwards.' The group was nodding. Yes, they could picture the scene. 'Her face was like a squashed pear,' Jacob says. 'Like a pear so ripe that when you pick it out from the fruit basket its soft fleshy skin collapses slightly.' The group are glancing at each other now. They listen with uncertainty. 'I couldn't stop looking at her,' Jacob continues. 'It was that damn lime green fleece she was wearing. It kept catching my eye. And every time I looked at her squashed face and crooked smile I had to pull my attention away. I had to stare at my feet or out of the window – although, damn it, her reflection was always there in that window for my eyes to be drawn towards. And she kept *laughing*. She was with her carer, a black woman wearing a rasta hat, and this carer kept making jokes. And whenever the disabled woman laughed, her mouth stretched open and showed all her squint narrow teeth twisting out from her gums.' Jacob looks around at the awestruck and unnerved faces of his audience. 'I found myself really *fucking* resenting her. Her mushy-pear face, her crooked smile, her fluorescent lime green fleece. And that damned carer making her laugh. I resented them both for drawing attention to their situation when it wasn't *right* for me to stare.'

The balding, born-to-write, slightly camp man with his round face burning red clears his throat and swallows a little nervously. He says softly, 'Merton, you really shouldn't say these things.'

A wry smile lifts one corner of Jacob's mouth. 'No?' He drains the rest of his ale in one short swig. 'I'm only indirectly answering a question.' He sets the pint glass onto the table with a *thuck*. 'That damn lime green woman. She rolled off the bus with the electrics in her wheelchair humming and her carer still making her laugh, laugh, laugh, and you know what I thought? I thought now *that's* where I should be sitting. In that very same position where her wheelchair had just been. Facing a bus-load of everybodies, ugly, gawping, smushy-faced, stinking like a catheter bag and *fucking laughing*, while the rest of the bus, damn them, pretend to look every which way, but never at me.' Jacob is standing now, he is readying himself to leave, he has pulled on his long grey coat. '*Expositus vulgaris,*' he says, 'that's what my project is about. Now if you'll excuse me, I have someone else to be.'

A different year, a different time, a different place, a different name. In 2004 he was Otto, a purple-bearded pagan dabbling in the occult. In 2005 he was theatre fanatic Benny Silverside. In 2006 he was known as both Simeon Lear the historian and Keith the archaeologist. In 2007 he was Isaac Featherstone, Teddy Two-Fingers and Graymalkin the street preacher. In 2008 he was Lambert the Christian and Teza the Buddhist. In 2009 he was Kenny Berk, Lindsay Ray, Trevor Bolter. In 2010 he was philosopher Eric Germain Huber and then later simply Archie the alcoholic.

Rest assured, Mother, I am in good health and have found a way to live a life somewhat contented. There is no need to search for me any longer.

J.L.

And with each different name comes a different obsession.

'Is *that* the epiphany?'

'I don't expect you to understand, Solace.'

'*Understand?* What's there to understand? "Theory of Obsession", my ass, Jacob. It's the biggest pile of bum I've ever heard! So let me get this straight, you're just going to move from place to place pretending to be different people?'

'It's not "pretending".'

'Well yeah, Jacob, I hate to break it to you, but it is.'

*

2011. Elsewhere, dear reader. An old man is sitting at a kitchen table while a woman, much younger than he is (she's in her thirties) with candyfloss pink, ponytailed hair, prepares to make two cups of tea. The old man has white hair and thick eyebrows that tuft into tiny devil horns. He has both hands flat on the kitchen table, his fingers twitch and tap out an inaudible rhythm.

The woman has her back turned to the old man. She sidestep-slides from cupboard to mug to kettle to fridge. She is slim. She is wearing black leggings. She scratches behind her ear where the tight pink ponytail pulls at the fair roots of her hair.

The old man is watching the woman's posterior. He is thinking about his wife and her fleshy thighs. The pink-haired woman is so slim her thighs do not touch. When she bends he can see the short slit, the groove, where her tight leggings hug her genitalia. The words 'second skin' come into his head. Then 'foreskin'. Then he is thinking about his own genitals, his sagging balls, the loss of hair, balding back to prepubescent, and his erection, half an inch shorter than it used to be.

When making tea the woman puts the milk in with the bag before pouring the water. Now the words 'generational differences' form in the old man's head as the electric roar and pop of a stainless steel kettle fills the room. He is the sort of person who stews his tea for three minutes in a pot; milk in jug, sugar in bowl, cups and saucers, spoon. Tea tastes better in a china cup. Never a mug. No, never a mug.

Outside in the garden a man and boy are playing football. They've set up dribbling drills together. The boy has to manoeuvre the ball between rocks and then shoot at the improvised jumper-post goal. Every so often the old man can hear the young boy's voice call for the ball: 'Dad, here, Dad, Dad!' or he can see the boy celebrate scoring with an air-pumping of the fist.

The pink-haired woman sets a mug of tea down in front of the old man. 'Generational differences,' she says. The man pricks his ears, raises his eyebrows. 'My grandma would've killed me if I'd offered her tea in a mug.' She sits down opposite with her own tea and sips through the steaming heat. The bangles on her wrist slide down her arm, clacking together. She has a nose piercing. It glints emerald green in the sunlight. From beneath the short sleeves of her T-shirt the old man can see the snaking black ink of a tattoo.

He smiles and thanks the woman. He feels an urge to explain in a lighthearted way that tea just tastes better in china. But he says nothing. He is a stranger in this house and does not want to sound critical. Instead his eyes search out the ticking of a wall clock. It is an amusing wall clock with all the digits piled at the bottom of its face as though they've been shaken from their number-hooks.

Time out. Time and again. A race against time. A matter of time.

'I don't mean to sound blunt,' says the woman, 'but if you're stuck for conversation then let's talk about Jacob. That's why you're here after all, isn't it?'

Elsewhere, dear reader. 'Elsewhere'. It is an interesting concept. Have you ever stopped to wonder what the world is made up of? Only two things. There is 'Here' and there is 'Elsewhere'. Elsewhere is the far more interesting of the two. Elsewhere is where *everything* happens all at once. It has endless possibilities. 'Here' is tiny in comparison with its limitations of the present; it contains but a thimbleful of actions. But Here is a truism. Elsewhere speculation.

'Nothing is real unless it's observed, Gifford.' An elderly gentleman dressed in tweed stands pontificating next to an open fireplace. He gesticulates, cigar in hand. '*You* know that with all your interest in science. But surely then the question has to be raised that for the universe to exist there must be someone or something "outside" observing it?'

Sitting in a leather armchair, dimly lit by a Tiffany lamp, is Jacob, though you'll notice he looks quite different. His top teeth jut out over his bottom lip and he is thinner and more awkward than ever, unable to make eye contact. 'And that is your argument for the existence of God?' he speaks quietly and with a lisp. 'But aren't *humans* the observers you seek?' He pauses regularly to swallow excess saliva caused by those ugly false teeth. 'The universe exists . . .' pause '. . . because *we* are watching it. And perhaps . . .' pause '. . . *we* only exist because we are watching each other.'

The pink-haired woman sets her own mug down on the kitchen table. 'I don't know where he is, if that's what you want to know.' She turns her face towards the window, to where her son still plays with the ball in the garden. 'I haven't seen Jacob in, what, ten years or more.' The woman strokes her long slim fingers over the mug she is drinking from. It has a Manchester United FC badge printed on its side and the words 'Red Devils' underneath. She strokes the mug absentmindedly as though massaging it for warmth. The old man sitting opposite notices how the index finger circles and caresses the word 'Devils' like a tell-tale tic of the subconscious. 'Better to keep it that way,' she continues. 'There's not a day that goes by when I don't think about him, Mr Benson, but I'll not see him again. Not if I can help it. I hope you can appreciate that.'

6

'I often have a dream,' Jacob tells the girl curled under his arm, 'that I wake up one morning and nobody can see me. Have you ever had that before? Not superhuman invisible, it's more that people just don't believe I'm there any more. I can push a woman in the street and she'll think she's lost her balance. I can talk to a man and he'll flick his hand up to his ear as though my voice is a buzzing fly. It doesn't matter if I kick or scream or tear at the world around me, people continue to believe I'm not there. I don't exist.'

Lucy's shift has ended. It is 10 p.m. and still light. The darker rain clouds have cleared and now the evening sun seeps through the remaining white in little golden pools of light. The edges of the sky are turning pink. The puddles trickle towards the drains. Lucy has walked home; she doesn't live far. She is letting herself in now through the narrow front door that opens onto the stairwell that leads up to the flat. Her mother is sitting on the sofa in the living room, watching television. She looks up when Lucy enters. 'Lucy Lu.'

'Hey, Mum.'

'How's work?'

'Fine.' Lucy goes to the fridge. She takes out some orange juice and drinks it straight from the carton. 'Sal says hi.' Her mother is watching the *EastEnders* omnibus recorded from that afternoon. Lucy swigs some more orange juice before placing it back in the fridge door. 'Sal's finally managed to get a new lodger for the room,' she calls through to her mother.

'That's good.'

Lucy is staring in at the brightly lit fridge shelves. A pack of bacon. A Scotch egg. Some tomatoes. Milk. Orange juice. She is not thinking about the things she is looking at, she is thinking about Jacob, the man she hasn't met yet. Lucy wants to talk about him to her mother, but there is nothing to say. She swings the fridge door closed. It makes a dull *fumph*.

Lucy's mother is sprawled out on the two-seater sofa. She is leaning her elbow on the armrest, her hand propping up

69

her head. Her bare feet are on the cushions and they are curling and uncurling rhythmically in their comfort, toenails painted a shimmering pink. She senses Lucy standing nearby and turns to look up at her. 'You want to sit down, Luce?'

'Nah.'

Her mother points at the television screen. 'Tamwar and Afia have banned their family from attending the wedding ceremony.'

'Oh?' Lucy doesn't care. 'Where's Anya?'

'In the Writer's Block.' Her mother rolls her eyes. 'Tread carefully, Lu. I heard some strange noises coming from there not so long ago.'

The Writer's Block: a converted cupboard at the top of the stairs. It fits a desk, one chair and two shelves of books. A bare lightbulb dangles from its fitting. Papers and notes and quotes and photos hang from strings tied like washing lines from wall to wall. Anya, Lucy's 'other' mother, works here. We can hear her muttering as Lucy approaches the closed cupboard door. 'Ani?' she calls quietly.

The tapping of computer keys stops.

'Just thought I'd say goodnight . . .' says Lucy.

She can hear movement from inside, the chair being pushed back, a shuffling sound. 'Lucy?' The name is whispered through the keyhole. 'Lucy, is that you?'

Lucy smiles.

'If it's you then you must hurry your ear to this keyhole at once; I have something to tell you.'

'It's me, Ani.' Lucy sits herself down, cross-legged, her head resting against the door. She closes her eyes. 'Do you want to tell me a story?'

'No,' says the voice. 'I wish to prophesy.'

'Oh?'

'Yes, listen closely, for I am the Oracle in the Keyhole, and I have seen in a vision that tonight you will have a dream and in that dream you will meet a man. A man with many heads.'

'Sounds weird.'

'Yes. Very weird. There will be ugly heads, angry heads, snooty heads, murderous heads, heads so stinking and foul you'll want to retch. But be prepared, Lucy! For you will fall instantly in love with the central head, the most *beautiful* and *kind* head. He will look at you with his flashing blue eyes and flick his blond princely locks and say to you, 'Lucy, my sweet Lucy . . . where have thou been all my days?' There is a pause. 'Lucy . . . ?' The voice pauses again. 'I don't think you're taking me seriously, Lucy – I can hear you laughing.'

'Oh, Ani . . .'

'Shhh! Now listen carefully, incline your ear, for this tale comes with a warning. Now you've heard the age-old expression, "love is blind", yes? Well indeed, you will experience it, for the deeper you stare into the eyes of the handsome head, the more you will lose sight of the other ugly heads, until very soon you will only be able to see the beautiful princely figure, smiling at you with his warm eyes and rosy cheeks. But woe! Should you ever attempt to kiss your love, the ugly heads will reappear and gnash their teeth and tear your face off!'

'Is this your way of telling me not to rush into anything "hasty", Ani?'

'Shhh!' says the voice. 'There is more to tell. Listen closely, Lucy, for if you wish to win the heart of your prince

71

you must first learn to love all of the other ugly heads, each and every one of them. No easy task! For how do you love such vile and violent creatures that want to gnaw you like an old piece of bone?'

'Anya, you're going to give me nightmares.'

'I pray the nightmares remain only in your dreams, Lu.'

'Aye well, I'd rather not have them at all,' but Lucy is smiling as she says this. 'Goodnight, Ani.' She is on her feet. 'I'll see you in the morning.'

'The Oracle in the Keyhole says goodnight!' calls the voice. 'And the Oracle in the Keyhole says, "I love you and all your many heads".'

The Westbry Family Trio: the three joke together that it sounds like a band. Alison Westbry on the harp strings of Mother, Anya on the bass beats of Other, Lucy Lu on vocals, 'wailing her loves and woes like a blues diva'. But where is the story here? This family is *happy*, this family *works*, they love each other. Someone write in a murder or scandalous love affair! Quick, oh Lord, before our reader loses interest!

Lucy's bedroom is a small converted attic with a skylight. The walls have recently been painted a soft grey; you can still smell the emulsion. The curtains have also been changed from a pastel blue covered in stars and rainbows to a deep red. There are new black shelves fixed to the walls with metal brackets. The shelves are lined with books, ornaments, an oversized alarm clock. On a beanbag there is a pile of teddies that look sat upon and forgotten.

This recent face-lift had been her mother's idea. It had been suggested to Lucy on her sixteenth birthday. 'You know, if you ever feel as though you're too old for rainbows and stars,' she'd said, 'you're more than welcome to redecorate. Any colour you want. I'll give you the money for the paint and a new set of curtains.' Her mother had considered this act of lenience as giving her daughter ample opportunity to express herself. 'It's important, though, isn't it?' she'd remarked to Anya over coffee. 'She's at that age when kids try desperately to make sense of themselves. To figure out where they fit in. That's what they say, isn't it?'

'Do we ever grow out of that stage?' Anya had replied.

Lucy throws herself onto the single bed. She sighs. Then yawns. She turns onto her side, placing her face onto her open palm. Next to her on the pillow is a stuffed rabbit named Wabbit. She reaches out and presses her finger against its nose and says, 'I am your muse. You should love your muse.'

Wabbit stares back with her one plastic beady eye.

'You're supposed to say, *Love is tainted*,' she tells the rabbit. '*Love is imperfect. Love is not good enough for you.*'

Wabbit remains mute. Her face is slightly squashed to one side where she was so often thrust down the side of Lucy's pram in her earliest years.

Lucy stares quietly at Wabbit. She sucks back the saliva that has pooled in the corner of her mouth. How funny that Anya would talk of meeting a man and falling in love, she thinks, for hadn't she met the new lodger at Pauper's Inn? Well, not *met*, as such, but in some way they had connected, through the green jotter. And yet of course the 'central head', the 'prince' in Anya's story was so clearly based on Billy, with his blond hair and blue eyes, that Lucy couldn't help but suspect Anya's hidden morals and warnings.

Lucy is thinking now about sex, about Billy and the way he touched her thigh. She is thinking about her friends at school and how they say it hurts the first time. Ellie Banks has already done it with Graham Cherrington, so she would know.

Lucy is back on her feet. She has clicked shut the door. She begins to undress, letting her clothes drop onto the floor in a heap. On her naked right ankle there are two small red marks where she nicked herself shaving for the first time. She pauses to look at the wounds. Her eyes travel to her pubic hair. She is thinking of the line from the green jotter, though she can't quite remember it. *What virgin would think of her hair there . . . as anything other than natural?*

On her desk there is a mirror. Lucy stands naked in front of it. She is studying her face, her round eyes and cheeks, the colour and shape of her lips. Her fingers trace over her clavicles. She presses together her pointed pyramidal breasts to form a cleavage of sorts. She pouts her lips, leans forward a little. She tries to look 'smouldering', but there is something missing; Lucy can't see it, but she can sense it. What is it? She tries standing in different poses, but not one of them looks 'sexy'. Not really. And then she brings to mind the painting in the jotter, the blonde woman. *Dear Solace . . . it is almost your spitting image, your reflection, don't you think?* Lucy remembers how the woman was pointing towards her left breast, and this Lucy does with a loose wrist. But she can't remember what the other hand was doing. Lucy tries holding her hip, then stroking her belly, then letting her arm hang limply at her side. None of them is right. Eventually she gives up and turns away from her reflection. She steps into her pale pink and white stripy pyjama bottoms left on her bed that morning, and pulls the matching shirt over her head.

1992. We are going back again, dear reader. To another time and another looking glass. It would be three years yet before the infant Lucy Westbry is born, but here is our Jacob Little, thirteen years old. He is kneeling in a bathroom in front of a full-length mirror, his palms pressing against the glass, his fingers spread wide. He is staring with a quiet ferocity into the eyes of his reflection. His thin lips are mouth-muttering words we can barely hear. We should get closer, like they do in a film, zooming in from behind the kneeling boy, closer and closer to focus on the fast-moving lips of his reflection.

'How long would it take to shift shape?

    'How long would it take to shift shape?'

A quiet tapping comes from the frosted-glass window on the bathroom door. 'Jacob?' The sound of his mother's voice breaks the boy's spell. 'Jacob? You've been in there ever such a long time.' Her knocks become louder. 'Jacob?'

Jacob clenches his teeth. He looks at the watch he's placed on the basket of towels.

'Jacob?'

'I'm fine, Mum,' he says. 'I'm doing an experiment.'

On the other side of the door Jacob's mother is leaning

close to the glass to hear her son. A small grey woman with a wide shallow forehead and pointed chin. Nervous looking. She has shadowy eyes set back into her skull and prominent cheekbones. Thin lips. Narrow nose. Her greying hair is dull and limp, cut into a short bob around the ears. Without a smile this woman looks solemn and fretful, and it's the woman's own awareness of this that over the years has left those thin lips with a permanent upward curl to the corners. A fixed slight smile. She is unaware, however, of how this slight smile unnerves many who meet her for the first time. She is unaware even of how it has unnerved her son over the years, who in silent rebellion rarely ever smiles. Like the polar opposite of his mother's lips, his are fixed in a slight curve down.

'What sort of experiment?' His mother is apprehensive. She worries only in part that she's interrupted her son during masturbation; in truth she worries more that he is up to something more disturbing. Mutilating insects? Mutilating himself? Her son is a quiet and pensive teenager. A loner. She believes he's bullied at school but keeps it secret. She's had no evidence of this, but she believes it intuitively. For wasn't she a quiet and pensive teenager? A loner? And wasn't she so often bullied throughout her school years? 'You've been in there for almost two hours, Jacob.'

'Yes,' says Jacob. 'It's an experiment. I'm seeing how long it takes before my face turns into somebody else's face.'

His mother rests her forehead against the glass on the door. 'Oh, Jacob,' she is talking softly. 'I think you should come out now.'

'It *is* possible though, isn't it, Mum? If I look long enough. I think my chin has already become a little more pointed. And my eyes seem a darker brown.'

The following year, when Jacob was fourteen, he wrote a short story for an English assignment. It was about a man who stared at himself for so long in the mirror that his appearance changed. His hair grew long, his face lost weight, his cheekbones became more pronounced, his nose took on a more elegant appearance, until eventually it was a woman staring back at him – a beautiful woman – not himself. The man fell in love with the illusion. He spent hours every night talking to the woman in the mirror, courting her, until eventually he plucked up the courage to kiss the glass. The cool soft lips of the lady: his own lips pressing against the lips of his reflection. A twisted tale of Narcissus.

His teacher read the story out loud in class. A highly accomplished, thought-provoking piece of writing, she said. He was given an A+. A gold star. A first. But that, of course, did not stop the snickering and stares of the other kids in the room. And in the corridors between classes boys would pucker up as they walked past him. They'd make kissing noises. 'Jacob likes snogging himself in the mirror,' they teased.

Jacob burned the story in the garden. His mother had watched him through the kitchen window. She didn't know what it was Jacob was burning, only that he seemed distressed. The pages were full of handwriting. She thought maybe it was a journal, a diary of confessions that he didn't want anyone else to read. Jacob held the flaming pages by the corner, like a boy holding a dead rat by the tail. He let go only when the fire started licking at his own skin. He dropped it into the grass and watched the words turn to a soft grey ash.

Time flies.
The time is ripe.
Time and a half.
Time is against you.
Time heals all wounds.

The pink-haired woman has turned her face into the warm daylight that comes in through the kitchen window. She has closed her eyes. With her elbows on the table she holds her mug of tea with the fingertips of both hands.

'I heard she hanged herself,' she says. 'His mother.'

The old man has finished his tea. He stares into the bottom of his mug where the flotsam of the biscuits he dunked sit, pale and brown. The room is silent apart from the ticking wall clock and from outside the boy calling, 'Dad! Here!' There is laughter followed by the toe-punt of a ball.

'Yes,' says the old man.

The woman nods. She lifts her mug of tea to her lips and drains the lukewarm remains. 'She was an odd sort,' she says. She taps her fingernails against her now empty mug. 'She always thought Jacob was a genius. Did she say the same to you? Every time I met Olivia Little she'd find some way to slip it into the conversation. *Did you know my son's a genius? He has an IQ of 160, you know.* And then, within moments, she'd . . . I don't know . . . she'd lose her senses, become manic. She'd tell me her son was a madman, suicidal, in need of help. She'd get on her knees and beg me to find him.' The tapping of the woman's nails against the mug seem to keep a strange rhythm with the wall clock and its unhinged numbers. It distracts the old man, who is fast becoming fuddled by what he is hearing, so much so that the tapping and ticking become louder than the words.

'You must think I'm heartless,' she says, *tap tap*, 'to not seem to,' *tick*, 'about her death,' *tap tick*. 'You must think me,' *tap tap, tick tap*. 'But please understand,' *tap tap, tick tap*, 'the woman was mad.' *Tap tick, tap tick.*

7

Jacob tickles the girl.

                                The girl squeals.

She slaps at his hands.

The tormented laughter
          reels up and out from inside her chest.

'Oh, would you stop?' she squeals.

                            'Please. Oh *stop*. Please.'

Adult Jacob is asleep. He is lying on that lumpy single mattress in his newly rented room above Pauper's Inn. He is sprawled in an ungainly fashion, wearing only greyish-white Y-fronts. His pasty body is thin, his chest bare apart from a few curling hairs around the nipples. His bones jut from beneath his skin, ribs rising and falling as he breathes. He is lying with one arm curled above his head, the other flung wide. His armpit hair is thick and long. Beneath the underwear his cock bulges, semi-erect. There is a bluish bruise on his left shin, small and circular.

Despite the open window this room smells of cigarettes, alcohol, body odour, slightly of flatulence, with a hint of semen. On the floor next to the bed there is a bottle of whisky, three shots short of empty. There is an ashtray half filled with the stumps of rolled cigarettes; a pouch of tobacco, some papers, a box of filters, a lighter. There are screwed-up pieces of tissue by the sleeping Jacob's feet. And scattered like a deck of cards there are the many printed pictures of *Honeymoon Nude*. Solace.

The contents of the holdall have been spilled across the room. Three shirts. A pair of jeans. A brown T-shirt. An orange plastic bag of socks and underwear. A book with scraps of paper marking its pages. Nietzsche, *Thus Spoke Zarathustra*.

Jacob is using the clothes he wore the day before as a pillow. The green jotter that Lucy read is amongst the pile of clothes. More interestingly there is a new green jotter. It is on the mattress under Jacob's right knee. A leaky pen is nearby. The ink has smeared into the mattress, a stain to join the other stains. Might you like to know what has been written? I could tell you. Or better still, I could show you. Let us go back to the early hours of the morning. Please, allow me.

Bish . . .

    bash . . .

  bosh . . .

It is 3 a.m. Jacob, drunk, is kneeling on the floor, pulling everything out from the red and blue holdall. He is not doing this aggressively, he is only mildly annoyed. He seems to be looking for something, but through poor drunken coordination he does not feel inclined to rummage, it is easier to haul everything out.

The green jotter, the new one, is in his hand. There is a towel beside him and a bottle of all-in-one shampoo and shower gel 'for men'. Still he searches in the bag until his hand closes around a pen. It spots his fingers with bluish-black ink. 'Aw, fuck.' Jacob's head is heavy and seems to sway with its drunken weight. He closes his eyes. Opens them. 'Get up, get up . . .' the words slur from those thin lips. 'Get up, get up, whoever you are . . .' and this seems to make the drunk Jacob laugh. His head flops back, then to the side and then rooouund in a slow circular movement. 'Get up!' he says again, more aggressively. 'Get up, idiot!' He pulls the towel and shower gel into his arms. He clutches the green jotter and pen. He forces himself to his feet and walks – nay, staggers – with a forward-leaning propulsion out of the bedroom, up the hallway and into the bathroom. The door he slams behind him. The sound ricochets like a shot through the house.

Big Sal is asleep. She does not hear it.

'Shhh!' Jacob has dropped the items he is carrying onto the bathroom floor. He is pressing a finger to his lips. 'Shhh!' He moves to the sink, a solid surface. He grips. Onto. Its cool edges. He peers at his reflection in the mirrored medicine cabinet. Head cocked, shoulders hunched. 'Damn it,' he says to his reflection. 'Damn it an' . . . damn you, Solace.' His lips curl into a pained grimace. Jacob turns on the tap, wets his hand with the cold water, rubs it over his face. He drinks. Leaning a little too close, he clashes his teeth against the metal. 'Fuck!' He drinks more water. Splashes his face. 'Bath,' he says to the face in the mirror. 'Bath.' And so he sways to the tub. 'Bath.' The word is continually repeated as Jacob turns the taps. No water comes out. No hot. No cold. 'Bath,' he drawls. He is frowning down at the enamel tub as though it has insulted him. He tries the taps again. 'Damn thing . . . plumber . . . fat woman . . .'

Jacob picks up the green jotter and the leaky pen and climbs into the bath regardless of the lack of water. He lies there fully clothed, staring up at the walls, the peeling paint, the cobweb in the corner stretching down to the shower curtain rail. There are little black bodies of dead flies wrapped up and rotting in that old dusty grey web.

Jacob begins to write. Not fluently. He seems to struggle with the words – after all, he is. Ridiculously. Drunk. *I have lived here before.* He stops after this sentence. A pause to inwardly hiccup. He glances all around him, then continues writing. Every sentence requires the same effort. The words are slowly forced onto the paper.

I have lived here before. In another city
                                    perhaps,
but I recognise without a doubt these walls, peeling
PUTRID pink in colour, black lumped with damp and
mould. And these ill-
                    fitted frosted
windows. And the cracked full-length mirror. FUCK.
This toilet, this sink, this BATH with its dirty grey ring
of limescale and chipped fucking enamel. This dusty
laminated tile flooring. Wood effect.
        It's the same.
                ALWAYS THE SAME.
I needn't look in the corners. I know there will be hair
and dust forming clumps.
And there will be that
thick layer of grey
running all along the skirting of the room.
I can feel the sticky grit of mouthwash remains
CONGEALING
        amid dust
on top of the mirrored cabinet
above the sink,
and I haven't even reached my finger for it yet.
                                    I will
of course.
It will be confirmation that YES,
I am here again.
        Moved city but not moved on.
The same. Always the same.
Just as Solace said it would be.

Sitting in the empty bathtub, Jacob's drunken head wobbles on his neck. His body rocks slightly. His movements jerk as he attempts to find his. Centre. Of. Gravity. 'Damn you, *demon*,' he gasps. 'Damn you, hellion of the night! Sneaking into my loneliest loneliness . . .' With his right hand he has taken hold of his left wrist. He is staring at it closely. His thumb runs across a small scar the length and width of a razor blade. 'The same . . .' the drunk Jacob mutter-slurs into his wrist. 'Always . . . the same. Just as you said it would be.'

It is 1 p.m. the following afternoon. A fly has come in through the bedroom window and is buzzing about. Four smaller flies flitter around and land on the ceiling. Outside the sky is clear and there is a breeze, cooler than the day before. You can hear the sound of passing cars from the street below, a distant siren, the squawk of gulls.

The fly lands on Jacob's leg. It crawls up the inside to where the right knee bends. Jacob's leg twitches away from the tickling sucker feet of the fly, a jerk that whisks the little black body back into flight.

Downstairs, Big Sal is in the kitchen, frying bacon on an electric stove. The spit and sizzle and smell fill the room. In the corner, mounted on the wall, there is a small black and white monitor linked to a CCTV camera. It points towards the door of the pub and takes in part of the bar and most of its floor space. She can see Alex, her part-time barman, leaning with elbows on the counter flicking through a magazine. Big Sal takes the frying pan off the heat and starts buttering her bread. From the bar she can hear voices. Her eyes glance up at the monitor. Lucy, dressed in school uniform, black trousers and white polo shirt, is talking to Alex. Big Sal pinches the greasy hot bacon with her fingers and places it on the buttered bread.

'Aye,' she calls out into the corridor when she hears Lucy's footsteps. 'I see ye, Lucy Westbry.'

'You spying on me, Sal?'

Big Sal smiles and nods towards the monitor. 'Pass the ketchup, love.'

Lucy is in the kitchen. She opens the cupboard door by her head.

'Seems I can't keep ye away,' Sal says to the girl. 'Comin' round here on your lunch hour now, eh?'

Lucy passes the fat woman the squeezy bottle of red. 'I left my book,' she says. The book is by the microwave. Lucy skips over to it, picks it up, fans through the pages and waves it at Sal.

'I thought that must be yours,' Sal says.

'*Wuthering Heights*,' Lucy says.

'For school?'

'No. Just . . .' she shrugs, 'cos.'

Sal is sitting now at the kitchen table. She is tucking in to her bacon butty. 'Never read it.' She nods towards the packet of bacon left open on the kitchen unit. 'Help yourself if you're hungry, my lass.'

Lucy is pleased. She's been looking for a way to prolong the visit.

Big Sal gestures at Lucy to hand her the book. The corner of the cover is torn and the spine creased. Sal reads the back. *Cathy and Heathcliff have been inseparable ever since they were children. Growing up together . . . blah blah . . . nothing can break the fierce bond between them*

. . . blah blah . . . *passionate nature . . . fatal decision . . . violence . . . destruction . . . revenge.*

'It's about love,' says Lucy. She is watching Sal reading the blurb. The soft sizzle and smell of cooking bacon once more in the air.

'Huh,' says Sal. 'That's the one word they haven't used on the back.'

'Well, they don't tell you Cathy's a bitch and Heathcliff's a thug either, but that's the way it is.'

'Sounds like you dinna think much of it.'

'The opposite,' Lucy says, flipping the frying meat. 'I love it. I'm bored of reading novels where the heros are so *perfect* and the love is so . . .' She circles the greasy spatula in the air, searching for the right word. 'You know . . .'

Sal's lips are wrapped around her sandwich, her teeth tearing another bite of bacon. As she pulls away, a gloop of ketchup is left in the corner of her mouth. She wipes it with a finger and pops the finger between her lips. 'Romantic?' she suggests. Her mouth is full yet she pushes the word out.

Lucy isn't sure if 'romantic' was the word she was looking for. She remains quiet for a moment, staring into the spitting pan. Her mind strays away from love to the smells that she knows will cling to her school uniform. She will sit in her afternoon classes smelling of bacon. It will be on her during double art and German. *Entschuldigung, ich rieche nach Speck.*

She turns off the hob and puts together her sandwich. Two slices of bacon, a squirt of ketchup. She presses the pieces of white flimsy bread together. 'Predictable,' she says suddenly. The word has come to her. 'In books and films love is always so *predictable*. But not in this one.' She is sitting at the table now and nods towards *Wuthering*

Heights. 'The love between Cathy and Heathcliff is raw, obsessive. It's unstoppable. Uncontainable. It *traps* them. It's more like *torture* than the soft, squidgy, predictable love you read about in other books.'

'It doesn't sound very pleasant.'

'It's not pleasant,' Lucy says. 'It's painful.' She quietly picks up the book and fans through the pages. She chews her mouthful of food. Swallows. With a page selected she tells Sal to listen and begins to read.

*'I cannot express it; but surely you and every body
have a notion that there is, or should be, an existence
of yours beyond you. What were the use of my creation if I were entirely contained here? My great
miseries in this world have been Heathcliff's miseries,
and I watched and felt each from the beginning; my
great thought in living is himself. If all else perished,
and he remained, I should still continue to be; and if
all else remained, and he were annihilated, the
Universe would turn to a mighty stranger. I should not
seem a part of it . . . I am Heathcliff – he's always,
always in my mind . . .'*

Lucy puts the book down. She has read it well. With an air of drama.

There is a silence between the pair . . .

And then Big Sal begins to laugh. A boisterous guffaw. 'I'm sorry, my love . . .'

The corner of Lucy's mouth rises into an uncertain smile. She isn't sure whether Big Sal is laughing at her or at the reading. Either way, she doesn't understand the joke.

'It's just . . .' Her laughter pushes the breath out of her. She is wheezing with chuckles. 'It's just I canna imagine me sayin' anything like that about my Bev.' She tries it out loud. 'I *am* Beverley – he's always, always in my mind . . .' She laughs again, so much so that small tears squeeze out from the corners of her eyes and she wipes them away with a finger.

Lucy is smiling, but not laughing.

'Och, dinna mind me,' Sal says. 'Whack the kettle on, my love, let's have a cup o' tea.'

Lucy is back on her feet, brushing crumbs from her hands onto her black trousers. She thinks of Bev as she checks the kettle has enough water and switches it on. She imagines Bev working on the rigs and wonders when he is next due leave. She doesn't like him. Never has done. Meathead is what she calls him. *I am Meathead – Meathead is always, always in my mind*. Big Sal is right, you couldn't say such things about Beverley. And this makes Lucy sad. For Sal.

'So, if you don't mind me askin',' Sal interrupts her thoughts, 'havin' no' read the book, what's the problem?'

'The problem?' Lucy is dropping teabags into mugs.

'Aye, well, if they love each other so much, why no' just crack on and be together? What's the fuss?'

'Oh,' says Lucy, turning towards the fridge. 'Well, Cathy ends up marrying someone else.' As she says it something on the fridge door catches her eye. Sticking out from beneath a small star magnet is the picture of the blonde woman from the green jotter, Solace, nudely pointing inwards at herself. The sight of it freezes Lucy. She pulls the card from beneath the magnet.

'Lucy?'

The girl turns.

'Why?' Sal asks.

'Why what?'

'Why did she marry someone else?'

'Oh.' Lucy taps the card against her hand. 'For money,' she says. 'Linton is rich and well educated. Heathcliff has nothing.' She shrugs. 'Told you Cathy was a bitch.' She holds the card up to Sal. 'Where did you get this?' she asks.

'Jacob, the new lodger.'

'He gave it to you?'

'He's looking for some woman, an ex-girlfriend o' his. She looks like that. Apparently.'

'Oh.'

'Know anyone who looks like that?'

Lucy shakes her head. She notices how the woman's left hand in the painting is resting lightly above her navel, fingers brushing her skin. She seems a little awkward standing there, Lucy thinks. A little self-conscious. She hadn't noticed it the first time she'd seen the painting, but now, in the bright kitchen light, without the words from the jotter written underneath . . .

'Luuuucy,' Sal is cooing her name.

Lucy blinks over at Big Sal sitting at the square table.

'You're away with the fairies, lass.'

'Oh,' says Lucy. The sound hangs in the air after it leaves her lips. She is suddenly and strangely aware of how much she's used that 'nothing' word in a short space of time. Oh, oh, oh. She says it again, softer, as though it were an echo of the former 'Oh,' though this time she continues her sentence, 'I was just thinking about art. We're doing

90

a project on painting the nude.' This is a lie. In class they are painting still-life. 'Do you mind if I take this?' Lucy flaps the card in the air. 'As part of my study?'

'On ye go, lass.' Sal seems indifferent. 'I think it's odd lookin', myself.'

During this conversation, or the first part at least, the moment where Lucy enters the kitchen and asks Big Sal, 'You spying on me?' There, at this point, Jacob is beginning to stir. He is waking up. And while Lucy is slapping slices of cold meat into the frying pan, talking to Sal about the book and cooking her lunch, Jacob is pulling the brown T-shirt over his pasty body, a pair of jeans onto his legs, rooting around for some socks in that orange plastic bag. As Lucy is circling the greasy spatula in the air, Jacob shuffles towards the bathroom. 'Love is so . . . you know . . .' and Jacob unbuttons his jeans. 'Romantic?' He pisses into the toilet, head back, staring at the ceiling above him. He can smell the bacon wafting up the stairs, down the hallway and through the open door of the bathroom. He sighs. '*Predictable*,' Lucy says with sudden conviction. Jacob shakes. Spots of urine flick onto the toilet seat and onto the floor. He studies his face in the mirror. Grimaces. He looks hungover. His pupils are tiny black dots, his skin dark underneath his eyes. He rubs a hand over his patchy beard before running the tap and splashing his face with cold water. By the time Lucy has put together her sandwich and taken the first bite, Jacob has finished brushing his teeth with the squashed bristles of a greying toothbrush and left the bathroom. He returns to his bedroom and collects his long coat. He is walking down the stairs just as Lucy chews, swallows and says to Sal, 'Listen to this.' Jacob stops at the bottom of the stairway. He listens. He leans slightly to peer round the corner. The kitchen door is open and Lucy is sitting at the table. Watch her face, dear reader, the changing expressions as she recites. She does not simply say the words, she acts them. Her eyes are wide, part panic-stricken, part begging as she says the words '. . . surely you and every body have a notion that there is, or should be, an existence of yours beyond you.' Frowning with aggressive sincerity as she talks of misery, perishing, annihilation. Desperate, almost fearful, as she says those words, 'I *am* Heathcliff – he's always, always in my mind . . .' Quite the actor, our Lucy Westbry.

And then comes Big Sal's guffaw.

Jacob slips across the hallway and into the bar while Lucy's back is turned. She is checking the weight of the kettle and picking two mugs from the mug-tree.

In the corner of the kitchen where that little black and white monitor is mounted, we can see the new lodger, Jacob Little, enter the screen. He stops near Alex, the barman, and nods a greeting. They exchange a few words. Alex has his hand on the magazine, midway through turning a page. The old monitor flickers. Neither Big Sal nor Lucy notice the exchange between lodger and barman; they are not watching the camera, they are talking about the book. The voices of the two men are drowned by the boiling kettle.

Lucy has spotted the card pinned to the fridge. At this exact moment Jacob pulls an identical card from his jacket pocket. He hands it to Alex who is now standing up straight, the magazine temporarily forgotten. Their movements are jerky on the screen.

'Where did you get this?' Lucy holds up the card.

'Jacob, the new lodger.'

'He gave it to you?'

'He's looking for some woman, an ex-girlfriend o' his. She looks like that. Apparently.'

'Oh.'

'Know anyone who looks like that?'

Lucy shakes her head.

On the monitor, Jacob is leaving the pub. Alex watches him, the card still in his hands. Though the monitor is poor we can just make out the image of the *Honeymoon Nude*, or at least her ghostly shape and wispy hair. A pale spirit of a figure on a shadowy background. When the door swings shut and Jacob can no longer be seen, Alex looks down at the painting in his hands.

'I think it's odd lookin', myself,' Sal says.

And Lucy's eyes swing up towards the monitor.

8

Daylight is shining through the tiny pinprick holes in the faded brown curtains, peppering the limp material with bright, pretty specks. 'Like star constellations,' the girl says. 'I like that,' and she shifts a little onto her back so she can see it better. 'Even something so obviously ugly has its element of beauty,' she says.

There is a cafe across the road from Pauper's Inn. You might remember it from before. Piccalitos. It sounds Italian, but the decor is American with bright red PVC eating booths and neon signs on the walls saying ENJOY, WELCOME, SMILE. It sells panini and freshly filled baguettes and homemade burgers with chunky potato wedges. There is a girl behind the counter wearing a half-apron and a red polo shirt with Piccalitos sewn above her left breast. Her hair is tied up into a ponytail. She is leaning back against the unit and the massive espresso machine, examining her nails. Her lips move as she sings quietly along to the radio.

Outside there are two women lounging with a frappuccino and a skinny latte. They seem in good humour, talking casually and smiling into the sun. They have pulled the small round table away from the shade of the building. The girl behind the counter looks up when one of the women – the one drinking the frappuccino – laughs raucously, tossing back her head and touching her friend lightly on the shoulder. The girl is still mutter-singing along with the radio. Her eyes leave the two women and follow the backs of passing pedestrians. A man stops, looks at the menu, shades his eyes as he presses his face close to the glass to look in. The girl looks back at her nails.

Enter Jacob, grey-skinned and unshaven. The girl glances up when she hears the sound of feet on lino and a voice cracked with phlegm say, 'Good morning.' He clears his throat and tries again. 'Good morning,' but the young barista is already grimacing. She can smell old cigarettes and alcohol. She stands up straight, ready to serve, but her face is not open or friendly as it usually is. She doesn't smile at the man in front of her.

'What can I get ye?' she asks.

Jacob, his hand trembling slightly, sets a five-pound note on the counter.

'I wonder if I might have some change,' he says. 'For the phone box.'

The girl raises an eyebrow. She is wondering how it is this man doesn't have a mobile. 'I'm afraid we canna open the till wi'out a sale,' she drawls, her accent thick. She tells herself the man must be a tramp. He certainly *looks* like a tramp. She feels for her own mobile in her pocket.

'Right.' Jacob looks above the girl's head at the chalkboard menu. 'I'll have a coffee then.'

'To take away?'

'Yes.'

'Milk?'

'Black. One sugar.'

'The sugar is just on the side there.' The girl nods over to the little containers stuffed with sachets of white and brown sugar; another container filled with stirring sticks. He seems too polite for a tramp, she thinks. Maybe he's been mugged? It doesn't matter, she's already decided she doesn't like him and doesn't want to help. There's something odd about him. Uncomfortable. Awkward. The girl moves off to make the coffee, twisting levers, pushing buttons, letting out steam from the big metal coffee-making machine. She glances back at the man. He is pulling the collar of his coat away from his neck. Weird, she thinks. Why wear a coat on a day like this? Their eyes meet briefly. Both look away.

The two women outside are also intrigued by the odd man in the long coat. They are leaning back in their seats, peering through the window. When Jacob turns his face towards them one woman looks quickly away, while the other narrows her eyes and looks all the more determinedly. Jacob shuffles his feet. He places both hands on the counter. He looks at the saucer with its handwritten sign requesting tips. 'We don't pay our staff nearly enough . . .' it says. There are a few coins inside.

'Here y'are.' The girl places a cardboard cup of black in front of Jacob. 'One eighty, then.' And Jacob releases the five-pound note he'd pinned to the counter with a finger.

'Will tens and twenties do ye?' She drills the sale through the till. Jacob looks at her strangely, as though he doesn't know what she's talking about. 'For the phone,' she says, as the drawer pops out and strikes her lightly on the stomach.

'Oh, yes,' he says. 'Thank you.'

The girl nods. She hands him a fistful of change.

'Goodbye,' Jacob says.

'Yeah,' the girl forces a smile against her will, 'bye.'

Outside, Jacob stops briefly. He looks up and down the street, one hand holding the coffee, the other hand rattling the change he poured into his jacket pocket. It's a shame he's stopped here at this moment. It's a shame because it's given the two women sipping their coffee an opportunity to allow their prickly distaste of the man to develop into snide curiosity. His hesitation allows them to speak.

'Excuse me.' It is the glaring woman drinking the frappuccino. 'Excuse me, hello? You there . . .' Jacob doesn't turn. 'Skinny man with the floppy hair.' Frappuccino has a sneering look of girlish glee about her. When Jacob eventually turns to look her way, she nudges her friend, who has an expectant smile curling her thick lips. 'If you don't mind us asking, why are you wearing that ridiculous coat on this scorching hot day?' Skinny Latte giggles at her friend's nerve and encourages her with a knee-poke. 'I mean, you're obviously *uncomfortable*, so why don't you take it off?'

Jacob says nothing at first. He simply looks at the pair.

Frappuccino is a brunette with a big bust and a hooked nose. Skinny Latte is rotund, blonde, thick-lipped and wide-mouthed. Both are in their mid- to late thirties and heavily made up; both are sporting large beaded necklaces and hooped earrings. Sneering Frappuccino wears a stripy sailor's top and high-belted denim shorts. Plump Skinny Latte wears black leggings and a long, baggy, sequinned T-shirt pulled over her behind as though it's a skirt.

'I need this jacket,' Jacob replies finally, 'to hide my enormous erect penis.'

The two women's faces drop from teasing smiles to looks of disgust. 'Is that supposed to be funny?'

'That's disgusting.'

'You pervert!'

Jacob walks off.

Elsewhere. More specifically, a flat in the south of England. More specifically still, the very same flat Jacob stormed out of eleven years ago. There is a man sitting on a sofa watching daytime television. His name is Michael. He is Caucasian, early thirties, completely bald. Not a bad-looking chap by all accounts. Average height, not overweight, he has the correct body mass index of 175. He has prominent facial features and dark eyes that his girlfriend used to say – when they first started dating – were 'dreamy'. I won't describe him in much more detail as he is wholly and completely irrelevant to the telling of this story apart from two occasions. After these two scenes, you will not read about him again, nor, I'm sure, ever think about him. Poor Michael. But he is just one of life's many small encounters that we experience and then promptly forget.

SCENE ONE: Michael sitting on the sofa. He has one arm resting over the top of his bald head, the other hand over his crotch. The changing light and colour of the television screen can be seen flitting over Michael's face as the programme switches camera angle. He is watching a show about the world's deadliest creatures. '*Warning to all women. Do not kiss! This isn't the kind of frog that will turn into a prince! The poison dart frog carries enough neurotoxin to kill ten humans . . .*'

The front door opens and in spills Michael's girlfriend, carrying several bags of food shopping. She looks hot and flustered from climbing the stairs. 'Michael,' her voice is sharp and irritable, 'I've been trying to ring you.'

'Oh.' Michael quickly extracts his mobile phone from his trouser pocket. Three missed calls. 'I'm sorry,' he says. 'It was on silent.'

'Well, *why* is it on silent?' His girlfriend is dumping bags on the kitchen unit. 'What's the point in having it on *silent*?'

Michael is on his feet. 'I had a meeting with the boss yesterday.'

'Yesterday morning. You didn't think to switch it off *silent* after that?'

'Well . . . no.' He is moving towards the open door to the kitchen where he can see his girlfriend viciously unpacking carrier bags. The landline telephone starts to ring. Michael ignores it. 'Do you need a hand?'

'Oh no, Michael, I'm absolutely *fine*. I've managed so far on my own, I think I'll manage to finish the rest, don't you?'

Michael rubs his face with his hands. The landline still rings. *Brrrp. Brrrp.* 'Here,' he says, 'why don't you let me unpack the rest? I'll make you some tea.'

'Just . . . leave it alone, Michael. This kitchen is too small for both of us.'

Michael returns to the sofa. He slumps back into the soft cushions. The flickering lights of the television screen return to his empty face. The phone still rings. Three more times. *Brrrp. Brrrp. Brrrp.* Then stops. Under Michael's right eye a nerve begins to twitch.

'What,' his girlfriend hollers from the kitchen, 'are you completely incapable of answering a phone even when it *does* ring now?' And so ends scene one.

*

Jacob leaves the phone box. He pauses momentarily outside the booth, hands in his pockets. A woman out walking her Jack Russell passes by. Her eyes glance over Jacob, then away, then back again. She recognises the man in the long coat standing by the public telephone box. She doesn't know from where. She smiles when their eyes meet and Jacob nods his head in greeting. The woman returns the nod. She says, 'Lovely morning.' Jacob agrees. The woman bows her head to break eye contact. She mutters, 'Come on, Charlie,' to her dog and tugs a little at the lead.

Jacob begins to walk back the way he came but stops short when he sees the two women at the cafe still sitting at their table outside. The brunette also notices Jacob and nudges her friend. They fix him with identical looks of disdain. Jacob promptly turns into an alleyway.

The route he has taken leads out into a small playground. We have been here before. It is the park we walked past only last night. Now it is empty of youths and young children. The rusty swing remains unswung and the seesaw silent of squeaks and creaks. It is hauntingly quiet and yet almost humming with its own potential movement and sound. Jacob pauses on seeing the empty park. His eyes focus on one of its benches.

This park is surrounded by blocks of flats and narrow offshoot alleyways. It is sheltered from the wind and in part from the sun. Jacob sits on a bench in the shade. He pulls out a piece of scrap paper from his pocket and stares at it. There is an address scrawled across it and a telephone number.

Over by one of the alley walls there is a young girl. Ten years old. Blonde hair cropped short. Dirt is smeared across her chin. There are grazes on both her white knees. She is wearing grey shorts with grass stains on the bum. Her long white socks are pushed down around her ankles. She has a pair of tatty plimsolls on her feet. She looks like a boy.

Jacob has not seen this girl, but the girl has seen Jacob. She is peering over at the strange man sitting alone in the empty park. The young girl presses her fingers against the stone wall, feeling into its cracks. She is making an absentminded repetitive noise under her breath, 'Chu chu chu chu . . .' like the noise young children make when they play at war games. Her fingers pull at the crumbling lime mortar and moss. She watches as the strange man wearing the long coat closes his eyes and allows his head to flop back. 'Chu chu chu chu,' the girl whispers. And then stops. She pushes out her bottom lip. Just as she does so a larger piece of mortar comes away from underneath her fingers and falls with a small shower of dust to the ground. She gasps at the noise and hurriedly presses her body against the wall as the strange man turns his attention towards her.

Nothing happens.

The young girl can smell the fusty moss and mortar in amongst the stone. The wall is cold against her cheek. Perhaps the man didn't see her, she thinks. She pushes her whole body against the wall, as flat as she can make it. She feels the hard surface on her chest and her thighs and her 'secret bits'.

If I was a superhero I'd be able to walk through walls. I'd be able to fly. I'd be able to turn invisible. And I'd be so clever I wouldn't have to go to school. That's how it would be if I was a superhero.

She peers around the edge of the wall to spy on the man. He is still there. Sitting silently.

If I was a superhero Mum wouldn't have to work any more and Grandma wouldn't be sick and me and God would hang out showing each other tricks, like who could throw stones the furthest or fly faster than an aeroplane. I wouldn't have to pretend to be best friends with Mary McInnes any more and I could pinch Daniel Prophet back three times as hard and make him cry.

The young girl clears her throat. She wants the man to look at her again, but he doesn't. He's too busy staring at his hands. The girl kicks the broken piece of mortar out from the alleyway into the open. Still the man doesn't look up.

'Chu chu chu chu . . .' The girl makes her noise. She cocks her head to one side to observe the stranger on the bench. She wonders how much trouble she'll be in at school if she goes back late. Would the teachers tell her mum? She continues making her noise, but louder this time. She wants the man to look up.

He doesn't.

The girl glances around the playground. Now she makes a new sound whenever her eyes fall across an object. Roundabout. Zzzip. Swing. Zzzip. Seesaw. Zzzip. Climbing frame. Zzzip. Her laser vision rests on the slide. Zzzip. It has a roof shelter. Yes, the perfect hiding place. And so her feet are thrown into sudden motion. She runs fast, jumping the sandpit, across the loose bark, past the swing, flying up the slide, her plimsolls slapping hard on the metal and the noise smacking from wall to wall, echoing up and down the alleyways. Zzziiip!

She's not supposed to talk to strangers. Her father tells her the world is full of bad people who want to do bad things. She wonders whether this man is one of those people. One of the baddies. The young girl clears her throat.

'Excuse me . . .'

The man does not look up.

'Excuse me . . . Mister . . .' Her dad also tells her Uncle Ronnie is a vampire and eats little children if they don't go to bed on time. 'Excuse me . . . You over there . . .' Her dad must think she's *really* stupid. 'Hey!'

The man looks up.

'Are you a paedophile?'

'I'm sorry?'

'A paedophile,' the girl repeats.

The man is silent.

'Dad says I should be careful,' the girl continues. 'He says the world is full of rapists and kidnappers and murderers. And paedophiles.'

'I see,' says the man.

The girl suddenly ducks from view behind the wood panelling. She presses her eye up to a spy-hole to study the man in secret. He looks hungry, she thinks. And sad. And lonely. He looks like he doesn't have many friends. Temporarily she forgets about the man to pick at a scab on her shin and think about her mother's 'down days', when she comes home from school and finds her sitting on the sofa, in the dark, with shoulders slumping forward, her eyes staring out, full of nothing. The same way this man is sitting now.

Her eye returns to the spy-hole. 'You look depressed,' she announces.

These words seem to have a strange effect on the man. He sits up straight, hands on lap, ears pricked. He is suddenly very alert. 'What did you say?' He searches keenly for the girl hiding behind the wood panelling.

'You look . . .' the girl presses her lips against the hole and speaks loud and clear, 'depressed.'

The man spots the spy-hole. 'Come out,' he says. 'Let me see you.'

'No.'

'Why not?'

'Because you haven't answered my question.'

'What question is that?'

The girl presses her lips against the spy-hole once more. 'Are. You. A. Paedophile?'

'No,' says the man.

'A rapist?'

'No.'

'Kidnapper?'

'No.'

'Murderer?'

'No.'

The girl pauses. She screws up her mouth as she tries to think. 'Well, what about a *thief*?' she asks finally.

'I'm not a thief,' says the man. 'I'm not anything.'

'Well then,' says the girl, 'I'm allowed to speak to you.' She reaches over to the fireman's pole beside the slide's ladder and grapple-hooks her body close. She slides jerkily, skin squeaking against metal, her feet quickly padding down on the loose bark covering the play area. 'My name's Max,' she says. It is not her real name, it is the name she has chosen for herself. Last week she and some other girls at school decided to create a secret club together and everyone had to pick a new nickname. There was Bubble and Pinky and Kitten and Sweets. She'd wanted 'Max', but all the girls laughed. 'You can't have Max. That's a *boy's* name!'

'If I can't be called Max then I don't want to play.'

'This isn't a *game*, Lizzy. This is a *secret club*.'

They'd argued. Her temper had flared. She'd spat on one of the girl's shoe buckles and announced she didn't want to be part of their stupid secret club anyway. 'Sounds babyish to me.' At lunchtime she'd fought with the brother of the girl she'd spat on. He was a year older than her. He came up to her when she was watching the year sevens play touch rugby and without warning pushed her over. She quickly got to her feet and kicked him in the shins. He smacked her on the shoulder. She smacked him squarely on the jaw. They'd wrestled, teeth gnashing, arms flailing, legs kicking, and both ended up in the headmaster's office.

'Max,' says the man on the bench.

The girl, we will call her Max and not Lizzy, is watching the man carefully. She is looking for hesitation or an expression that might suggest the man disbelieves her. She can feel the lie herself, creeping through those tiny hairs that grow all over her body. It's making her itch. It's always like this, whenever she lies. She feels so very different that she's certain markings must appear all over her face and a flashing sign above her head with the word 'LIAR' blazing out.

But the man simply says, 'Pleased to meet you.'

He sounds different, Max thinks. His words are pronounced carefully. He doesn't drop his 't's. Max's mum is forever telling her off for such lazy speak. Especially at church. God frowns upon those who speak sloppily.

'You have a funny accent,' Max tells the man.

'Thank you,' he says.

Max laughs.

'Why are you laughing?' asks the man.

'Because you're not supposed to say "thank you".'

'No?' The man's eyes are bright now. 'What is it I'm supposed to say?'

Max screws up her lips. 'Well,' she says, 'I don't know everything yet. I'm only ten.'

It is now the man's turn to laugh. The corners of his mouth curl upwards, only slightly, and a short chuckling sound slips from between his thin lips. Jacob. Laughing.

'Oh,' says Max, she feels emboldened by the man's good humour, 'you also have funny teeth.'

'Yes,' replies the man. 'My teeth serve as a reminder to ten-year-olds never to forget to brush daily.'

Max stares. She is thinking about brushing her teeth. She is standing by a lamppost, her arms linked around the metal pole. Now she begins to swing herself round. 'I brush my teeth every day,' she tells the man. 'Once in the morning and once in the evening.'

'Keep up the good work,' he says.

Max stops swinging. She leaves the lamppost to join the man on the bench. She immediately adopts the same pose as him, sitting with back straight and hands on lap. She can smell the stale smoke from the man's clothes and wrinkles up her nose. She does not comment on this, however (that would be rude).

'You haven't told me *your* name.' She allows her legs to swing.

'No,' the man says. 'I haven't.'

'Why not?'

'Because you haven't asked.'

'Well,' Max says, 'I'm asking now.'

But the man is quiet.

'So?' Max asks. 'What's your name?'

And then the man does a very strange thing. He sighs, loudly and at length. His body slumps against the back of the bench. His arms go limp, his hands slide from his lap.

'My name . . .' he mutters, but follows it with nothing.

'What,' Max asks, 'you don't know your own name?'

The man shrugs.

'But everyone has a name,' Max says.

'I've had many,' the man says. 'But none of them are right.'

'So make one up!' It seems so simple to the ten-year-old. She almost wants to tell the sad-looking man that her name isn't Max at all. It's Elizabeth Mary Duda. The surname is Polish. They make fun of her at school, singing that silly rhyme, 'Lizzy wants to be a boy, doo-daa, doo-daa.' But Max doesn't care. She likes the name. She likes the idea that her great-grandparents were from another country far away. She's seen Poland on the map. She's memorised the countries around it. Germany, Czech Republic, Slovakia, Ukraine, Belarus, Lithuania. One day she will go there. She will go to all those countries. She'll travel the world.

But she doesn't tell the sad man her real name. Why? Because the man believes she is a boy – Max is sure of it. He's not treating her the same way adults treat girls. He's talking to her differently. He would have told her by now how pretty her face is if only he knew she was a girl. Or he'd ask her why she's so mucky. That's not very ladylike, he might say. It's not very *nice* to be so dirty. But he doesn't say these things. He thinks Max is a boy and boys can be as mucky as they please. This excites young Max, it pleases her, she doesn't want it to stop.

Max wriggles on the seat next to the man. She is getting restless after sitting still for so long. 'Do you want me to help you?' she asks. 'I can help you find your name.'

The man pauses before answering. 'Yes. I'd like that very much.'

So she jumps to her feet. 'Let me think,' she tells the man. She begins to pace around the edge of the park, hands clasped firmly behind her back. She sucks her bottom lip in concentration. 'I'm a private detective,' she says. 'Your name has gone missing and I'm going to help find it.' She picks up some loose bark from the ground. Discards it. She touches the metal slide. The climbing frame. The seesaw.

'Are you Sherlock Holmes?' the man asks.

'No,' says the girl. 'I'm Max. I'm a private detective. And I can walk through walls and turn invisible.' She spins the roundabout. She pushes the swing. She spots something grey lying in amongst the bark and at once leaps for it. Whatever this 'something' is, she hides it from view. She studies it privately, peeking at her secret through cupped hands. 'Yes!' She turns with a cry of jubilation and approaches the nameless man on the bench. 'It's a clue,' she says and holds out her hand. Balancing on her palm is a stone.

The man picks it up. He peers at it. 'A stone,' he says.

'That's right,' Max says.

'Does that mean my name is Stone?'

'Perhaps,' says Max. 'I'm not sure. But I think we're one step closer. Don't you?'

'I think you're right,' says the man.

The stone is typically stone-like: grey with speckled light and dark marks. Mostly smooth. Rough on one corner. Quite unremarkable.

'I found it by the swings,' Max says.

'You should write it all down,' the man says. 'A good detective keeps very precise notes.'

'You're right,' says Max. 'I'll write it all down.'

'And keep the evidence safe.' The man hands back the stone. 'With any luck, we'll get to the bottom of this mystery.'

'The mystery of the man with no name,' says Max.

For the last half an hour Michael (do you remember Michael?) has been lying on the sofa with his arms folded angrily around his body. He is still watching the television, but now he glares at the screen. The programme on the world's deadliest creatures has finished. Adverts blare out. Mortgages, phones, car insurance, sofa sales. His girlfriend is hoovering in the bedroom. He can hear the furniture being pulled away from the wall and the dragging of the hoover-brush against the carpet. This act is an attack on Michael, or so Michael thinks. He hoovered only two days ago.

The phone rings.

Michael eyes it warily. He doesn't want to answer it. It's

probably an automated call trying to sell something. He hates those automated calls. They infuriate him more than the salesmen. You can't be rude to a robot. He lets it ring, wondering if the noise can be heard in the bedroom over the hoover. Surely not. But it would be worse if his girlfriend stormed through and answered the damn thing herself. He listens carefully. There is the sound of banging coming from the bedroom. The wardrobe doors perhaps? The chest of drawers? Michael decides the phone can't be heard and allows it to ring off.

Then it starts again.

'For *fuck's* sake.' He sits up. The phone brrrips merrily at him from the end table. 'Hello?' Michael presses the receiver against his ear. 'Sorry, what?' He picks up the remote and mutes the television. 'Who?' His face screws up in confusion. 'I'm sorry, I think you've got the wrong number.' He hangs up. Michael sighs. He pulls a cushion onto his stomach and flops back into his lying position on the sofa. The hoover stops. The phone rings. 'Fuck me.'

From the bedroom his girlfriend hollers, 'Jesus, Michael, will you get the bloody phone!'

'I'm *getting* the bloody phone!'

Jacob is in the phone box feeding twenty-pence pieces into the coin slot. He is listening to the dial tone.

VOICE: *(irritable and abrupt)* Yes?
JACOB: It's me again.
VOICE: Right. Well. You've still got the wrong number.
JACOB: No, I have the right number.

VOICE: Listen, mate, you've got the *wrong* number. Nobody called Solace lives here.

JACOB: But they used to.

VOICE: And?

JACOB: So I've got the *right* number. I meant to dial this number.

VOICE: *(pause)* Who is this?

JACOB: Just a friend. I'm sorry, I don't mean to trouble you. I was just wondering if perhaps you knew where Solace has moved to?

VOICE: Well, I don't. Sorry.

JACOB: Is there any way you could find out?

VOICE: No.

JACOB: No forwarding address?

VOICE: No.

JACOB: Right.

VOICE: I'm sorry, I can't help you.

JACOB: Can't or won't?

VOICE: Both. You're beginning to annoy me.

JACOB: I see. *(feeds money into coin slot)* One more thing.

VOICE: What?

JACOB: I don't suppose . . . *(trails off)*

VOICE: Don't suppose what?

JACOB: I don't suppose you could suggest where to look?

VOICE: *(silence)*

JACOB: Hello?

VOICE: What do you mean?

JACOB: I mean, I'm looking for Solace. An old friend. She used to live at your address, now she doesn't and . . . well, I don't know where else to look. I was wondering if you had any suggestions?

VOICE: Are you serious?

JACOB: Deadly serious.

VOICE: *(there is a pause before soft chuckling can be heard)* Oh, I get it. You want to find 'Solace' and you need a suggestion of where to look. This is a joke, right?

JACOB: No joke.

VOICE: Are you calling from the radio?

JACOB: I'm afraid not.

VOICE: *(hesitating)* OK, listen, mate, I don't know what's going on here, but this sounds a hell of a lot like some bullshit stunt they pull on the radio. If that's the case, I'm not interested. Seriously. If this is a wind-up you can hang up now. *(pause)* Are you still there?

JACOB: Yes.

VOICE: Right.

JACOB: I'm not from the radio. I'm just looking for my friend. She used to live where you live now.

VOICE: *(sighs)* Fine. Let me tell you what I know. My girlfriend and I have been living in this flat for just over a year. Before us there was a bunch of students. The landlord said they were a pain in his ass and wanted a professional couple to move in. That's all I know.

JACOB: Students?

VOICE: That's right.

JACOB: Do you know anything about them?

VOICE: No.

JACOB: Were they male or female?

VOICE: They were students, that's all I know. Listen, why

113

don't you contact the landlord if you're trying to track your friend down?

JACOB: *(pleased)* Of course! That's a good suggestion. Thank you.

VOICE: Have you got his number?

JACOB: No.

VOICE: Right. Hang on. *(the phone is put down. In the distance a female voice can be heard, 'Who is it, Michael?' and a male voice reply, 'A wrong number.' Female voice, 'Well if it's a wrong number why haven't you hung up?' Male voice, 'Oh God, just . . . because, OK? Just because.' The receiver is once more picked up)* Right.

JACOB: *(searching in jacket pockets)* Right.

VOICE: *(reads number out)*

JACOB: No, I'm sorry, you'll have to give that to me again. I wasn't ready.

VOICE: *(reads number out)*

JACOB: No, wait. Please. *(frantically searching through pockets. The receiver is wedged between shoulder and ear. He finally pulls out a pencil)* Ah, OK.

VOICE: Are you ready now?

JACOB: One moment, I'm just looking for something to write on. *(spots the disposable cup of coffee still full from earlier that morning on the ground. He empties it. The blackish brown liquid splashes all over his shoe and on his trousers)* Oh, blast!

VOICE: Is there a problem?

JACOB: *(shaking trouser leg)* No. No problem. *(flattens*

cup and leans on metal shelf next to phone)
Right. I'm ready now.

VOICE: Good. *(reads number)*

JACOB: Oh. *(lets out a distraught, strangled, high-pitched groan)*

VOICE: What's wrong?

JACOB: The pencil. I'm sorry. It won't write on the cup. *(he knocks the flattened cup to the floor)* It has a plastic coating. The cup. And the pencil won't . . . Oh, never mind. I *am* sorry. I know this is beginning to get tedious but you'll have to give me that number again.

VOICE: *(annoyed)* Now?

JACOB: Yes. Now.

VOICE: *(reads out number)*

JACOB: *(licks his finger and writes it into the grime on the telephone box window)*

VOICE: So? Have you got it?

JACOB: Yes.

VOICE: Can I go now?

JACOB: Yes. Thank you. You've been most helpful.

There is a click as Michael hangs up. END SCENE TWO.

Jacob allows the hum of the line to sound before slowly replacing the receiver. His hand rests on the metal shelf as he turns to the number smeared into the window. And then, inexplicably, he begins to laugh. Quiet to begin with, growing in depth. He leans back against one side of the phone box and lets this laughter roll out from within him. People pass by and frown or pull quizzical faces. One woman raises her eyebrows and smiles. She sees a skinny floppy-haired man wearing a long coat, laughing to himself in a phone box. It amuses her. Another woman looks on distastefully and mutters the word, 'drunkard'.

9

'What's in a name?' Jacob says to the girl. 'People might call me Jacob, but what is it really? It's just a label, an agreed description, a social necessity. It is only ever a name, this "Jacob", for there isn't really a person here. There is no *one* in me at all. Can't you see? I am large. I contain multitudes.'

Away now. I want to take you to a brightly lit room where an old man sits bent over his desk. This old man is called Mr Benson. Yes, we have already met him, drinking tea with the pink-haired woman. Seventy-six years old. Retired. Father of two. Grandfather of one. Here he sits piecing together the fine intricate parts of a watch movement. The barrel, the springs, the wheels and gears, the pallets, pins and jewels. And all around him there is the tick, tock, tack and clack of a wall covered with clock faces and swaying pendulums, a metronomic cacophony. Next to his desk there is a shelf lined with shoeboxes and even from these there comes the soft clickering of many a watch ticking.

tickety-tickety-tickety-bok-bok-click-click-click-dong-
clicketyticketytocktock-tick tock-tick-tock-tick-tock.

'How can you even bear it?' His eldest daughter will not even enter this room. She says the noise fills her head so much she can no longer think. 'I don't understand how you can sit in here all day.' But it is not the ticking that troubles old Mr Benson, it is the silence beneath it. The ticklessness that drifts from the boxes of broken clocks and watches waiting to be fixed. It is their sound that unnerves the old man.

With a loupe fastened to his spectacles, Mr Benson squints down and tweezers at each tiny gear, picking it up and carefully setting it into the timepiece he is working on. An old pocket watch. His wife is in the kitchen making flapjacks. He can smell the warm sugary scent from here. She always bakes when visitors are to be expected and today both his daughters are joining them for supper and of course his grandson will be with them, only five months old.

Ah, yes, his grandson! Already that boy has cheated time. Born premature, he is older than he should be by just over a month. The smallest baby Mr Benson has ever seen. That is why he calls him Planck, after the smallest known measurement of time in physics. One planck unit is to a second what a second is to hundreds of billions of years. Trillions even; Mr Benson isn't sure of the specifics.

'Please, Father, don't call him *Planck*. His name is Thomas.' In his mind Mr Benson can hear the plea of his youngest daughter and it makes him smile. Later, when he takes the boy into his arms, he'll tell him a story. It'll make his daughter groan but he'll tell it anyway. A story about the most wonderful clock. 'Once upon a time there was an old watchmaker who believed he could make the cleverest clock. A clock that proved time doesn't exist at all. A clock that both ticked and didn't tick at the same time. A quantum clock that held everything past, present and future in one dimensionless point.'

From the hallway he can hear the phone ring.

'Hello?' His wife's soft voice drifts underneath the door. 'Certainly. One moment.' There is a quiet knocking. 'Stan,' and the door is pushed open, 'it's for you.'

'Who is it?'

'I don't know, dear.'

Mr Benson sets his tweezers down on his desk and pushes the hinged loupe away from his eye. The muscles in his back have seized from sitting bent for so long. He groans as he gets up, rolling his shoulders and stretching his neck.

In the hallway his wife hands him the phone and closes the door to his study. The tickings from inside dull to a muffle.

'Benson speaking.' Mr Benson watches his wife's back as she returns to the kitchen. A man's voice announces he is calling with regard to an ex-tenant, a girl named Solace.

'She lived in your property some eleven or twelve years ago.'

'Who?'

'Solace.'

'Solace?'

'That's right.'

'I can't say I know anyone called Solace. Twelve years ago, you say?'

'Yes.'

'Long time is twelve years.'

'I suppose it is.'

'Quite an unusual name. I think I'd remember it.'

'She lived with two other tenants. Two young men. One of them was called Jacob Little.'

Mr Benson raises a hand to his forehead.

'Hello?'

'I know Jacob Little.' He massages his temples. 'May I ask who's calling?'

'Yes,' says the voice. 'My name is Stone. I'm a private detective.'

When her husband finally comes off the phone, Mrs Benson, who has been listening behind the kitchen door, wipes her hands on her apron and moves over to the table in the centre of the room. She tidies the newspaper and all its supplements into a neat pile. 'Who was that, dear?' she calls.

Her husband joins her in the kitchen. He sits, almost slumps, heavily into one of the chairs. He looks more pale than usual underneath his flock of grey-white hair. His thick, tufty eyebrows are twizzled into points. His spectacles have slipped down his nose with the weight of the loupe. Expecting bad news, Mrs Benson takes the seat opposite. 'What is it, Stan?' She clasps her hands into a tight prayer position.

Her husband removes his glasses and cleans them with a handkerchief. 'You'll remember, of course,' he says, 'the tenant Jacob Little?'

Mrs Benson sets her jaw and pinches her thin lips together. 'The boy who went missing,' she says. 'Of course I remember him.'

'Well, it seems he is still missing. And despite his mother's passing, someone is still searching for him.'

'I see.' Mrs Benson tightens her grip on her fingers. She twists them a little. 'Who?' she asks 'A relation?'

'I don't know. The man on the phone claimed to be a private detective, called Stone. But who has employed him, he didn't say.'

'A private detective? Well, what did he want to speak to you for?'

'He's following a lead.'

Mrs Benson watches as her husband lets out a long sigh and rubs his eyes with finger and thumb. 'That boy will continue to haunt me until the day I die,' he says.

'It's not the boy that haunts you.' Mrs Benson's tone is sharp, much sharper than she meant it to be.

'Please, Ada. It's not the time.'

'No,' she says, but despite herself her hands are shaking.

Jacob Little, yes, of course she remembers the tenant. She remembers him well even though she only met him twice. Once in passing on the day he first moved into the flat they let, and then again on the day he lost his key and needed a spare. He'd phoned ahead to explain the situation and then showed up at the door. Her husband had just popped out to the shops. Jacob Little had waited in the living room. He'd sat in her armchair and she gave him tea, offered him biscuits. He was a well-spoken boy. She remembers thinking how polite he seemed. And so young. Yet there was something strange about him, an awkwardness in the way he sat and the way he held himself. And he rarely smiled.

She remembers he asked her about the noise. The ticking.

'Noise?' Mrs Benson hadn't realised what he was talking about at first. 'Oh, that! The clocks. My husband is a collector. It's his hobby. He's become very good over the years at fixing broken clocks and watches. He finds them at car-boot sales and flea markets and charity shops.' She was gushing, she could hear herself, but made no effort to stop. She always gushed whenever she felt unsettled in new company. 'The trouble is he tends to keep them all. Hence the ticking. His study is next door.'

'Why does he keep them all?' Jacob asked.

'Why? Well, now,' Mrs Benson smiled from behind her teacup, 'that is a very good question and one my daughters and I often ask. Though I should think you are better equipped to answer it than we are, Jacob. Being a man yourself.'

'I'm not sure that being a man has anything to do with it,' he said.

'No?'

'No. We do not all have the same mind.'

'Of course not.' She remembers how his reply flustered her so and how the colour rose to her cheeks. 'Perhaps I would do better to ask a fellow clock collector.'

'Or maybe you should ask Mr Benson.'

'Quite.'

Mrs Benson had felt relieved when her husband finally returned. She'd made her excuses and left the two alone, but not before she'd heard Jacob Little request to see the study. 'If it's not too much trouble,' he'd said. And the two men had removed themselves to the incessantly ticking room.

Yes, Mrs Benson remembers it well. She remembers how her husband and this young tenant had remained in the study for quite some time. She had wondered what on earth they could be talking about. What could they possibly have in common? She also remembers how relieved she'd felt when Jacob Little finally left. There was just something about the boy. Something strange. She didn't . . . *trust* him. But it is not the thought of Jacob Little now that has set Mrs Benson on edge. It is the thought of that woman. That odd little grey woman with the empty eyes and the forever-smile on her lips. Jacob Little's mother.

The spectacles have been replaced on old Mr Benson's nose. 'Tell me, Ada, do you remember the name of the other chap who lived at the flat? Brian or Bertie or Billy . . .'

'Benjamin?'

'Barry . . . no, Barnaby . . .'

'Bruce?'

'No, now what *was* his name? I can't for the life of me remember.'

'You're getting old, dear.'

'Yes, well, it doesn't matter now. I'm sure I've written it down somewhere. But did you know there was a girl who lived there too?'

'There was?'

'Apparently so. A girl named Solace. And this Private Detective Stone seems to think that if he finds this girl, who is of course now a woman, he'll also find Jacob Little.'

'I see.' Mrs Benson rests a hand on her chest. 'Well, there's nothing *we* can do.' She taps at her breastbone nervously. 'Stan?' But her husband turns his face from her and closes his eyes. 'Well, what did you tell him? We don't know anything about this girl he's looking for. We didn't even know she was staying with those boys.'

'No,' he says. 'Or rather, I don't know.'

'Oh *really*, Stan. What on earth do you mean?'

'I mean . . .' He sighs. 'I might know something.'

Mr Benson returns to his study. The tickety clickety tack tock tock room. It is coming up for the hour. Many of these clocks will start bonging, several will cuckoo cuckoo, there's even one clock that moos and a small dairy cow is thrust out from behind tiny plastic shed doors. Mr Benson walks to his desk and the shelf of shoeboxes, and picks out a box from the collection. One that doesn't tick. He sits down at his desk, rests the shoebox on his lap and lifts the lid.

Inside is a French Champlevé enamel repeating carriage clock. Late nineteenth century. Greek-key shaped handle. Moulded brass cornicing. Bevelled glass panelling. It is supported by four Corinthian columns on a plinth base, finely decorated with a floral, almost oriental, design.

Colours red, white, black and green on a pale blue background. It has a white dial with Arabic numerals and blued steel spade hands. It is, in a word, beautiful. The twin-barrel movement is signed and numbered. EM & CO. It has a bimetallic balance and a silvered lever platform escapement, which *would* strike and repeat on a coiled steel gong, if only it wasn't broken. If only. It wasn't. Broken.

The note had been left on top. Five simple words. *Stanley. It just stopped ticking.* Mr Benson closes his eyes when he reads them. His mouth turns down. He swallows. It is her bare feet and ankles that haunt him. The way they'd hung from beneath her long nightdress. Delicate toes pointing down towards the carpet, stiff and mottled dark purple where the blood had pooled. A bruised colour. Those dainty little feet. It is not the neck with its welts and strangled skin, or the red swollen tongue bulging from the mouth, or the open, empty, panic-stricken eyes. It is not even the smell of the soiled nightdress, the excrement on the floor, the urine that had trickled down her legs. It is the feet. Those perfect little feet and that ugly colour.

Mr Benson takes a deep breath and puts the note to one side. He focuses his attention instead on the clock. Oh, that beautiful clock! He allows himself to remember the first time he set eyes on it, at 23 Gunney Drive in Olivia Little's front room. It was working then. He remembers the soft metallic sound of its gong striking five and the short grey woman standing by her window, weeping.

The situation had been most uncomfortable. The story in full. Mr Benson had come strictly on business to speak to Olivia Little about her son, Jacob. He hadn't paid his rent for three months and now it seemed he'd completely disappeared. Mr Benson had visited the rented property and spoken with B—, the joint tenant. From him the old man could glean only the smallest of facts – a planck fact, if you will. Jacob had packed a bag one day and left. No note. No indication of whether he was coming back. Nothing. And so, in a sense, Mr Benson had driven to 23 Gunney Drive with the intention of playing bailiff. After all, Mrs Olivia Little had been Jacob's guarantor and three months' rent is a lot of money.

He had not anticipated, however, Mrs Little's emotional or mental state. When Mr Benson had announced on the doorstep that he was Jacob's landlord, the small grey woman had gripped him by his lapels and shaken him. 'Tell me he's come back! Have you seen him? Have you seen my Jacob?' And when Mr Benson had apologised, conceded that no, he had not seen or heard from Jacob for quite some time and indeed, that was the reason for his visit, the woman had broken away from him with a sharp wail as though he'd struck her.

'He's gone! He's gone!' She'd turned and staggered back into the dark hallway, hands pushing off the walls for support. 'He's gone and I just don't know what to do.' She'd disappeared through a door.

Mr Benson had stood outside, staring into the hallway. His eyes rested on what looked like a large stone garden ornament, a lion lying on the red carpet. A garden ornament? In the hallway? He listened for movement from within. 'Mrs Little?' There was no reply. 'Mrs Little, should I come in?' And then, the strange woman, she'd reappeared with a forced smile on her lips, drying her eyes.

'Oh, how rude of me,' she'd said. 'Please excuse me, it's just . . . well, I'm not quite myself these days. Please, come in. Let me make you some tea.'

And that was how he'd come to be sitting in Olivia Little's front room, on a sofa, too soft, his bottom sinking beyond the broken springs, when the beautiful carriage clock on the mantelpiece struck five. In his hands he held a cup and saucer. He sipped at the much-too-milky tea. So milky it was almost white. And cold. He'd requested no sugar and got what tasted like two.

Mrs Little was pressing crumpled kitchen roll into her eyes. Her shoulders shook with silent sobs. A peculiar woman, both in behaviour and physical appearance. She was short and frail; her movements were timid. She curled her rounded shoulders inwards in a way that put Mr Benson in mind of a dog waiting to be kicked. Her hair was cut into an unfortunate style, a short mushroom-like bob, which emphasised the negative traits of her heart-shaped face. The shallow forehead, the pointed chin, the unusual length of her slanting jawline.

She'd told Mr Benson her version of events. Yes, Jacob had shown up four months previously. February. He'd arrived with only one bag and announced his plan to stay for a while. He gave no reason. Mrs Little had tried to find out if there had been some problem with accommodation or an argument with a friend that had triggered the sudden upheaval. Jacob was not one for spontaneous visits, you see, especially not lengthy ones. But Jacob had insisted there was nothing to worry about. No, nothing at all. In fact, he seemed oddly cheerful.

'I thought he must've met someone. A girl. My son isn't known to laugh and smile like that.'

'Had he?'

'No. He said no.'

'Did he tell you why he was so happy?'

'Oh, some philosophical breakthrough. Something life-changing, he said. Ground-breaking. An epiphany. I'd never seen him so . . .' Mrs Little had paused before breathing out the word, '. . . manic.' She'd turned suddenly to Mr Benson. 'Do you know my son, Mr Benson? Do you know he is a genius? He has an IQ of 160.'

'No, I didn't know that.'

'He's a thinker, Mr Benson. A philosopher. You might not believe me when I say it, but he was born that way. Even as a baby he was quiet. Pensive. He often had the look of an old man frowning. And as a child he got into this strange habit of pacing. He never played like other children, he just paced around. Head down and hands clasped behind his back. I don't know where he learned it from. His father never paced. I never paced. Not like that. And then as a teenager he'd spend hours of an evening just sitting on the front doorstep. Thinking. Thinking. Always thinking. Or muttering to himself. I often heard him muttering.'

'How strange.'

'Not really. Not when you think about it. My son is not like other people. He lives in his mind. His body might be in this world, but *he* is not. And when a man lives in his mind, Mr Benson, there is nobody else to talk to. Only himself.'

Mr Benson remembered admiring the profundity of this. He also remembered dreading every sip of that cup of tea. And that clock. He had to resist the temptation to pull himself free from the hungry maw of the sunken settee and inspect its movement, see its stamp. An antique, he was certain. He'd wanted to ask Mrs Little how she'd come to own such a fine thing. A family heirloom, perhaps? Or a lucky purchase at a car-boot sale? He couldn't ask, of course. Not while Mrs Little was sobbing. Nor could he possibly ask the distraught woman for the overdue rent. How could he?

'Mad. My son is mad, Mr Benson. A perfect genius who was perfectly mad. I'd hear him talking to his reflection in mirrors as though it were a different person. He'd write on the walls or draw rude pictures of, well, I can't even say. Men and women without any clothes on. And he had the most frustrating habit of turning back clocks. Always he would turn back the clocks whenever he passed them in the house. And always to the same time. Four thirty.'

'Mrs Little, you say your son is missing . . .'

'Not missing,' she corrected. 'He's gone. *Gone*.' And she hoo-hooed noisily into her torn scrap of tissue. 'He left a note. Here. See for yourself.' And she produced a note from her cardigan pocket, folded neatly into four, with the word *Mother* written on the front.

Please understand, Mother, my actions bear no reflection on you, but I have to leave and I do not wish you to look for me.

Jacob

'It's my fault,' said the woman. 'It's my fault. I'm such a timid wretch and it angers him so. It's my fault, Mr Benson. I should have let him be, but I didn't. I couldn't. You don't understand. He's everything to me.'

'Now now, there there.' His words, he knew, were hollow, but he had to say them, if only to fill his own awkward silence. So the young man had left of his own volition? What could be done about such a thing? He wondered whether he should get up and stand beside the crying woman. He wondered if that was what his wife would do in such a situation. He could rest a comforting hand on her shoulder. Would that help? It didn't seem right somehow. 'Do you have a friend, Mrs Little? Someone you can talk to? I could call them for you. I think you need a good friend to stay with you awhile.'

'No, please.' Mrs Little was quick to become panicked. 'Oh dear. Oh. You want to leave, don't you? I can see this must be awful for you.' She laughs bleary-eyed at him with a hint of hysteria. 'You don't know me from Adam and yet you're sitting here listening to me witter on. I know. I know, it's very strange. But Mr Benson, please, I beg you not to go. Don't leave me here.'

'My dear, I don't quite know what you want me to do.'

'Just. Talk to me.'

The note Jacob had left was in the shoebox underneath the carriage clock. There was also the postcard Jacob had sent two years later from Wells. *I have found a way to live a life somewhat contented. There is no need to search for me any longer.* Mr Benson studied the back-slanting hand carefully. He remembered an article he'd once read on Morettian graphology and the psychology behind hand-writing. Perfectly ludicrous, of course. Pseudoscientific piffle. But it seemed he'd retained the information anyway. Something about the Forward Slant being emotionally self-expressive and the Back Slant being masked, concealed, unwilling to admit to its own interpersonal needs as necessary. Both pursuing the same goal of sentimentality, seeking something on which to 'lavish its affection', but Forward is more open, Back is more closed. Hogwash. Why did his brain even deem it worthy to store such information?

Underneath the carriage clock there are the police letters, the notes, the missing poster with Jacob's thin, unsmiling face on the front, Olivia Little's will, her death certificate, a sealed envelope with the words '*For my son*' written in a haphazard hand. And then there is the photograph. The one he was looking for. It is of a young woman – a blonde, wispy-haired woman – holding a baby in her arms. On the back someone has penned an address, and below it, in block capitals, the word 'SOLACE'.

THE MIDDLE

There it is.

Oh, that wicked footage!

Did he jump? Did he slip? Was he pushed? The rumours are rife. He didn't want to die, people say. Why would he flail his legs about like that, or hold his arms up to his face if he'd *wanted* to die? More questionably, why wouldn't he have chosen a taller building? Why wouldn't he have made absolutely certain there was nothing below that could cushion his fall? The hushed debate is whispered behind palms and closed doors. Even Lucy Westbry, in three years' time, will hit the hashtag #jumpingman. '*Poor bastard wants to end it all*.' And the blurred image of a man as he crashes into a skip filled with building debris. The thump echoes around the derelict warehouse and the girl filming lets out a meek and breathless 'fuck me'.

But not yet. No, not yet. After all, young Lucy Westbry has only just begun to slide the slippery slope towards falling in love with this man she has not even met. Yet. The scandalous love affair! It is still to come. She, a mere sixteen-year-old girl, and Jacob, a man of thirty-three.

But she *will* lose her virginity to him. Even now, before anything has happened, we know it. And somehow so does she.

Lucy is sitting on the windowsill in her small attic bedroom. One foot is on the floor, the other is on the ledge, knee bent. In her hands she holds the painting *Honeymoon Nude*. Solace. But Lucy is not looking at the painting. She is staring out at the wet world. Rain, rain, go away, come again another day, little Lucy wants to play. She is watching the people in the street below dashing for shelter or scuttling with heads covered by umbrellas, newspapers, hoods, or the backs of jumpers stretched like a Muslim woman's hijab. It's raining, it's pouring, the old man is snoring.

In her pocket, her phone vibrates and whistles for attention. A text message from Billy.

> ORANGE TWO FOR ONE
> @ ODEON. MY TREAT.

Lucy sighs and presses her forehead against the cold windowpane. Doctor Foster went to Gloucester in a shower of rain. Her thumbs quickly tap out a response on the touch-screen keypad.

> Sorry billy. Not 2nite. 2 much homework.
> Plus, u looked out the window?
> Its pissin out there! What, you want
> my hair 2 go frizzy? x

She gets up from her semi-seat on the sill and moves over to the mirror where she tacks the painting of Solace to the glass. It joins a postcard of a beach in Tenerife, some yellow smiley-faced stickers and a few cuttings from magazines of famous actors and singers. There is also a photograph of the Westbry Family Trio, each member pulling a face for the camera.

Lucy takes down the photograph and looks closely first at her mother's face, then at her own. You can see the resemblance. Nose, eyes, lips, they're the same, but not ears and jaw. Those come from the unknown side of Lucy's genetic make-up, Sperm Donor Dad, the side Lucy has begun to question of late whenever she looks in the mirror. Her eyes drift over then to Anya blowing out her cheeks. Fun-loving Anya, punky, alternative with spiked hair flaming red on top of an otherwise completely shaved head. 'Does it never make you sad, Ani,' she had asked her once, 'that I'm not half of your genetic make-up as well? I mean, do you not wish I could have been blood related to you too?'

And Ani had replied quickly, as though perhaps she'd been expecting such a question for years, 'But Lucy, you *are* half of me. Not genetically maybe, but if it wasn't for your mother and I loving each other, *you* would never have been born.'

Lucy tacks the photo back onto the mirror next to Solace. Her phone vibrates and whistles.

SERIOUSLY? YOU CARE MORE
ABOUT YOUR HAIR THAN ME?

'Oh Jesus, Billy, it was a joke. A *joke*.' She directs these words at the phone in her hand. 'Bloody hell! Comedy retard.' And she slaps the mobile onto the desk. No, that's not enough; she picks it up and holds down the power button. OFF.

Itsy bitsy spider climbed up the water spout, down came the rain and washed the spider out.

She is thinking again of sex. She has been thinking about it a lot of late. At the beginning of the week her class had been divided into two different rooms, the boys from the girls, to practise putting condoms onto bananas. 'Squeeze the bubble on top so it doesn't burst and roll the ring down the shaft of the banana.' The girls had all giggled and nudged one another. 'For goodness' sake, girls, how old are you? This is an important life lesson you're learning here.' But Lucy couldn't help but giggle with her friends and grimace at the slimy feel of the pink latex.

'Did you know,' her friend Ness had told her at lunchtime, 'Mark Douglas is saying Sally Muir allowed him to put his fingers right up inside her? They were playing a game at a party – *Truth, Dare, Double-dare, Love, Kiss or Hate*. He said it was "warm and wet".'

'That's gross,' Lucy had said.

'Aye, well, Sally Muir says it's all bullshit and that she wouldn't let Mark Douglas blow on her through a straw let alone poke her with his grubby little fingers, but she can't stop the rumours.' Ness had shrugged. 'You know there are some people who say she gives blow-jobs in the park for a fiver.'

'Really?'

'Nah,' Ness had said. 'I reckon she gives them away for free.'

Now, Lucy flops onto the bed next to Wabbit and stares up at the slanting ceiling. The pattering and fierce spats of rain smack like BB pellets against the skylight above her.

They say it hurts the first time. Some say it even bleeds. Doesn't something have to tear? Some flap of skin? The hymen. If that's the case then Lucy would rather do it herself. She's been thinking about this all for some time, almost every night. Why not just do it herself? Break herself in like a pair of new shoes. No, that's a bad analogy. Regardless, she *could* do it. Why not? And then, that morning after showering, she'd noticed the deodorant bottle.

Lucy reaches under her pillow and pulls out the roll-on tube of deodorant. It has a rounded lid, like the tip of a man's cock. It has been under her pillow since that morning.

Well?

She didn't want the first time to hurt, did she?

Lucy picks up Wabbit, and kisses her firmly on her squashed little face. 'Sorry, Wabbit, but this isn't for your innocent eye to see.' And she pushes the soft toy into the stuffy darkness of the nether-pillow.

10

'If you could be somebody famous, who would you be and why?' The girl who is curled under Jacob's arm has her hand resting on his chest. She is pressing her fingers lightly against his pale skin as though pressing the keys on a piano. She looks up when Jacob does not answer. His eyes are closed. 'Jakey?'

'I don't want to play that game,' he says.

In another bedroom, in a small city house amidst those labyrinth alleyways and stone walls with the playground in its centre, Elizabeth Mary Duda, known to us as Max, is fishing for a shoebox of toys she keeps underneath her bed. This room is a mess, clothes spilling out from the chest of drawers and forming piles on the floor alongside scatterings of books and toys and papers with treasure maps drawn on them. One particularly large pile of clothes has a Barbie doll sticking out from the top – '*Giant's Mountain*', Max calls it – and nearby an army truck has parked up and all its GI Joe soldiers have spilled out and formed a base camp in the trouser leg of a pair of jeans.

Max, still rooting for the shoebox underneath the bed, nearly kicks over the *Tower of Blyton*, a stack of *Famous Five* books where two figurines from the enemy camp keep lookout. They are planning their ambush. They will soon radio over to the line of soldiers ready to charge, a disparate group of random toys that want to claim the Head of Barbie for themselves. Looking at Barbie more closely now, you can see this game has been popular for some time. Her head lolls loosely to one side and bits of her hair have been cut or pulled out. There is a crudely drawn Frankenstein scar under her left cheekbone and a small hole at the back of her skull where her head was once pushed onto a spike.

But all military operations have been temporarily postponed. Max is busy on her new project. Not far from the *Tower of Blyton* lies the stone that Max found earlier that afternoon in the park, and next to it a notepad. On this notepad Max has written in her childish hand a phone number. It is the same number that was smeared into the grime on the telephone box window. Max had followed the 'nameless man', like any true detective would. She'd followed him and watched as he phoned someone, then struggled to write something on a coffee cup, then licked his finger and smudged a number onto the grubby windowpane. She'd even watched him as he'd hung up and laughed hysterically. After the second phone call, Max had moved quickly. With the nameless man walking off out of sight she'd called the number written on the window and spent her last fifty-pence piece talking to an old man on the other end. The conversation had gone something like this:

MAX: Excuse me, sir, but did my dad just phone you up?
MAN: Well now, that depends on whether your dad is a certain Mr Stone?
MAX: Yes. That's him. Did he tell you where he was going?
MAN: I'm afraid not.
MAX: Or what he was doing?
MAN: I'm not sure I'm at liberty to say. Your father was calling me with regard to work.
MAX: Oh.
MAN: But . . . *(hesitates)* I wonder if you might pass on a message to him?
MAX: OK.
MAN: Can you tell him that Mr Benson might know something more about Solace. He should call me back.

MAX: OK.
MAN: Thank you.
MAX: Bye.

So on the notepad underneath the number, Max has written the words MR BENSIN KNOWS SOMETHING ABOUT SOLIS. It's a codeword, 'SOLIS', that much is obvious, and Max would have to somehow decipher what it means.

She finds the shoebox and empties its contents onto her bed. Marbles and pieces of Lego fall out, two cars and some farm animals she'd long forgotten about. She sits on the floor with the empty box and with a black marker pen writes on its lid:

EVIDENCE
KEEP OUT!

She places the stone inside the box along with the notepad, and from her school satchel she pulls out the disposable coffee cup the nameless man dropped onto the floor of the telephone box. She hadn't been sure whether the coffee cup was a clue or not, but decided to take it anyway. If nothing else it looked better to have an evidence box with more contents inside.

At Pauper's Inn, the rain has driven some very wet passers-by into the pub to shake off their umbrellas and dry out their feet. Many of the tables have small groups or couples sitting at them. All the spare stools have been laden with rain jackets. One woman, not local, comes in and walks straight to the bar. She requests coffee or tea or anything *hot*. 'So this is the Scottish summer?' she asks, rubbing her pinkening fingers together. Big Sal, not impolitely, laughs at her. She calls to Alex to make the woman a hot toddy. 'That'll warm ye,' she says.

In one corner some local boys are setting up a band. Two fiddlers, a guitarist, a boy with a bodhrán and another on a penny whistle. A girl nearby sits on a table. She waits for the band to tune their instruments. The boy on the bodhrán says something to her, but by now the small pub has a buzz about it, the banter and laughter lifting the air, and the girl can't hear. She holds a hand to her ear. The boy repeats. The girl nods. 'Aye,' she says. We do not need to know what is being said. We watch and wait, as many of the tables do amidst their conversations. There is the anticipation of music. Outside an A-frame has been set on the pavement. The words COME INSIDE OUT THE RAIN, CEILIDH HERE TONIGHT in red and blue and yellow chalk. The writing is slowly disappearing with the wet on the blackboard surface.

The beat of the bodhrán calls for quiet at the bar. Some people nod in the direction of the band. Others hush-hush or 'wheesht' their conversation. A standing group has already begun to form a semi-circle around the musicians. Hands clasping their wine glasses, pints of lager, tumblers of whisky. The girl begins to port-a-beul in Gaelic, a slow singing in time to the beat, and the cold and wet woman nursing her hot toddy says to her companion how fortunate that the rain would take them both to a ceilidh. 'Aye, lady,' says a stranger standing close by, 'you'll never be far from the music up here.' And all hands keep time, tapping fingers on thighs, feet keeping the beat on the floor, as the bodhrán speeds up and the girl sings out words nonsensical in sound, fast and falling with rolling rhotic trills and breathy consonants. Someone lets out a whoop. Another whistles. And as though it were a cue, the fiddlers bring their instruments to their chins and all begin to play.

The music travels through the doorway that leads into the hall and up the narrow staircase and underneath the closed door of Jacob Little's rented room. The laughter travels too. Jacob will be able to hear it rising above the muffled banter below. He'll be able to feel the vibration of the beat in the floorboards and walls. He is sitting on the bare mattress on the floor. He is wearing his brown T-shirt and cords. He looks strangely buckled with his long legs knotted together and body curving slightly, accentuating his emaciated stomach. With one hand he holds a green jotter to his knee, the other holds both a pen and a cigarette, but he is neither smoking nor writing. The cigarette is turning to ash and soon it will break and fall to the floor. There. See. It falls.

In the jotter we can see that Jacob was writing a list of names. We should recognise them. Wilhelm and Merton, Lambert and Otto, Gifford and Lear. Beside each name – Archie, Isaac, Lindsay Ray – there is a word, a subject even. These words have been columnised under the heading OBSESSION: 'Art', 'Literature', 'History', 'The Occult'. One name, Teddy Two-Fingers, has the word 'Origami' written in the column next to it. Isaac has the word 'Gardening'. Kenny has 'Bike Mechanics'. Dates, places, names and obsessions. The identities Jacob has created in his past.

*

'The trouble with Jacob, Mr Benson, is he wants to be everyone but himself.' The pink-haired woman is pulling a cigarette out of a new packet of twenty. 'Can't say I blame him.' She taps the back of her hand with the butt end, glancing out of the window into the garden where her husband and son still play. 'Do you mind if I smoke?' she asks. She doesn't wait for an answer but leans back in her seat to open a cupboard and pull out an ashtray. 'I don't usually smoke in the house,' she says.

'We can go outside,' says Mr Benson. 'I don't mind.'

'No,' says the pink-haired woman. 'I'd rather not.' She lights her cigarette with a match. Mr Benson watches the flame take and the glow of red as the woman inhales. 'It was his mother who fucked him up. That's what I say.' And she exhales a long jet of smoke into the air. 'Her and her step-son.'

'Step-son?'

'Oh? She didn't tell you about Adam?' The pink-haired woman shrugs and makes a face to show she isn't surprised. 'Well maybe you don't know then that Olivia Little was never married to Jacob's father? They were lovers who lived separately. But when Jacob's father died,' she pauses, 'bowel cancer,' she says, 'his son came to live with them for a while. Maybe a year or so.'

'I didn't know that.'

'No.' She draws on her cigarette and exhales again. 'Well, if Jacob's word is to be trusted – and in truth, Mr Benson, I'm not entirely sure it is – the boy was a bit of a shit. He used to, well, "bully" Jacob.'

'How so?'

'He accused him of being nuts,' and she taps at her temple with her right index finger.

Mr Benson has become aware that his lips are dry. He licks at them discreetly with his tongue. He picks up his mug to moisten them with a mouthful of tea, but the mug is empty. The pink-haired woman offers him another cup.

'No,' says Mr Benson. 'No, thank you.'

So she stays sitting where she is, this woman we may presume to be Solace, continuing to smoke, tapping ash into the crystal ashtray on the table. She carries on with her story. 'When this boy, Adam, moved in, Olivia Little told him that Jacob was "mad", a "loner", an "eccentric". I mean, how messed up is that? Describing your own son to the new kid like that? Jacob had been hiding upstairs on the landing when she'd said all this. He'd been watching the new boy with all his bags stand in the hallway below. He heard his mother say something along the lines of, "He'll probably not want to be friends with you, Adam, he finds it difficult talking to people." I guess Jacob felt pretty shit about himself at that point. And scared. Right? I mean, I guess that's why he remembered it so well. Needless to say the two didn't get off to a flying start. This new kid, well, he was pretty angry about his dad dying. Grieving. Whatever. And he took it out on Jacob.'

'How old were they both?'

'Jacob was young. Maybe nine or ten. This new kid was older. A teenager. Maybe fifteen? I don't know, I can't remember. He did tell me, but . . .' She shrugs. 'You only remember so much,' she says. 'Anyway. This new kid used to play tricks on Jacob. Tricks to make his mother think he really *was* mad. I remember Jake telling me this one story about the time his mother came home from shopping. It had been raining and Jakey knew how flustered his mother got in wet weather. It made her sob. So he waited for her to come in with all the bags – and sure enough she was sobbing – and she dumped all these shopping bags in the front doorway to be sorted. Jacob stood back, waiting for her to stop crying. He knew that to interfere would make her cry even harder. Unfortunately he was standing next to this table where a large fancy jug was placed. Well, you can probably guess what happens next before I even say it. The new kid comes out and pulls the jug off the table which smashes onto the head of a really ugly stone lion garden ornament which just happens to be in their hallway – and then the new kid just vanishes. Runs off. And there's Jacob standing in the hallway with his mother's favourite jug in pieces around his feet, the wild flowers that she picked are all limp in amongst the broken pottery and the water is seeping into that nasty red carpet like a bad accident.' She stops to take a breath. She flicks her cigarette. 'I love telling a good story,' she says.

'Did that actually happen?'

The woman shrugs. 'I hope so. It's quite dramatic.'

'So Jacob got the blame?'

'Yeah. Well. There you have just one of many stories. This new kid would do all sorts of things. He'd spit on the walls around the house and tell Olivia he'd seen Jacob do it. He'd hide things in her bed – like worms or dead insects. He'd piss in the corner of a room so the urine would soak into the carpet and smell. He did all these things and somehow blamed it on Jacob.'

Old Mr Benson chews on his bottom lip. 'Did he used to wind back all the clocks?' he asks.

'What, to four thirty?' the pink-haired woman finishes Mr Benson's thought.

'That was Adam?'

'It was all Adam, Mr Benson. All of it.' She wags a finger in the air. 'Oh, here's a good one,' she says. 'He used to tip out the ashtrays onto the carpet and claim he'd seen Jacob play with the stubs as though they were little toy people.'

'Why would this child do such a thing?'

'Kids are cruel,' she says. 'But do you wanna know what really fucked up Jacob? I mean more than just taking the blame for all the shit that went on? This kid, Adam, he'd go to Jacob in his room when he was completely alone, pin him to the floor or to the bed or to the wall, and shout at him, 'What the *hell* were you thinking? Olivia is so upset. You're always, always upsetting Olivia and she's been so kind to me.' The pink-haired woman stops. She raises her eyebrows and nods at Mr Benson. Her expression says 'unbelievable maybe, but it happened'. 'And poor Jacob would cry,' she says. 'He'd say he didn't do it . . . and Adam would call him a liar . . . and Jacob would say he wasn't lying . . .' she is telling the story now as if it were all predictable and very boring. 'And then Adam would ruffle him up a bit, you know, to teach him a lesson.'

'This is a horrible story,' Mr Benson says.

'The best stories often are,' the woman replies.

'Well.' Mr Benson isn't sure any more whether he likes the woman sitting across from him. She seems very brash, he decides, and swears too much. But whether he likes her or not is beside the point. It is her home he is in, after all, and something – he would later wonder at length what it was – compels him to stay. 'I can only hope for a happy ending,' he says.

'No offence, Mr Benson,' the pink-haired woman replies, 'but have you met Jacob?'

Below Jacob, the ceilidh continues. A piper has joined in. There is clapping and whooping and stomping and laughter. Jacob still sits in the same position as before, on the soiled mattress with his jotter on his lap. The remains of the cigarette he was smoking have been stubbed onto the floor, making another bloom-hole in the carpet. The window, still wedged open, is letting in gusts of wet wind. Raindrops pool together and form tiny puddles on the wood of the sash frame. The soft hair all over Jacob's skinny pale arms stands on end, his skin goosepimpled against the cold.

11

'You know, people often tell me that I'm so quiet,' Jacob says to the girl curled under his arm. 'But there was one year I didn't say anything at all. I just woke up one morning and realised I had nothing more to say. Just like that. For a whole year.' He pauses. 'You want to know what it was like?' he asks. 'I'll tell you what it was like. It was *loud*. When I stopped talking everything started to shout. And I mean *everything*. The cars, the roads, the trees, the sky, the birds, the wind, the sun. *Everything*. That's why I started to speak again. The world was just too damn noisy.'

Once upon a time, there was a teacher called Mr Forbes. He was an older gentleman, tall with grey, stuck-out Einstein hair and gangly limbs. Everyone, even the other teachers, likened this kindly man to a tree, his thin body a trunk, arms for branches and hair like a burst of leaves; and pupils soon nicknamed him the Whomping Willow, for the time he'd lost his patience with an unruly class and struck down hard onto a table. WHOMP! It was Mr Forbes who taught the teenage Jacob Little philosophy and religious studies at school, and it is to a certain one of his philosophical lessons that this anecdote pertains.

WHO AM I?

Mr Forbes chalked the words up onto the blackboard. 'The question seems very simple,' he said. 'I am Mr Forbes. But what's really in a name?'

For this story to be truly effective *you*, the reader, should imagine yourself sitting in this classroom with its many large windows letting in light. Cloud gazing. Staring at hands. Doodling on pencil cases. SANDY B. LOVES JAMIE T. 4 EVA. You can even smell the classroom smells. Pencil shavings, the blackboard and chalk, the paper, the jotters, an old apple core in somebody's bag, Irma Crowe's armpits because no one had the guts to tell her she stank.

Jacob is sitting at the table on the other side of the room. His floppy hair looks greasy and there is a stain on the chest of his school jumper. On his forehead there are the swollen bright spots of puberty. He keeps his head down.

'So who am I?' The lanky Mr Forbes struts around the classroom. 'It turns out to be quite a difficult question to answer.' He points a finger at the chubby boy sitting opposite Jacob. '*You*,' he says. 'Who are you?'

And the chubby boy replies, 'Stuart Grantham, sir.'

'Good,' answers Mr Forbes. 'So let's work on a little thought experiment, shall we, Stuart? Say your parents had named you Peter when you were born. You grow up living and experiencing everything you have already lived through and experienced, in exactly the same way, right up to this very moment. Here. Now. In this classroom. But you wouldn't be Stuart Grantham any more, would you? You'd be Peter Grantham. But does having a different name make you a different person?'

'Uh . . . no?'

'Right, then we must come back to the original question. Who are you?'

Poor Stuart Grantham. He stares at Mr Forbes, his pink lips forming into a gormless 'O' and the soft downy facial hair on his top lip looking silvery-white under the beam of the overhead strip-lights.

'We're not just a name . . .' someone else finally ventures. 'We're more than just a name. We have a personality.'

'Good, Celia. Anyone else?'

'Genetics, sir?'

'Are we our memories?'

And Mr Forbes writes all the words on the blackboard underneath his question. PERSONALITY, MEMORIES, GENES, FAMILY, FRIENDS, UPBRINGING, CULTURE, GENDER, EXPERIENCES, PAST, PRESENT, FUTURE.

Later, after school, Jacob Little runs home, and without even shouting hello to his mother, locks himself in the bathroom with his typewriter. This is what he writes.

WHO AM I?

You tell me I am my experiences, my thoughts, my memories, my emotions, the decisions I make and the consequences that arise because of them. You tell me I am the people I know. The language I learn. The books that I read and the films that I watch. You say I am everything I've ever seen, heard, touched, tasted. I am my parents, my peers, my genetics, my gender, my culture, my upbringing, my morals. Or so you say. I am what I know. And also what I don't know. What I've experienced and what I am yet to experience. I am defined by my past, but also the possibilities of a future. But all said and done, it seems I exist only because *you* say I do.

Jacob Little rereads what he's written and smiles. It pleases him. He was silent throughout the entire lesson, but listened to every word. *You*, on the other hand, *you* drifted off, *you* lost concentration. You kept fiddling with your pencil case and rubbing your eraser hard on the surface of the desk whenever teacher wasn't looking, trying to get its grey grubby skin back to pristine white. And when Mr Forbes asked everyone to close their eyes and imagine themselves floating alone in space, where there is no sound, no gravity, no light

154

to see by, *you* were one of the gigglers. Mr Forbes continued as though he hadn't heard. Would you still be able to think? he asked. Would you still hear the voice in your head? Who *is* that voice? What *is* consciousness? Is it the same thing as the 'soul'? Does the soul even exist?

Jacob had almost bitten through the skin of his bottom lip he was concentrating so hard on everything that was said. It was the first time he'd ever heard of Avicenna and the 'floating man' experiment, but not the first time he'd imagined it. For years, as far back as he could remember, his mind had been consumed by the thought, 'If I wasn't here, right now, in this body, where and what would I be?' And these thoughts would make his head spin so much he'd feel both sick and afraid. He knew it was impossible to exist beyond his body – and yet his body felt alien to him. Disjointed. Unconnected. He'd decided in amidst all that teenage angst that consciousness was nothing but a freak byproduct of the brain, a mutation that had grown like a tumour. Out of hand. The parasite 'self' feeding off the rest of him, getting fat with all the blood and thoughts and experiences it consumed. But it wasn't real. It was an illusion. A clever trick of the mind.

```
If it weren't for the existence of others,
I wouldn't exist at all.
```

He wanted to tell Mr Forbes all of this. He'd never told anyone before, but Mr Forbes seemed like he might understand. And so the young Jacob Little typed his passage out twice with the intention of giving a copy to his teacher the following day. He folded the A4 piece of paper neatly into four and spent over an hour in front of the bathroom mirror, practising how he would approach the teacher. 'Mr Forbes, I really enjoyed your lesson yesterday.' Jacob Little studied the way his lips moved and his keen facial expressions. He wanted to see *exactly* what Mr Forbes would see when he approached him. 'Mr Forbes, I've written this in answer to your question. I've taken books out of the library. Books on philosophy.'

But the next morning at school there were wild rumours racing through the corridors. Mr Forbes was dead. Dead. Dead as a dodo, they said. There'd been an accident. He'd been hit by a . . . what was that? He'd been hit by a car? He'd been crossing the road with the green man flashing, but the car hadn't stopped. It honked its horn. It tried to brake, but too late. A black car. No, was it blue? Or green? It didn't matter. The car was going too fast, it went through the red light. It hit Mr Forbes and sent him flying. WHOMP. Body on bonnet and windscreen and over the roof, rolling, rolling. That's what they said. And who was the driver? Some kid who'd just passed his test. Someone from that very school. Davie Miller? Lawrence Smith? The rumours charged around the schoolyard, through the halls, in the canteen, behind toilet cubicle doors. Everywhere Jacob walked he heard Mr Forbes was dead. The words filled the entire school, along with the nervous excitement of pack animal youth when faced with a death, perhaps for the first time. While the older boys and girls donned appropriately sombre faces and shook their heads forlornly, the younger years clustered and gossiped and made crass jokes.

The rumours were confirmed at assembly. Mr Forbes

had been knocked down and killed the night before. No more details given. And in Jacob's pocket, the neatly folded philosophical enquiry remained.

WHO AM I ?

In his jotter, Jacob the man allows the question mark to be bigger than the words. He lets it curl more at the top, he accentuates the curve and boldens the dot. He had, once upon a time, related this memory of his teacher's death to Solace, he'd told her about the young group of girls, new first-year pupils, who'd sat on a bench in the hall after the assembly was over, holding each other in a firm group hug, sobbing and sobbing, tears pouring in long grizzly lines down their cheeks. He'd told her how the broken staccato noise of their sobs spread up and down the hallway, like the rumours had before assembly. And how like a chain reaction more girls began to sob. Some even rushed towards the group hug and spread their arms around it or wove themselves into it. The hysteria spread further, until everyone in the school had heard about the sobbing girls and was making their way towards the hall. The corridors became crammed as people tried to get a peek. The noise was unbearable, the hubbub of chatter and giggles and questions and concern mixed with the wails from the hall which had grown in pitch and boomed all around them. More people began to cry. Not just girls, even boys began to shed a tear – although true to form most were just nudging each other and pointing. Teachers tried to bring order. They shouted loudly to get back to registration class. They began peeling people from the crowd and ushering them away. Jacob Little's shoulder had been gripped roughly by one irritated teacher and he was hauled over to the doors, 'Get to class, boy. Do you hear?' As though the entire thing had been *his* fault.

And Solace, well, she had been strangely excited by the story, as though simply by hearing about those sobbing girls she was touched by a fraction of the hysteria.

'And what happened next?' she asked.

'Everyone went back to their registration class.'

'Is that it?'

'Anticlimactic, I know.'

'But what about the girls?'

'I believe they got told off.'

'Christ, that's harsh. Their teacher just died.'

Jacob had tried to explain that actually they weren't crying for Mr Forbes at all. They never had been. The young girls were crying because they thought that's what they were supposed to do. Cry when someone died. In fact, Jacob continued to explain, some of the new first-year pupils in the very centre of that hug hadn't even *met* Mr Forbes. And then as the hysteria grew it became even less about him. Nobody was thinking about the dead teacher any more. They were all just infected by the sound as though it were a virus. Some cried and didn't know why they were crying. Others cried while thinking about their own worries.

'But not one of them was thinking about Forbes,' Jacob had said to Solace. 'I didn't go back to registration class. I left school that day and used my lunch money to get a train ticket to Bristol.'

'You rebel,' Solace had said.

Jacob didn't tell her, however, that he'd ended up at the Clifton Suspension Bridge staring at the jagged cliffs and the river and the muddied embankment far below. He didn't tell her that he held out his arms like a bird so he could feel the soft breeze against his palms, ruffling the sleeves of his school sweater. He didn't tell her he'd imagined himself falling and as he fell, in his mind, he thought about Forbes. No tears, just thoughts. And he'd taken the piece of paper out from his pocket with the carefully typed words, tore it into tiny, tiny pieces and let them blow and flutter over the side of the bridge, small specks of white spiralling towards the brown, sluggish river below. He didn't tell her any of that. But he did say that with regard to his first ever 'philosophical enquiry', that perhaps it was better Mr Forbes hadn't seen it. Stuart Grantham had got it right, he'd said. In answer to the question WHO ARE YOU?, staring up at Mr Forbes, tongue-tied and filled with angst at being singled out in front of the whole class, Stuart Grantham had said nothing. And Mr Forbes had let the air fill with his silence.

12

Jacob cups her breasts in his hands and squeezes. He presses his lips against her soft skin and circles her nipples with his tongue. The breath between them grows heavier. The girl gasps. He holds the inside of her thigh and pushes her legs apart gently. 'Shhh,' he says when the girl tries to speak. 'Not now. Don't say anything. Now is not the time.'

Big Sal is lying fat and fatigued on the sofa, sprawled and semi-clad, her mouth gaping, head lolling, drooling ever so slightly into her palm and over her wrist. She is drunken-dozing. Midway through undressing for bed, she'd slumped onto the sofa and rested her heavy head back and then . . . sleep. In her mind the ceilidh continues. The fast fiddling and the bodhrán beating and the high-pitched penny whistle chirruping a tune like the Pied Piper in command of his dancing rats. The singing girl with her short golden curls gets to her feet and slip-steps and skip-changes and pas de basques around in a circle. 'Dance!' she whoops at the standing crowd. 'Dance!' And she grabs at hands and elbows to pull them in. Even Big Sal dances; she gets off her barstool and jigs her body in time to the music, she shuffles and keeps the beat, hand tapping her thigh. The locals all call out and cheer at her, they cry above heads, 'See here, see! The music has got to Big Sal!', 'Dance for us, Sal!', and Sal bends and grinds and sways in time. 'It'll aye be a grand night, boys, if the good lady is on her feet.' And see, dear reader? There is not a drop of sweat on her. Her lungs are full of breath. As Big Sal dances and the boys all clap and whistle she can feel the weight lift from her body, the fat peel away. She is free, she is free! And as fit as the fiddler himself!

Lucy Westbry, she too is asleep, head sinking in soft pillows, wearing her pink and white rock-candy pyjamas and dreaming a different dream. She is at the school prom, wearing her blue dress and pearl earrings, slow dancing with Billy. She often has this dream and it plays out just as she remembers it, he with his hands on her waist, she with her hands on his shoulders. They sway and waddle in tight little circles, around and around and around. She knew they would kiss at the end of the song. That is what always happens. Sure enough, when the song draws to silence Billy moves closer, Lucy leans forward, only their clumsy lips and open mouths and wet tongues never meet; instead there is the barking and clawing and gnashing of teeth as Billy's face blurs and a hundred heads come screaming and spitting to surround Lucy.

She wakes. Sitting bolt upright and breathing heavily. She looks around in the gloom, the curtains backlit by the golden glow of the streetlights, her furniture black lumps shaping the dark. Lucy sighs as she allows herself to fall back into her pillows. 'Damn it, Ani. I knew that would happen,' she says.

Young Elizabeth Mary Duda, our good friend Max, is not asleep. She is lying in her bed listening to the pigeons outside her window. It is early morning, the dawn is just breaking, the night sky is brightening into an inky blue. Our Max is deep in thought. About God.

A girl from youth club had told her that Jesus spoke to people through the birds. That was why Max had dropped torn bread and seeds into the guttering outside her window. Now she is listening hard as two feral pigeons coo and bicker and peck at each other over the scraps scattered across the roof tiles.

Max gets out of bed to watch them. Her cropped blonde hair is sticking out in tufts. Her *Pokémon* pyjama top is only half tucked into her bottoms. She leans her elbows on the windowsill and rests her chin in her hands. 'Don't fight, wee pigeons. There's plenty of food for both of you,' she says. But the two pigeons continue to peck and coo at each other. Their sharp beaks nip at the bread and seeds and then at each other's feathers. Max is concentrating on the sounds they are making. 'If Jesus speaks to us through birds,' she wonders, 'how am I supposed to understand?'

Max yawns. It is early. The pigeons woke her. As the colours break across the sky with pink traces amongst the clouds, Max's mind wanders. She thinks about all the fairytales and stories where animals can speak and humans can understand them. *Little Red Riding Hood*, *The Three Bears*, *Cinderella*, *The Jungle Book*, the Narnia stories . . . There's a lot! Even in the Bible, didn't the snake speak to Eve? And isn't there a talking donkey?

She thinks about her mother's framed painting, in the hallway, of St Francis of Assisi, arms outstretched in prayer and the birds and beasts of the wood gathered all around his feet. St Francis could talk to the animals, why couldn't she? If she was a superhero *that* would be her greatest power.

Max turns away from the window with another yawn and shuffles back to her bed. She sends out a little prayer. 'God,' she says, 'when you talk to me I hope you'll speak in English. It will be a lot easier. Love you!' These words at the end are automatically tagged on, like the end of her phone calls to her father. 'Oh! And Amen,' she adds, because everyone knows the prayer won't be sent if not properly stamped.

Such beautiful innocence! It will be almost sad when thoughts of the strange-looking nameless man return to worry this young mind.

Mrs Ada Benson lies alone on one side of a large double bed. She is awake. In the warmth of the room she has pushed back the floral duvet to around her waist and kicked free her bare feet and legs from the goose down. Her right hand has reached out into the space her husband has left, her palm smoothing over the sleep-creases of the bed sheet.

Mrs Ada Benson stares up at the light fitting with its pretty shade and tassels hanging from the ceiling. She is aware of the birdsong coming in through the open window, but she is not listening to it. Not like she might normally listen in the morning. Her face is straight-lipped and wearied.

Outside in the garden, Mr Benson stands in his dark blue dressing gown and matching slippers. He is completely still, hands in pockets. He is breathing in the honeysuckle scent and staring at the yellow blossom climbing and winding its way through the wooden garden arch. Somewhere a bee hums. Mr Benson takes out his hand from his pocket and brings it to his forehead, massaging his temples and running his finger and thumb back and forth across his thick eyebrows. He breathes in deeply, eyes closed, and exhales with a sigh.

Once upon a time there was an old watchmaker
who believed he could make the cleverest clock.
A clock that proved time doesn't exist at all.
A clock that both ticked
        and didn't tick at the same time.

164

A quantum clock
that held everything past, present and future
in one dimensionless point.

Mr Benson is remembering the day he and Jacob sat together in his clock workshop, the day Jacob had locked himself out of the flat. How was it that despite being surrounded by all those ticking clocks, Mr Benson had lost track of time? They had spoken for hours. Or at least Mr Benson had spoken. Jacob, in truth, had said very little. Such an unusual young man! He'd listened with such active interest to everything Mr Benson had said about clocks and watches and time. He'd listened so intensely, in fact, biting down on his bottom lip, that when he'd relaxed Mr Benson could see toothmarks in the soft skin. 'You remind me of my old school teacher,' Jacob had said when he was leaving. 'You're just like him.'

The bee hums somewhere closer now. Or perhaps it is a different bee. Mr Benson with head bowed is looking down at his feet. With both hands back in his dressing-gown pockets he slips out of his slippers and stands on the soft green lawn. For a moment he does nothing but concentrate on the feel of the grass underneath his feet and in between his toes. Then he allows himself to imagine those old toes and nails growing into roots and digging into the surface of the lawn, burrowing down into the soil, deeper and deeper. He imagines his spine twisting like the trunk of an old tree, his arms reaching out like branches and his skin browning to cracked rough bark in the sun. This is how old Mr Benson often imagines his end. Never in his study where he whiles away the hours collecting time and giving old broken clocks the ability to tick again. His imagined end is always in this garden. And he always turns into a tree.

'Stan?' The soft voice of his wife interrupts his thoughts. Mr Benson turns to see Ada standing a few paces behind him. She too is in her dressing gown, pale pink. She is tying the cord tighter around her waist. 'Come inside, Stan,' her voice is gently teasing. 'What on earth will the neighbours think if they see us standing out here in our nightclothes?'

Mr Benson smiles. He lets out a 'Huh!' of laughter, but the good feeling is short lived, the smile disappears as he turns his face to look back at the honeysuckle. 'Oh, Ada,' he says. He bows his head. 'I'm an old fool of a man.' He looks back at his wife to see her reaction. Her smile is tight-lipped. Her eyes are watery with sad concern.

'Please, Stan,' she says. 'Come inside. I'll put a pot on.'

13

'Are you hungry, Jake?' The girl pokes
Jacob in the side. 'Jakey? Fancy a Chinese?
I don't mind going out for one.'

A different year, a different time, a different place. 22 September 2004, the autumnal equinox. Chalked onto the floorboards of a town's scout hut is a five-pointed star. Coloured tea-lights and candles dimly light the hall and we can see through the murk, sitting with crossed legs at each point of the pentagram, there are five robed individuals, arms outstretched and fingers touching as they softly chant. Jacob is among them, known to this group as Otto. He sits on the western point. We cannot see his face shadowed in the hood of his long ceremonial robe, but we can see the wiry point of his purple beard.

A bell is rung.

The chanting stops.

'The wheel has once more turned,' a voice speaks out, 'and the change of season begins.'

An altar is decorated with red cloth and scattered with seeds and pine cones and ivy vines. Incense is burning.

'Light and dark, day and night, O Lord and Lady, we worship you and the internal balance of nature. Life leads to death and death to new life. We give thanks.' A bell is rung again, three times. 'We welcome the darkening of days,' the voice says.

'Tell me, Mr Benson, what do you know about Jacob?' The pink-haired woman clasps her hands in front of her and rests them on the table. 'I'd imagine only what his mother told you. And what was that? That he was mad? Clinically insane?'

'She worried about him,' the old man replies.

'She smothered him.'

'She believed he would hurt himself. He had suicidal tendencies.'

'Please, Mr Benson, I experienced Jacob's "suicidal tendencies" first hand. Nothing more than a scratch on his wrist. I could have done more damage by beating him round the head with a pillow.' The pink-haired woman breaks her hands free from their clasp and taps her long nails against the surface of the kitchen table. 'I wonder if Olivia told you about Jacob's "epiphany"?' she asks. 'His grand lightbulb "eureka!" moment? No? Then please, you're in for a treat! Would you like another cup of tea, Mr Benson?' She stands, not waiting for a reply, to refill and switch on the kettle. 'Let me set the scene,' she says with an air of drama. 'There he was, lying in a bath surrounded by all those lovely warm bubbles, meditating on that interminable question – what *is* the point? Is life really *this* meaningless? And he was on the very edge of doing it; the knife-edge, quite literally. He was going to see it through, Mr Benson, he was going to kill himself. He had the razor blade digging into his wrist. Not too hard. Of course not too hard. He wanted to feel the sharp point of the blade first. A taster. Maybe dig a little deeper and watch a bead of blood bubble up and out of his body. It was only natural, don't you think? After all, he'd been planning it for weeks. Psyching himself up. You wouldn't want to rush into these things, would you? Let careful planning become sloppy. He wanted it to be perfect. He wanted it to be dramatic. He wanted it to be beautiful.'

'Did Jacob tell you all this?'

'Please, Mr Benson, wait for it. We're getting to the best bit.' The pink-haired woman raises her voice to compete with the growing rumble of the kettle. 'So naturally Jacob's "suicide" wasn't quite as beautiful as he'd hoped. For one thing there was nothing romantic or beautiful about the bathroom, with its peeling wallpaper and damp dirty mould and ill-fitting frosted windows. (No offence, Mr Benson, but I hope you've given that flat a face-lift since we moved out.) And for another thing, the point of the blade digging into Jacob's wrist hurt – and that was some-thing Jacob simply hadn't accounted for. Pain. So he stopped. He sat up. He had a re-think. It was while re-thinking his sorry life and all its meaninglessness that he realised for those last few weeks, with all his careful planning and obsessing over suicide, spending every waking moment dreaming of his final breath, he'd actually been somewhat content. He'd given himself a purpose. Not the healthiest purpose, I'll grant you that, but a purpose none-theless. And thus began Jacob's obsession with obsessions. Eureka!' Solace leans across the kitchen table, reaching with her long thin arms to take hold of Mr Benson's mug. 'I know,' she says, 'I was disappointed too. Archimedes' bath-time eureka moment was by far more inspiring.'

'I'm not sure I follow,' the old man says.

'That's probably because you're trying to intellectualise something incredibly basic, Mr Benson.' Steam pours from the spout of the metal kettle. 'Don't try so hard. Jacob really isn't the genius his mother made him out to be.' The kettle clicks off. The bubbles die down to a simmer. 'Milk no sugar, right?'

'Thank you,' says Mr Benson.

'My pleasure.'

And in a few swift moments a fresh, hot mug of tea is presented to the old man.

A different year, a different time, a different place. June 2005. There is a polite, formal buzz in the air, the chinking of glasses, restrained laughter. We are standing at a theatre bar, waiting for our interval drinks and watching the throng of smart-casual theatregoers milling about and making conversation. Jacob is here. Of course he is. But you won't recognise him. Look, over there, standing at the far end of the bar. See the grey-haired man with the dicky bow? The man with weight to his cheeks and a gut that pillows out (just a little) from underneath his collared flower-print shirt? That's Jacob. Transformed by weight, wig and glasses. Although perhaps you *would* recognise him. By the long grey coat that is tucked neatly over his arm; or by the way he is staring empty-eyed into his drink.

'Benny, Benny!' a voice booms from across the room, and a fat bald-headed man appears with the command of a red-faced ringmaster. Jacob looks up. He smooths down his shirt and straightens his tie. He *smiles*. It is an awkward uncomfortable twist of a smile, but it's a smile nonetheless. 'How are you, my fine fellow? It's good to see you.' Followed by much back-slapping and hand-shaking. 'You've met my wife, Agatha? Agatha, this is Benny Silverside, playwright and theatre critic for *Total Theatre and Preview*. And how have you been finding the Candelabra Theatre Company's modern interpretation of Brecht's *Threepenny Opera*? No, wait, don't answer that, first let me buy you a drink.'

'You're very kind, Mr Metcalf. Mine is a sherry.'

*

'So this epiphany,' Mr Benson pulls the mug closer to him, 'is simply that man must make his own purpose in life?'

'You've got it.' The pink-haired woman leans back against the kitchen unit. 'I told you it was basic. But what's interesting about this epiphany is Jacob's interpretation of it. Potential ultimate control over "who" he is.' She slurp-sips at her own hot mug of tea. 'I mean, OK, I thought he really was nuts when he first told me about all this, but now I see it from his point of view. This "epiphany" allows him to mould new identities for himself by changing his "purpose", as you say. Or, as he says, "obsession". *The self in despair wants to be master of itself or to create itself*, as Kierkegaard once said. So yeah, you know, I can see how it was a real breakthrough for him. I mean, think about it: throughout his childhood his mother insisted he was mad, a loner, Billy-no-mates. Then there was Adam with all his trickeries, messing with his mind. Jacob began to believe he really *was* crazy. He even started acting crazy. He became more and more withdrawn. He always muttered to himself. Without warning he would laugh loudly and aggressively. There was even one year he stopped talking altogether.'

'Yes, I heard about that.'

The pink-haired woman nods. She slurps again at her tea. 'He became an oddball, Mr Benson. We all would under those conditions. But at least when I first met him he was an oddball with an interesting philosophy. Not this banal "Theory of Obsession", that didn't come until much later. When I first met Jacob he used to talk about his "Theory of Others". He believed Identity was not some-thing we chose for ourselves, nor was it something that

172

grew organically as we got older. It was something gifted to us. By others. Jacob used to imagine Identity as a kind of malleable gloop that could be manipulated by the people around us; never fixed, but changing with every situation and circumstance. It's a frightening thought, Mr Benson. Unnerving, don't you agree? I mean, how does it make you feel to think you're not actually in control of who you are? You're just a *reaction* to the environment around you, or a *reflection* of how other people see you.'

'I'm not sure I agree.'

'Oh, you don't have to. But it explains a lot about Jacob, don't you think?' The pink-haired woman reaches for a large square tin next to the kettle. 'I don't know, maybe it's all a load of nonsense, but there's some little gem of truth hiding in there. I can see it glittering.' She pops open the tin and places it on the table. 'Biscuit, Mr Benson?'

14

'If you could be somebody famous, who would you be and why?' The girl who is curled under Jacob's arm stares up at the ceiling.

'You've asked me that before,' Jacob says.

'You never answered,' she replies.

On 1 July the schools break up for summer and it's to this day that we will fast forward. Max, with her school rucksack swinging off one shoulder, is running home as soon as she leaves the school gates. Some friendly voices call out to her, 'Lizzy, wait up!' but she turns on her heels and shouts back that she can't stop, she has things to do, important things. She runs almost all the way home with the empty tupperware inside her lunchbox rattling with every bouncing step. She lets herself into the house with her own key.

Her mother has left a note on the table in the hallway: LIZZY, I'M CLEANING THE CHURCH. MEET ME THERE. Max reads the note, but doesn't touch it. She doesn't want to leave any fingerprints. She dumps her schoolbag at the bottom of the staircase and runs up to her bedroom to get changed. She pulls on her Teenage Mutant Hero Turtle jeans, a bright yellow T-shirt and the stonewashed jean jacket her father gave her on her last birthday. 'Max,' she says to her reflection in the hallway mirror. Really she *does* look like a boy. She returns to her room to pick up her evidence box and to put on her base-ball cap. Dark red in colour, it is a little too big for her small head, but she wants to wear it anyway. 'Detective Max Duda.' The name suits her more than Elizabeth Mary. '*Jak się masz?*' she says to her reflection. '*Mam na imię* Detective Max Duda.' She has started to teach herself Polish.

At the bottom of the stairs Max empties her schoolbag. The tupperware and exercise jotters she just leaves on the floor in the hallway and in her bag she puts the evidence box. It is a lot fuller after several days of collecting treasures. Max had found a broken earring, a baby's dummy, a rubber ball with a love heart printed onto it and a fifty-cent coin her mum told her was from Europe. All these items, Max had decided, were 'clues' that would eventually help solve the 'Man With No Name' mystery. But her best clue yet, the 'lead' she was following, was her very own pocket bible.

Max is at the front door again; she pats her trouser pockets to make sure she has the key, and then she leaves, clicking the door shut behind her and swinging her rucksack back over her shoulder.

It was the priest who had given her the clue, or at least it was something he'd said during last Sunday's service. 'Times can be hard,' he'd said, 'and it is easy for our hearts to turn away from God at these times, it is easy for us to question His motive. What God is this, we ask, who does such wicked things? And yet when things run smoothly for us, we never question His work. We accept His graciousness with open arms. We accept unquestioningly. Why not then accept the challenges in life that God sets us?' The priest is a large, balding, square-faced man who shakes his hands at the congregation when he speaks. His presence is powerful. His voice booming. His arm gestures wide and sweeping. When he wants to make a particular point he leans forward on his lectern and presses his fingers into the hard wood. 'We. Must. Accept. Unquestioningly.' Max always feels as though the priest is telling her off during his sermons. She always keeps her back straight and sits on her hands whenever he speaks. 'But in these times of suffering,' he'd continued, 'we can find solace in God's love and solace in His word and scripture.'

'Solis?' Max had even said the word out loud – not so loud the priest could hear, but loud enough for her mother to glare. Solis in God's love. Solis in His word and scripture. She was sure she'd heard him right. Max had pinched her lips together and listened intently to the rest of the sermon, but there was no more mention of 'solis'.

'Hi, Christy.'

'Hey, Lizzy, have you come to choose your summer reading?'

'No.' The door of the local library closes behind Max. 'Can I use a computer?'

'Of course you can.'

Max chooses a computer from the cluster on the centre table. 'And by the way,' she says as she swizzles the mouse on its mouse mat, 'I've changed my name to Max.'

'Max?'

'Uh-huh.' Max clicks for the internet. 'I want to be called Max from now on. Not Lizzy.'

'Oh. OK,' Christy sounds uncertain. 'How come?'

'Just cos.'

From behind the reception desk Christy watches young Lizzy, now Max, type with index fingers on the computer keyboard. She glances over the ill-fitting jean jacket and the baseball cap with its overlapping popper-fastener pulled as tight as it will go (and still the cap is too big). Christy has always had a fondness for this curious young girl. She comes in two or three times a week, every week, to browse the shelves and select titles, seemingly at random, to sit and flick through on one of the massive brightly coloured beanbags in the Kids' Corner. Always polite. Always chirpy. Always alone.

Christy pushes her dark-rimmed glasses up to the top of her nose. They hadn't slipped down, this is an habitual action. She is remembering the day she asked Lizzy what her parents did, and the girl had replied, 'Oh, my dad is part Polish and my mum's a Christian.' It had made Christy laugh.

The library isn't busy. There is an old man looking in the local history section and a mother and daughter in the Kids' Corner. Christy slips out from behind the reception desk and walks over to the girl at the computer. 'So . . . Max . . .' she congratulates herself for remembering the name-change, kids can get funny if you don't play along with their games, 'what are you looking up?'

'Oh, just this thing . . .'

Christy pushes up her glasses and peers at the screen. The words 'SOLIS IN THE BIBLE' have been Googled, and underneath the search results:

Did you mean: ***souls in the bible***
silas in the bible   ***bullies in the bible***

'It's a code,' Lizzy explains. She has taken out a notebook from her schoolbag and is jotting down some of the links the search engine has thrown up. 'Solis,' she says. 'It's a codeword and I need to find out what it means.' Christy can see that in her shaky hand Lizzy has written the words *Dies Solis = (day of the sun)*.

'Is this homework?' Christy asks.

'Sort of,' Lizzy says.

'Is the word definitely . . .' and she frowns at the screen, 'solis?' Lizzy's hand has moved away from her notebook and is back on the mouse, navigating her way through more links. Christy can see now on the other page of the jotter the word CLUE has been written in big black capitals, followed by *Revrend Fransis = we can find solis in Gods love and solis in his words and* ~~scrips skrips~~ *the Bible.*

'Oh!' Christy reaches for the pen. 'I think you mean *solace*.' She writes it underneath the clue. 'S-O-L-A-C-E. It means . . .' and she pauses, her mouth jerking into a crooked pucker as she tries to think how best to explain the word. 'It means to find calm in something . . . or someone . . . when you're feeling upset. Here. Let me show you.' She leans over Lizzy to type the word into the search engine. 'There,' she says, as the definition comes up. 'Comfort or consolation in a time of distress or sadness. I was close, wasn't I?'

'And it's pronounced the same?' Lizzy's face looks flushed with excitement; she lifts her cap to see the screen better.

'That's right.'

But Christy has to break away from the girl and her code-cracking to sign out some books for the mother and daughter. A lost-looking backpacker comes in asking if he could use the internet, he's heard there is a hostel someplace nearby. A local resident pops in to return some late books and pay his fine. He stops to chat for a while. Then the telephone rings. By the time the next lull in Christy's workday comes, young Lizzy is packing away her notebook and pen. She logs off the computer.

'Have you cracked it?' Christy asks the girl as she is passing the desk. 'Have you solved the puzzle?'

'I'm one step closer,' says the girl.

Christy can see now she is clutching in her hand a black pocket bible with gilded page edges. 'I've gotta go meet my mum,' she says, but hesitates as though not wanting to leave. She stands hugging her book to her chest, a blush creeping into her white cheeks. 'Thanks for helping me, Christy,' and her face turns crimson as the words come out.

'Oh,' Christy nods with a smile, 'my pleasure . . . Max.'

15

The girl shifts onto her side and moves slightly away from Jacob. He opens one eye. 'Where are you going?' he asks.

'Nowhere,' she says. 'I just wanted to look at you.'

Jacob grunts and closes his eye again. 'Go to sleep,' he says.

When the school bell rings for the end of the day, Lucy isn't rushed like the rest of her class. She moves slowly, packing her pen, ruler, Tipp-Ex and rubber carefully into her pencil case, slipping her jotter into her workbook and sliding it into her satchel. All around her the sound of chatter fills the room, zips hurriedly closing rucksacks, the metal legs of chairs clattering against tables, the hurried shuffling of feet filing out into the corridor, but Lucy takes her time.

'Hey, Lucy, slow coach, hurry it up!' Her friend is waiting by the door. 'Billy said he'd drive us straight to the river.'

'I can't go,' Lucy says. 'Not any more.'

'What do you mean you can't go?'

'Mum wants me home, it's . . . Anya's birthday. We're having a special dinner.' Lucy shrugs. 'Sorry. I completely forgot about it. I'll come to the river another time. Maybe tomorrow.'

Her friend hesitates, unsure and disbelieving, before saying, 'Well, OK. I'll tell the others,' and then she disappears with a backward call of, 'Text me!'

Let's follow her, reader, this friend of Lucy's, as she moves with the crowd in the corridor through wide-open doors and down echoing stairs to the schoolyard outside, all jostling elbows and playful pushing. Someone punts a football and it skids across the concrete in front of her. There is laughter and the calling of names. The football is punted back by a squealing, giggling girl who makes a show of not being able to kick a ball. She covers her mouth in mock shock as it rolls off at an unaimed angle. A group

182

of boys tease her. Her friends laugh and wrap their arms around her. Lucy's friend hurries by.

Her name is Nessa, this girl; we have met her very briefly before. She is making her way to the car park where Billy is waiting in his Fiesta, peering out from behind the wheel. He frowns as Nessa walks past. 'Where's Lucy?' he mouths. She shrugs in response.

'She's not coming,' she says as she slips in next to him.

'What? Why not?'

'Her mum's cooking a special meal. For Anya.'

'Who the fuck is Anya?' This question is voiced from the backseat of the car where two of Billy's friends are sitting. Billy shakes his head dismissively and turns the key in the ignition. 'Whatever,' he says.

'Well what?' says the voice from the back. 'What's so special about Anya that she deserves such a special dinner?'

Nessa is looking at Billy, who is blushing fiercely.

'Well?'

When he doesn't answer, Nessa turns in her seat to look squarely at the two boys. 'Anya is Lucy's other mother,' she says. 'It's her birthday, so they're spending the evening together.'

'What do you mean, "other mother"?'

Nessa sighs and turns back into her seat. 'What do you mean, what do I mean? She has *two* mothers.' She eyes Billy again, who is pinch-lipped and crimson as he turns onto the road. 'They're lesbians,' she says, and as soon as the words are out they seem to expand. They fill the entire car.

'What the fuck?' says the voice in the back. 'Are you serious?'

Perhaps the scene that follows can be put down simply to unfortunate timing, but there is Lucy. She is walking along the same stretch of road Billy is travelling on. She walks with head bowed, studying her feet. Black skirt, white polo shirt, jumper tied around her waist. Before leaving the school she brushed her hair. No longer pony-tailed, its dark length falls over her shoulders and reaches down her back. Every so often she lifts the leather strap of her satchel to ease the textbook weight from her shoulder. Unfortunate timing. That's all. But there are the boys, eagerly rapping knuckles on the car window as they approach, hooting and whooping with such immoderate glee at this unexpected piece of information.

'Lesbians? Are you *serious*?'

'Quick! There she is! Wind down the window.'

Unfortunate timing. Lucy looks up as the sound of tapping and muffled hollering comes from behind her. It's Billy's car. It speeds up as it passes, but not quickly enough to distort the words whipping out from the wound-down window. '*Dyke daughter.*' The words slow Lucy almost to a standstill. Dyke daughter? She knows who the two boys are, friends of Billy's, appropriately nicknamed Pea Pod (he is small) and Goon (he is an idiot). Lucy doesn't feel offended, she feels stunned.

In her pocket her phone blips. A text message from Ness.

Ignore them. Goon is
SUCH a prick. xx

Lucy doesn't reply. She pockets the phone, readjusts the satchel strap on her shoulder and walks on, one foot quickly

184

in front of the other. She is numb. *Dyke daughter?* She notices the sound of her footsteps as they strike against the pavement, *clack-ick, clack-ick*. She looks down at her legs walking. Black buckle shoes and grey pavement. It is not until Lucy has turned the corner and walks a few more steps that she feels the heat in her face and the anger rising. No, it's humiliation, not anger. She feels the need to swear, but doesn't.

Fucking idiots can't think of anything more original to shout. I mean dyke daughter? What the hell is that? It's not even a proper insult.

Lucy holds up her hand, palm down, to watch her fingers quiver. She is actually *shaking*.

'Lucy? Is that you?'

Lucy has let herself into the flat.

'Lucy?'

'Yeah, Mum, it's me.'

'I'm in the kitchen.'

Lucy throws her satchel onto the sofa. She pulls off her shoes.

'Good last day?' Her mother is at the kitchen sink, her hands and arms plunged in washing-up suds. 'I thought you were going straight to the river after school?'

'I changed my mind.'

Her mother turns. She is wearing an apron that says 'Be nice to me or I'll poison your food'. She wipes the bubbles that cling to her hands on a tea-towel. 'You sound flat,' she says. And before Lucy can stop herself, before she even has time to think, she says the words, 'Billy and I have split up.' And then she's sobbing. Real tears welling up and dripping down her face. She's sobbing into her mother's arms, heaving in heavy gulps of air.

'Oh, Lucy.' Her mother is rubbing her back. 'What happened? Did he call things off? Oh dear. Oh, Lucy. I'm so sorry.'

Later, when Lucy is lying in bed reflecting back, she feels puzzled. Where did all that come from? Such an extreme emotional reaction and yet she'd felt oddly removed from the whole situation. The emotion hadn't felt like it belonged to her, somehow. It was as though she'd been trapped inside her own mind, looking out; and yet her body had responded to it all so physically. Her chest had felt tight, her throat constricted, her lungs couldn't seem to take in enough air.

More to the point, it had been a *lie*. Billy had not called things off. In fact he'd later sent a text message apologising on behalf of his stupid friends.

SORRY ABOUT GOON AND POD.
THEY R DICKHEADS. COME TO RIVER
AFTER DINNER? I CAN PICK U UP X

The kiss at the end was Nessa's touch. She knew her friend would have nagged Billy to send a text. Perhaps Billy had even been glad of her guidance? Lucy could well imagine Billy reading out the message to her friend and then Nessa asking, 'Is there a kiss? Let me see . . . no, Billy, sign off with a kiss. Don't you know anything about girls? Always sign off with a kiss.'

But that's just it: Billy really doesn't know anything about girls. He is clunky and awkward most of the time, yet has those strange flashes of sudden overwhelming self-assuredness that feels almost bullying. Lucy can't decide which side of this 'Billy' she finds less appealing. The fumbling inexperience or the bravado confidence. And why does he always text using block capitals? I mean, really, what is *wrong* with him?

'Or maybe there's something wrong with *me*?' She says this out loud to no one. The room responds with a deep silence. Even the ticking of her oversized alarm clock sounds empty. She gets to her feet and stands by the mirror. 'Who are you? What do you want?' She looks at her tired, tear-stricken face. 'I don't understand,' she tells it. 'Why are you here?' Her reflection looks pale. Her eyes look small and black. It's not her, she thinks. It doesn't look like her, not really; she doesn't recognise the reflection staring back. 'I'm changing,' she says to herself. 'That's what it is.' And somehow she knows that the change in her is rooted in the new lodger at Pauper's Inn.

Jacob Little. Almost an entire week has passed and still Lucy hasn't met him. She hasn't even *seen* him. All she's managed to obtain are scraps of passing opinion from Big Sal or Alex the barman.

'He's a bit odd though, isn't he, Sal? A bit awkward. It's like he doesn't really know how to work his own body. His movements seem kinda . . . out of rhythm, you know? And he's not really . . . well, *expressive*. He's the sorta guy who walks into a room and sucks out all the energy. You know what I mean? And I don't think I've seen him smile *once*.'

Whereas Big Sal had kept more to physical attributes. 'Skinny as a rake', 'terrible teeth'. 'I just wouldn't know what to do with a man like that . . . all sharp bones and no meat. I'd snap him like a twig.'

Such damning reports! But Lucy doesn't care.

'I'll tell ye what, Lucy, that man drinks like a fish and

smokes like a chimney. I went to his room only this mornin'
– to fix that damn window, mind – and there were empty
bottles all over the floor and an ashtray overflowin', butts
scattered everywhere. And aye, but he's a morose sort, is
he no'? There's a black cloud over that man's head. I can
see it!'

Surface detail. None of it matters. If only Big Sal had
seen the green jotter and had read what Lucy had read,
then she wouldn't be saying those things. *Love is tainted.
Love is imperfect. Love is not good enough for you.*

She turns away from the mirror and opens the skylight.
It is still light outside, the night is warm. Her friends, she
knows, will camp out by the river. They'll have made a fire
and pitched a tent. In previous years Lucy would have felt
left out had she not been there, but this year she feels
content alone in her bedroom. Yes, she is changing. She
can even *feel* it. There is a buzz underneath her skin.
Excitement. Anticipation. Restlessness. This summer something *big* is going to happen.

From the mirror she takes down the picture of the
Honeymoon Nude. Solace. Lying back on the bed, pillows
piled behind her, she traces the arching eyebrows of the
woman with her finger. 'Where are you?' she asks. 'Do you
know someone is looking for you? Do you know someone
loves you?' And absentmindedly she mimics the pose of
the woman in the painting, finger pointing inwards at
herself.

16

The girl kisses Jacob's chest, she licks his nipples, she presses her lips against every rib as she moves down. The tip of his cock brushes against her body. Purpling-bluish in colour, blood pulsing, veins thickening. It touches her breasts. The nape of her neck. And then her lips. She smells its skin. She smells the sex. She opens her mouth.

'Watch your teeth,' he says.

Come, let us take our fill of love until the morning.
Let us solace ourselves with loves.

(Proverbs 7:18)

I could strengthen you with my mouth,
and the solace of my lips would assuage your pain.

(Job 16:5)

Sex. That's what the Bible was talking about and that was why Max had flushed such a brilliant red on saying goodbye to Christy. Only moments before she'd been thinking about two naked bodies pressing close to each other and kissing. You had to be naked to have sex and you had to be kissing. And then Christy had smiled at her, 'Have you cracked it? Have you solved the puzzle?' Poor Max couldn't stop the blush from creeping up. It was like being caught out in her thoughts. 'I have covered my bed with coloured linens from Egypt. I have perfumed my bed with myrrh, aloes and cinnamon. Come, let's drink deep of love till morning; let's enjoy ourselves with love!' Those were the words in her pocket bible. Online they had been slightly different. 'Come, let us take our fill of love until the morning. Let us solace ourselves with loves.' But it all meant the same thing. Sex. The type adults did for fun, not just to make a baby.

Max runs all the way to the church. She slows down only as she passes through the gates into the grounds. 'Come, let's drink deep of love . . .' The drone of the hoover drifts out from inside the church. Max climbs the steps. She wonders what aloes are as she enters the nave. She imagines them to be something not unlike those small spiky things you press into oranges at Christmas time. Cloves. But you wouldn't want anything like *that* in your bed. 'With persuasive words she led him astray; she seduced him with her smooth talk.' In truth Max does not really understand what the words are trying to say, or what some of them mean. The topic is foreign to her, a concern for adults only, and yet she is excited by what she reads. The words contain secrets, tantalisingly close and yet just out of reach.

> *All at once he followed her*
> *like an ox going to slaughter,*
> *like a deer stepping into a noose*
> *till an arrow pierces his liver,*
> *like a bird darting into a snare,*
> *little knowing it will cost him his life.*

She is only ten years old, a competent reader, but still she will sound out those longer words with difficult spellings. Sla-ug-h-ter. She doesn't know where or what Sla-Ug-H-Ter is, only that an ox would go there. Max knows that an ox is a type of cow from the olden days. Perhaps Sla-Ug-H-Ter was where people from the Bible had their cattle show? She is thinking now of the cattle show she goes to every year with its funfair rides and all the stalls and candyfloss and the marching band. She thinks of the prize bulls all penned up waiting to be led around the showground by the farmers. The cattle show was a lot of fun.

Max has already walked past the stone font and has slipped into one of the rear pews. She reads and rereads the words. 'Then out came a woman to meet him, dressed like a prostitute and with crafty intent.'

Prostitutes are bad. Prostitutes are like paedophiles and murderers and thieves. Max isn't allowed to talk to them. So what are they doing in the Bible? Ox, deer, birds and prostitutes. She struggles to make sense of it all.

This moment will stay with Max forever. It is the moment she realises the Bible is full of the things left unsaid, it is full of violence and sex and death, not just miracles and magic and Noah's magnificent ark where the animals went in two by two, hurrah, hurrah! In future years Max will remember this as the moment she read the Bible for the first time and the moment it hooked her with its secrets.

The words.

Her mother has her back turned. She is hoovering the red carpet around the altar.

Max flicks through the tissue-thin pages of her bible to get to the book of Job. She knows the story from Sunday School. Job was a good man who loved God. One day, Satan said to God, 'You know, Job only loves you because you've been kind to him.' So God said to Satan, 'Very well, you can test him. Do as you will. Take away everything I've given him and we will see if he still loves and worships me.' So Satan kills all Job's sheep and cows and camels. He sends a terrible windstorm that sweeps away his children. And when Job hears about all this he tears off his robe and shaves his head and falls to the ground in worship. 'Naked I came from my mother's womb, and naked shall

I depart. The Lord gave and the Lord has taken away; may the name of the Lord be praised.'

So immersed is Max in her reading and so loud is the sound of the hoovering that she does not sense that someone – it is Reverend Francis – has walked into the nave and now stands by the stone font watching her. Dog-collared and all in black, he has one hand in his pocket and the other resting on his chest as though touched by the sight of the young girl in the oversized baseball cap reading her bible so intently. There is a kind smile on his meaty face. His eyes are bright.

'Oh!'

Max looks up as her mother lets out this breathy exclamation.

'I didn't hear you come in, Father.'

Max turns. She too feels something in her startle as she notices the priest. She shifts in her seat, the red creeping back into her cheeks. The hoover has been switched off and the stillness of the church has returned.

'I didn't mean to startle you, Aggie,' the reverend's voice is deep. 'Nor you, Lizzy.'

'Lizzy! Goodness me, look at you both creeping around like a pair of ghosts. How long have you been sitting there? Never mind.' She is unplugging the hoover. 'I've finished up here, let me just put this away.' And she is wrapping the cable around the body of the bright yellow vacuum with its smiling face printed on the side.

Max shifts again in her seat as the reverend joins her in the pew. He chooses to sit quite close. The wood creaks under his weight. He looks massive in the narrow space, his knees almost touching the embroidered kneeler hanging on the pew in front. Max breathes in his smell, not sweaty or dirty, but of warm soapy skin. 'Well,' he says, 'you're reading the Bible?' The reverend clasps his hands in his lap. 'May I ask which bit?' The sound of the cable slapping against the plastic body of the hoover echoes in the old church.

'The book of Job,' says Max.

Reverend Francis smiles. He corrects her pronunciation. '*Jobe*,' he says. 'Very good. May I ask which part?'

Max wants to shrug and she almost does, but then remembers her mother telling her it is rude to shrug. Instead she mutters, 'The devil is testing Job. And Job is angry at God.'

'You're reading an adult's bible. Don't you find the language difficult?'

'Sometimes.' Max looks over to where her mother is hulking the hoover towards the vestry. She does not smile when their eyes meet. She looks caught up in irritation. She nods viciously towards her daughter and mouths some angry words. All at once Max is aware of the baseball cap still on her head and quickly she swipes it off. 'Sorry, Reverend, I forgot to take my hat off.'

'Oh,' says the reverend, 'I wouldn't worry about that. Have you seen the hat the bishop wears when he comes to visit?' He lets out a brief laugh that quickly trails into silence. 'No, but of course it's respectful to take your hat off during the church service.'

They are silent for a while, listening to the clattering coming out from the vestry. Max imagines her mother struggling with the hoover and the overstocked cupboard, mops and broom handles falling everywhere. The reverend does not seem to notice the noise. He is lost in thought.

'Job is an interesting man, isn't he, Lizzy? He's so good and upright and turns away from evil. He loves God with all his heart. So why then is he angry with God? Why does he curse the day he was born?'

Max feels so very small next to this big man.

'Is it because Job no longer loves God?' The reverend's face is turned towards the high altar. 'Is it because he's angry? Sad?'

'He's in pain,' Max says. 'Satan has covered him in sores. It's a test.'

'Yes. That's right. He's suffering.'

Max follows the reverend's eyes to where they seem to rest on the stained-glass window. She looks at the purples and reds and yellows of the angels and the bearded men on their knees with halos over their heads and in the centre Jesus is carrying the cross, his head bleeding from the crown of thorns. Max is struck by the sadness of Jesus, his eyes cast down as his knees buckle under the heavy weight. She thinks how similar his long, gaunt face is to the nameless man's face.

'It must seem to you a very strange thing,' the reverend says, 'but even suffering is a gift from God. It is through the cross we are defined as Christians.'

Max's mother reappears from the vestry, closing the door quietly behind her. She brushes down her skirt and smiles at the reverend and this time at Max. 'Well,' she says, 'cleanliness *is* next to godliness,' and she laughs. It is forced and high-pitched and girlish. The reverend smiles politely. Max doesn't smile at all; she's heard her mother make this joke before.

Reverend Francis is standing up and shuffling sideways along the pew to meet Max's mother.

'You've done a grand job, Aggie.'

'Always a pleasure, Reverend.'

'Bless you.'

The reverend turns his attention back to Max and announces how very inspiring it is to see such a young face taking an active interest in Bible study.

'Yes, she's a good girl,' says Max's mother.

Max is not oblivious to these words, but she pretends to be. The compliments from both her mother and the priest have lifted her. She feels proud. She keeps her eyes on the pages of her bible and listens for a moment more, but the subject has changed. The two adults have moved onto church meetings, the parish newsletter, the weather.

'And how's Mary?'

'Oh, she's not doing so well, Reverend, but I suppose as well as to be expected.'

'My prayers are with her, Aggie.'

'Thank you, Reverend.'

Suffering is a gift from God? Max closes their voices off as she trains her eyes back onto the words she was reading. She is thinking about her sick grandmother, wheelchair-bound and droopy-faced, unable to hold a glass of water or drink through a straw without dribbling. Perhaps if her grandma was physically able she would strip off her cardigan, her blouse, her skirt and shave off her perm – just like Job – and worship God: 'Naked I came from my mother's womb, and naked shall I depart. The Lord gave and the Lord has taken away; may the name of the Lord be praised.'

Max wonders what, deep down, the nameless man is so sad about. Is he sad because he doesn't know who he is?

It doesn't seem *enough*, somehow. Not when Job lost his whole family, his house, his possessions, his health. Not when Jesus suffered death on a cross through betrayal. Not when her grandma is stuck in a wheelchair. The nameless man has just lost his name. That's all.

Perhaps it will all make sense when she pieces together the clues.

'I could strengthen you with my mouth, and the solace of my lips would assuage your pain.' She has flicked forward to Job 16:5. But this passage is not about kissing, as Max had previously thought. It's about talking. Poor Job, who is lying in pain and covered in sores, is complaining that his friends are not comforting him. 'Will your long-winded speeches never end? What ails you that you keep on arguing? I also could speak like you, if you were in my place; I could make fine speeches against you and shake my head at you. But my mouth would encourage you; comfort from my lips would bring you relief.'

In Max's version of the Bible there is no mention of the word 'solace', nor is there that difficult word 'assuage', which Max doesn't understand, but she promptly decides that the exact wording doesn't matter. It's the *stories* that hide the clues. She is sure the stories will help her discover who the nameless man is. Yes, and then Max will be able to cure his sadness.

'Lizzy,' her mother calls her, 'come on now, it's time to go.'

Max blinks up at her mother.

'Well, come on then,' and her mother gestures for her to hurry.

'Goodbye, Lizzy.'

'Bye, Reverend.' Max has closed the bible onto her thumb to mark her place. 'See you on Sunday,' she says as she slips out from the pew.

'Yes,' says the reverend. 'See you on Sunday.'

But before Sunday, dear reader, there is Saturday; and Saturday is most certainly worth a mention.

17

'Jesus, Jacob, did you just fart?' The girl quickly presses the sleeping bag close to their bodies. 'Aw Jesus, Jacob, it *reeks*.' And she rolls away from his arm, burying her face deep in the fabric. 'It smells like something has crawled into your arse and died. Jesus, Jacob. Open a window, would you?'

Saturday. *Things happen*, you see. Things that are relevant to this story. It is on this sunny Saturday that down by the river in an uncomfortably warm tent smelling of sleep and sweat and flatulence, Billy receives a text message. His two friends Pod and Goon lie sprawled in the heat on their sleeping bags. Nessa is outside, firing up the camping stove to make coffee. The text is from Lucy. It says:

> We need to talk, Billy.
> Let's meet later? x

'See this,' he calls out to Nessa. 'She's going to finish with me.'

Nessa takes the phone and reads the message. 'You don't know that, Billy,' she says.

'I do though, don't I?' The phone is handed back. 'It's obvious. What else does "we need to talk" mean?'

Nessa has returned her attention to the kettle and stove.

'Well?' asks Billy.

'Well, what?' Nessa says.

It is also on this Saturday that Mr Benson has arranged to meet the woman 'Solace'. The arrangement was made a few days before. Not having heard back from Detective Stone, Mr Benson decided to take the investigation into his own hands. He dialled the phone number written on the back of the photograph kept in the shoebox.

'Oh, hello there, my name is Mr Stanley Benson. I believe you were a tenant of mine some years ago?' And without his saying very much more, the woman on the other end of the phone agreed to meet him.

So it is on Saturday at 11.45 a.m., Mr Benson steps out from his house, squinting into the bright sun. He admires the weather. He enjoys its warmth and even closes his eyes and turns his face to bask in it, yet he feels restless. A nervous knot. His wife's dry-lipped kiss is still on his cheek. She didn't ask him where he was going, she simply stated her own plans for the day: meeting with the girls from the WI at lunch; might pop in to see Abigail and the baby, Thomas, at 3ish; she'll cook a ham for tea. She no doubt expected her husband to respond with his own plans, but Mr Benson only nodded. 'That all sounds fine, dear,' he said and then the two fell into a short silence.

'Right, well,' his wife said. 'I should go and get ready.'

Mr Benson closes the front door behind him, checking the latch has locked. It isn't that he doesn't want his wife to know where he's going, he just knows she wouldn't understand. 'Oh, why are you getting *involved*, Stan?' That's what she would say. 'Stop playing detective, it has nothing to do with you.' But it does, doesn't it? Somewhere along the line he has been inextricably linked to this storyline, he has been written in. And *look*, he has told himself time and again this week, look at what happened when he tried to escape. Olivia Little. *What if . . . ?*

Mr Benson feels for the keys in the pocket of his brown tweed jacket. He'll be too warm in this jacket, he knows that, but it's smart. And, well, his daughter has often told him that tweed is very 'in' at the moment. Very 'Doctor

Who'. Apparently the latest Doctor wears tweed. Despite his love of clocks, Mr Benson has never been much of a fan of the time-travelling man in his TARDIS, but he enjoys inserting into conversation whenever a reference to the programme is made that he remembers the show from its very humble beginnings in the sixties. 'Did you know,' he'll say, 'that the first episode was aired on Saturday 23 November 1963?' He would always pause to hear the 'Really?' from his audience or the exclamation of amazement that old Stanley Benson, always quiet in his room full of ticking clocks, would know such a fact. 'I'll tell you how I know such a thing,' he would say. 'It's because it was aired the day after the US President was assassinated. Kennedy. And I was visiting Harry Sanderson to watch the news on his box – because, see, we hadn't bought our own television at that point, we were a bit behind the times. And it was Harry who said to me I should fetch my young Julie to watch this time-travelling programme.'

As Mr Benson unlocks his car, the memory of his first television comes back to him. It comes with the image of his two young daughters, Julie and Abigail, sitting in front of the box pressing coloured sweetie wrappers from a tin of Cadbury Roses to their eyes. 'Look, Daddy, we have colour TV.'

How times have changed!

Mr Benson checks his mirrors as he sits down. He presses on each pedal. He pulls the lever underneath his seat to push himself back a bit, then forward a bit, then back again to perhaps exactly the same spot as he'd started in. He opens the glove compartment to make sure the map is there and to take out his driving glasses. These driving glasses are the same prescription as his everyday glasses, but he likes to make a distinction between the two. He rearranges himself on the seat. He pulls at the trouser material around his crotch area. All morning his underwear has kept twisting up between the cheeks of his rear; why hasn't he changed them? Momentarily he contemplates getting back out of the car to go inside and change his Y-fronts, but then dismisses the idea. He's in the car now, the key is in the ignition, he should just *go*. But he doesn't. Not straight away. He finds himself staring blankly at the rear of the parked car in front.

Saturday at Pauper's Inn. Big Sal is sitting on her barstool. She is flicking through a magazine and picking at a packet of chilli nuts. She is reading the article headlines. '*My carrot soup obsession turned my skin orange!*' '*He locked me in the basement because I didn't love him enough.*' '*My husband wants to become my wife!*'

It is midday. The pub is empty. The sound of Big Sal crunching on those crispy chilli nuts is loud in the still air. Beer flies spiral around the draught pumps.

'*I was so fat they had to break down the wall to get me out!*'

The pub door opens. It's Lucy. But it's Lucy with a difference.

'Hey, Sal.'

'Oh my God!' Big Sal's eyes widen. 'You've gone blonde!'

Lucy laughs as she walks in. She spins on her toes to show off her new barnet. 'Whaddya think?' she asks and pats playfully at the bottom of her hair to make it bounce.

'Has your mother seen it? Either of them?'

'Not yet.'

'Well . . .' Sal pauses. 'Well, well . . .'

Lucy laughs again. 'You're lost for words, Sal.'

'Aye, lass, that I am.'

'Well, I like it.' Lucy pulls herself up onto a barstool and helps herself to a chilli nut. 'I fancied a change.'

'It's certainly that.' Big Sal leans forward, elbows on the bar, as she studies the girl. 'And you're wearing make-up,' she says. 'What is this? I'd say you went to bed a girl and woke up a minx!' She laughs playfully as she looks over Lucy's darkened eyes and bronzed cheeks, her platinum hair, her closely fitted T-shirt, snug around her slender body and rounded breasts. The T-shirt is plain white, unobtrusive. It allows the eye to pick out the sparkle of a necklace resting on top of the material. 'Have you got a date later, by any chance?' she asks.

Lucy is smiling coyly. She takes another chilli nut and pops it in her mouth. 'Now that would be telling.'

'Ha!' Big Sal taps her nose. 'No more questions needed,' she says. It pleases Sal to think she and young Lucy have such a good rapport. She imagines herself as a sort of confidante, someone Lucy can speak freely to about things she wouldn't usually discuss with her mothers. 'Well, ye look stunnin',' she says. 'Ye'll aye, knock the puff out the boy when he sees ye!' And as Lucy blushes Sal hoots her delight at the ceiling. 'Well, there's no need to pinch yer cheeks to make 'em go red,' she says. She offers the girl a Coke, but it's refused.

'Sorry, Sal, I can't stay.' Lucy slips off the barstool onto her feet. 'I'm just nipping to the loo quickly. Is the new lodger in?'

Sal pulls a face to indicate she doesn't know. 'Haven't seen him,' she says. 'Why?'

'Because the mirror in his bathroom upstairs is bigger.'

'Ha!' Again Big Sal guffaws at the ceiling. 'But it might no' be big enough for the head o' a blonde bombshell!'

In the corridor out the back, at the bottom of the stairs, Lucy pauses. Her smile – and her blush – slowly fade as she rests her hand on the cool wood of the banister. She breathes in the fusty smells, the damp and the dusty carpets. Her stomach tightens with excited nervous knots. From the back pocket of her skinny blue jeans Lucy takes out the picture of Solace and studies it. She draws in a deep breath. 'This is it,' she says.

It wasn't that she was trying to *be* Solace, she would later tell herself. It was more that she wanted what Solace had. Love. Attention. To be the object of obsession. She wanted someone to search for her, to long for her. You must excuse such juvenile thought processes, dear reader. After all, Lucy is only just sixteen. In her mind Jacob Little has become her Heathcliff and she has become his Cathy. It's a role-playing game that she wants to act out and *that* is why she has transformed herself into a wispy blonde not dissimilar to the one in the painting she now holds. She has round eyes like Solace and bud-like lips. She is slender with squarish hips.

It is the dark eyebrows that betray her.

But what can be done about them?

On the landing at the top of the stairs Lucy slips the picture back into her pocket. She doesn't want Jacob to know she's seen it. Because that would be weird, right?

His door has been left ajar. As Lucy approaches with a creep in her step she can see a sliver of the room. A table has been placed by the sash window and on top of the table there are green jotters. Lots of them, *piles* of them, stacked high or spread out over the table. She notices too that there is a glass ashtray on top of some loose papers and inside this ashtray there is a lit cigarette, still spiralling smoke.

The sunlight slants through the window, cutting over the table surface and casting a warm line of light across the floor. *This is it*. At this point Lucy would never have predicted that she would have *gasped*, but gasp she did when a man, the lodger, our protagonist, Jacob Little, steps into the slanting sunlight to retrieve his burning cigarette. One sharp intake of breath later and Jacob is looking directly at Lucy.

'Hello,' he says.

'Hi,' she says.

In years to come Lucy will often wonder whether *this* was the point their love affair really began. This moment of knowing silence. Both holding each other's gaze. It is over in a second, but already the memory distorts in Lucy's brain. She'll remember the intensity between them as an almost audible buzz and the length of the gaze seeming like forever. It is not the case. A man says 'Hello', a nervous girl says 'Hi' and then she steps forward, but doesn't quite enter the room. That is what actually happens.

'I hope I'm not disturbing you?'

Jacob does not reply. He turns a little in the sun and stubs the cigarette out in the ashtray. Lucy can see at last what Alex meant when he described the lodger as 'awkward', someone who 'doesn't really know how to work his own body'. As Jacob stubs out his cigarette his free arm hangs limp like a spare part. His back looks stiff. He turns at the hips, feet still firmly planted, and gives his full concentration to the ashtray.

Lucy steps forward again, pushing the door a little wider to take in the rest of the room. The mattress is still bare of bedclothes. The sleeping bag is scrunched on top. A pile of clothes is where a pillow would usually be. Lucy can also see now that the boxes have been unpacked. There they are, flattened in the corner. And yet there is little to show of their contents apart from a pile of books next to the mattress, acting as a sort of bedside table, and on top of them an incense burner.

'Sal wasn't sure if you were in,' she says, her hand resting on the inside doorframe. 'I just came up to use . . .' She stops as she feels unexpected bumps against her fingertips. All around the doorframe the lodger has tacked dozens of one-penny pieces.

'My lucky pennies,' the man says.

'Oh,' and Lucy is inside the room, turning so she can look at the doorway in full.

'I've been collecting them for years,' he says. 'See a penny, pick it up, all day long you'll have good luck.'

It isn't just the doorframe, the rickety old wardrobe is also covered in copper pieces. Most are a dull dirtied brown, but the occasional shiny pinned-to-the-wall penny glints back in the bright sunlight.

'That's a lot of luck,' Lucy says. The words feel feeble and awkwardly polite. She stares at all the coins, aware she is giving them more awe than they are due, and yet feeling more comfortable gawping at them than turning to face the man still standing by the window. 'I'm sorry for barging in on you like this,' she says. She is expecting him to say something like, 'no need to be sorry', or 'don't worry about it', but he says nothing. 'I came up to use the loo,' she says, 'and saw your door open. I thought, well, isn't it strange we haven't met yet?'

'Is it strange?' the man asks.

'Well, no, I mean, kind of, don't you think? I mean, I work here. I'm a glass collector and I help Sal with a bit of cleaning. Just a part-time job, y'know? Until I figure out what I'm doing next.' She wonders how old she looks to him. Would he guess she is still at school? 'And you . . . well, you've been here for a while already.'

'Yes.'

'And I just thought, well, isn't it funny we haven't met yet.' Lucy presses her tongue against the inside of her top teeth. This wasn't going according to plan. She was bumbling and blustering. 'My name—' she starts, but the man interrupts her with an 'Ah, yes, wait.' He is pointing at her. 'You're the girl who brought my boxes up the stairs.'

'Yes,' sighs Lucy with relief.

'Yes,' nods Jacob. He is smiling now. It is an awkward smile, one that shows off his crooked teeth. He looks different from how she'd imagined. He is skinnier, taller and more bedraggled, but there is something striking about his face and something sad in his eyes that draws her in. 'Well, I'm pleased to be able to say thank you in person.' She likes his accent. It is fairytale English, well spoken, but not posh, the unassuming prince. 'Will you stop for some tea?' he asks.

'I wouldn't want to be any trouble,' she says.

'No trouble,' he says. There is a kettle on the floor in the corner of the room. There is a box of tea and two mugs. He walks over to it, bends down, switches the kettle on. Lucy notices the holes in the heels of his socks, the tatty hems of his trouser legs, the pale blue V-neck jumper losing its threads around the armpits. This man is so very unlike Billy. It pleases her.

Lucy smiles and turns to the table by the window. 'So,' she says, with a surge of new confidence, 'what are you working on?' She is acting too familiar and yet somehow she knows the man will accept it. She glances over the green jotters, her eyes falling on the open pages with that familiar handwriting. 'Looks like you write a lot,' she says.

'I do.'

'Anything in particular?'

'A novel,' he says.

'Oh?' Her eyes fall on one open page; it has a cut-out picture of an old man, loupe in his eye, bending over a workbench as he puts together the fine intricate pieces of a watch movement. Above the picture it says 'Charles Spencelayh; *The Watchmaker*; pencil and watercolour heightened with white'. Underneath the picture it says 'MR BENSON'.

'So what is your novel about?' Lucy asks.

'Life,' comes the short reply over the boil of the kettle. 'Do you take sugar?'

'No, thank you.'

On another page there is a cut-out picture of a fat woman sprawled naked on a misshapen sofa, cupping one of her massive breasts in her hand. Above the picture is written: Lucien Freud; oil on canvas; 1995; *Benefits Supervisor Sleeping*.

'Huh!' says Lucy. 'This one looks a bit like Sal.'

'The Lucien Freud?' Jacob asks. 'Yes, it does.' He is stirring milk into the tea. 'One of my favourite artists. He doesn't flatter his models, he paints them as they seem to be through his eyes. That's what I hope to do. With my novel.'

'Lucien Freud . . . I've heard of him.'

'He's very famous.'

'Is he the one who does all those paintings with the faces smeared and distorted?'

Jacob is standing up, a tea in each hand. 'I think,' he says, 'maybe you mean Francis Bacon.' He joins her by the table, setting the tea down and selecting another green jotter from the pile. Lucy can smell the sharp clean scent of aftershave as he fans through the pages. Didn't Big Sal tell her he had a beard? Unkempt and patchy? So he must've shaved. When Lucy glances up at him she can see his long gaunt face and chin, bristle-free. He has dark shadows underneath his small eyes. There is a slight crook in his nose. Perhaps he broke it once?

'Like this?' Jacob holds open the jotter. A phantom of a face stares back at her, the details smudged or scribbled over, the mouth gaping wide. '*Study for the Head of a Screaming Pope*,' says Jacob.

'Oh, yeah,' Lucy says. 'Maybe like that.'

'It is the blackness of his mouth I am drawn into,' says Jacob. 'It is like this man is filled with a void.' Underneath the painting Lucy sees a name written in block capitals. 'ADAM'.

Jacob snaps shut the jotter and returns it to the pile. 'You sure know a lot about art,' she says. She sounds American, she thinks. She is even maybe acting American, flirting like American girls might flirt. She has pulled back her shoulders to show off her breasts. 36B. Nipples erect. She is even bold enough now to face him, but focuses mostly on his chest, her eyes flitting up to his face only every so often. 'I like art,' she says and then feels herself blush. *God*, why can't she say something worth saying?

Perhaps Jacob can sense her discomfort. He moves away, over to the mattress, and sits down. 'Do you mind if I smoke?' he asks. He picks up the pouch of tobacco from the floor and pulls from its folds some loose papers.

Lucy shrugs. She hopes the shrug looks cool and laid back. She glances over the jotters again. There must be, what, fifty, maybe sixty green jotters? Maybe more. She doesn't want to seem nosey so her eyes skim over the open pages, never resting long enough to read the words.

'So,' she says, 'Sal mentioned you were looking for someone?'

'Yes,' he replies. 'A girl I used to know.' He licks the cigarette paper and folds it around the thin line of tobacco. 'This is her hometown.'

'I see.'

'Her name is Solace,' he says. 'Or at least, that's what I knew her as.' The cigarette is now between his lips. He picks the lighter up off the floor.

'Any luck finding her?' she asks.

'None,' he says, exhaling smoke. Lucy watches Jacob closely. She watches his movements with intrigue, each seeming to her wholly unique and belonging to this man only. The way he stretches across the mattress to retrieve something underneath the clothes heaped at one end. The way he blinks away the smoke of the cigarette gripped between his lips. The way he pushes himself back up into a sitting position, flipping the card in his hand round so that she can see the picture of the blonde nude.

'Solace,' he says, taking the cigarette out from his mouth.

And Lucy is walking over to the mattress, she is taking the picture from Jacob's hand. 'How funny,' she says. 'In a weird kind of way, she looks like *me*.'

18

'I'm going to write a novel about life,' Jacob tells the girl curled under his arm. 'I mean, I'm going to write a novel about how life *really* is. Pointless, relentless, full of encounters too insignificant to remember and completely irrelevant characters. A novel full of empty conversation and even emptier events. Unrelated. Fleeting. Ending in death. I'm going to write a novel that readers will *hate* and critics will ignore. A novel with unsympathetic inconsistent characters that change with every turn of the page. I'm going to write a novel that is chapterless, non-sequential, that subverts the damn institutionalised "narrative arc" of a story and its all-too-specific order of events; *fuck* conflict, *fuck* climax, *fuck* resolution. My novel will be mashed up smash from beginning to end. One long, battling conflict. Anticlimactic. No resolution. I'm going to write a novel *riddled* with cliches and *laden* with stereotypes.'

'Cool,' says the girl, 'can I be in it?'

Mr Benson is standing at the front door of a large red-brick new-build, semi-detached, in a quiet residential cul-de-sac. He is currently feeling a little unreal, as though he has just stepped into the advertisement poster for the Penny Tree Way development depicting its computer-generated red-brick homes and streets lined with sapling trees in cages. Such vivid colours and bright sunshine and blue sky with the occasional white puff of a cloud. And the day was just like that. Add the sound of a dog barking somewhere in the distance, and the squeak of swings from a nearby park, children laughing, birds singing, and you'd be standing right there with him.

He feels a little warm and uncomfortable, but this is due only in part to the tweed jacket. He feels more uncomfortable about the young boy standing in the next-door neighbour's tiled drive staring quietly at him. Mr Benson has already said hello to the young boy. How old? Maybe five or six? But the boy did not return his greeting. He simply stands and stares, one hand fiddling absentmindedly with his willy through the material of his trousers. He seems to be sucking on something. A sweet, perhaps.

Mr Benson is thinking of pear drops as he raises his hand and presses the doorbell again. He used to love pear drops as a child. And rhubarb and custard bonbons.

The boy is still staring. Still fiddling. Still sucking.

Mr Benson straightens his back and pulls at the hem of his jacket. He notes there is no car in the driveway.

He glances at his reflection in the slice of glass in the door and runs a hand through his greyish-white hair. He is thinking of 23 Gunney Drive and that first day he went to speak with Olivia Little about rent due. Her sad smiling face. Her hysteria. The milky, sugary tea and the fine clock on the mantelpiece. He is thinking about the purplish black of her hanging, swollen feet and ankles.

The clackity-clack of rapidly moving wheels over the concrete pavement makes Mr Benson turn his head. A young girl dressed in pink is scootering towards them. She notices Mr Benson and the boy who is still staring, still sucking. She comes to a halt. 'Toby,' she addresses the boy, 'are you coming to the park?'

The boy doesn't reply.

Mr Benson decides to address the girl: 'Excuse me, young lady, I don't suppose you know the people who live here? Have they gone out?'

The girl looks at the old man as if he is stupid. Then her expression changes to pity. She lets the scooter clatter to the pavement and walks over to where Mr Benson stands by the front door. 'You've gotta press *this*,' she says and pushes on the bell. 'See? Can you hear it ring inside?'

The fiddling, sucking boy has watched all this and now begins to laugh. Mr Benson can see the bright red of the hardboiled sweet in his wet mouth. The girl in pink frowns at the boy. 'Don't mind him,' she says to Mr Benson, 'he's a bit special.' She pats Mr Benson on the arm before running back over to her scooter. 'You're such an *idiot*, Toby,' and then she is off.

215

The boy still laughs. It is no longer natural laughter, he is forcing out his guffaws in loud bellyful 'HA HA HA!'s. He stamps his foot, he throws back his head, he slaps his thigh. Mr Benson watches the young boy with raised eyebrows. 'HA HA HA!' and the boy doubles over, holding his guts. 'HA HA HA!'

Mr Benson's mind has switched off to everything other than this unfolding debacle. He does not notice the shadows moving beyond the door. 'HA HA HA!' But he does hear the click of the latch as it turns and so looks up into the face of the young pink-haired woman who has answered, at last, the call of the bell.

She is frowning. She looks at Mr Benson and then at the laughing Toby who is stamping his feet on the drive. 'OI! TOBY!' The boy doesn't stop laughing. 'TOBY!' Nothing. The woman disappears but reappears almost instantly. She throws something at the boy – and not in a kindly manner – which hits the child on the arm and then falls onto the drive. The laughter stops as the boy retrieves whatever it is. 'I've got this great idea,' says the pink-haired woman. 'Why don't you go and laugh in the park, eh? Why don't you go and annoy someone your own age?'

It is a hardboiled sweet. Toby pops it into his mouth to join the first, then shrugs. 'Is Oscar coming out today?'

'No,' says the woman.

The boy shrugs again and shuffles off.

'God,' the woman at the door says, 'you've got to chase them off like feral cats around here.' She looks at Mr

Benson and smiles a half-smile. 'It's OK,' she says, 'I never aim for the head.'

Mr Benson cannot speak.

The woman raises her eyebrows. 'Right, well, the kettle's on. You should come in. It's Mr Benson, right?'

19

'Did you know,' the girl says, 'I've started to keep a diary. A journal, like you. I carry it around with me all the time. I write in it every day. But the weird thing is, I don't ever write down the truth. Because I'm scared, you see, that someone will read it. And because the truth isn't always very interesting. So I change bits. Do you do that? Do you change bits to sound better on paper?'

Elizabeth Mary Duda, our good friend Max, is sitting on her bedroom floor playing with two GI Joe soldiers. She is whispering a conversation between the plastic pair. A hurried, fervent conversation. It seems these two soldiers are about to part, one is to go on a dangerous mission and the other is to stay behind at the base. Max sets one of the soldier's hands onto the chest of the other. 'I'll be back soon,' she makes him say.

'Don't go,' says the other, 'it's too dangerous.'

'I have to.'

'But what if . . . ?'

'Don't think like that.'

The two soldiers kiss.

And because these toys have cleverly designed mobile joints and limbs, Max can wrap their arms around each other, she can cock their heads slightly to one side so that they can kiss fully on the mouth, their legs can intertwine.

'I love you,' says the soldier.

'I love you too,' says the other.

'I have laid my bed with aloes and myrrh,' says the first. 'And fine silks from Egypt.'

If Max's mother were passing the open door of this room now, she might smile at the sight of her daughter cross-legged on the floor, whispering play conversations between two toys. But then, of course, Max has her back to the door. Her mother would not be able to see that the two toys were being laid one on top of the other, bodies close and humping. She would not be able to see that it

219

was two male soldiers that were being made to love by the giant child controlling them.

She has changed, Max. Although it may not seem obvious to any passer-by or onlooker, she most certainly has changed, dramatically and irrevocably. It happened the day before in the church when the Reverend Francis complimented her. 'How very inspiring it is to see such a young face take an active interest in Bible study.'

'Yes,' her mother had said. 'She's a good girl.'

In future years, when Max is no longer calling herself Max, she'll tell people that it was on this day she realised, at least on some subconscious level, that her life would be dedicated to God. Her friends with an interest in psychology will suggest it was to do with that compliment. When a young mind receives praise, affection, attention, it will leave a lasting impression; it may even become an integral part of that individual's developing identity. In response Max will nod and say, 'Yes. You're right. And?' People will also say to her, 'Dedicated to God? But you're *gay*, aren't you?' In response Max will give the same reply, 'Yes. You're right. And?'

But right now, at this moment, in the bedroom of the ten-year-old girl, not even Max can sense the change that has happened inside her. She remains oblivious and quietly occupied with her toys, playing out this adult act in an attempt to understand.

She disentangles the two soldiers.

'I must go,' says one.

'May God be with you,' says the other.

'And also with you.'

She stops playing and lifts her head. From outside she

can hear the sound of a motorbike. She gets up off the floor and grabs her rucksack.

'Dad's here!'

Dear reader, you may be wondering how any of this is relevant. We have seemingly strayed from our protagonist and his storyline. But that is only because Max too has strayed. She has not thought about the nameless man since the day before when she noted the striking resemblance between him and the suffering Jesus. After that she had been swept up in a sea of compliments. On the way home her mother had expressed how very proud she was having such a pious daughter. 'The reverend sees a firm faith in you,' she'd said. 'The Lord is smiling kindly on us.' And they'd spent the evening in the living room together, her mother sitting in the armchair reading passages from the Bible and Max curled on the red shaggy rug listening until her eyes drooped. She had made her mother proud.

So now as Max rushes down the stairs to meet her father it is only the bible that is packed safely in her rucksack and not the evidence box. The mystery of the nameless man has been sidelined by the mystery of God. But we should forgive this girl her young mind and its fleeting occupations and obsessions. She is only ten years old, after all, and her story, we will eventually come to see, has relevance even in its apparent irrelevance.

Her mother, Aggie, has already opened the front door. She is stepping out onto the pavement. The road is overcast with the shadows of the houses around it. She pulls the cream cardigan she is wearing tighter around her body.

'Marek,' she says to the man as he gets off his bike. He takes off his helmet.

'Aggie,' he says. 'How are you?'

Max's mother pulls her cardigan tighter around her.

It doesn't matter, this not replying, because Max has pushed past and thrown herself into the arms of the man. Aggie's silence goes unnoticed as the man jokingly groans under the weight of his daughter. He lifts the girl up, right over his shoulder and then down again.

You should recognise him, this man. The leather waistcoat covered in pins, patches and badges. The thick red lips. The handlebar moustache. You've already met him, outside the pub near the brothel on a wet night, a summer storm. Do you remember? Jacob had stopped to speak with this man. To ask for a cigarette. Perhaps you should go back, dear reader, and read this scene again? Marek's behaviour may seem more interesting to you now. The way he pinched his rolled cigarette between his fingers, the way he spoke, the way he turned his face up to the grey sky, wishing for another pint and yet remaining outside with the strange man in search of his lost love. Max's father, Marek. Remember how he held both hands up in the air? 'I'm sorry,' he'd said, his gesture saying *I have nothing*. And those spots of rain that struck the card with its painting of a nude, he'd wiped the wet from her belly and breasts with the bottom of his T-shirt. A compassionate act, consoling. 'Solace,' he'd said for no particular reason. Do you remember?

Now this man is ruffling his daughter's hair. 'I thought we'd go to the river,' he says. 'Where's your helmet?'

Max whoops and runs back inside.

The two adults, Marek and Aggie, are left standing in silence.

'So.' Marek shifts his weight from one foot to the other. His legs creak in his leather trousers.

'Aye, well,' Aggie scoops a strand of her long fair hair behind her ear, 'I'll be back around three.'

'Oh.'

'You sound disappointed?'

'Oh no, it's just I was wondering if I could have Lizzy for the night?'

'She has church tomorrow.'

'I'll bring her back in time for church.'

'No,' Aggie says, 'I'd rather not.'

Marek pauses. 'For dinner, then. You'll let me treat her to dinner?'

Aggie sighs.

The two fall into silence again. Marek bows his head; he looks at the helmet in his hand. 'How's Mary?' he asks.

No reply.

'Look, Aggie . . .'

But Max has reappeared, her white helmet already on her head. 'Let's go!' she says and she runs to her father's motorbike. 'See you later, Mum! Say hello to Granny.'

20

'I hope you don't mind,' says the girl curled under Jacob's arm, 'but I thought I should wash some of your clothes. It's just, they were getting a bit fousty. A bit damp smelling. I took them to the launderette. I hope you don't mind.' She strokes the hair on Jacob's abdomen. 'They smell of sea breeze and summer meadows now.'

It is a beautiful day. Come, let's walk together through these city streets and let the summer sun warm the backs of our necks. Let's breathe in the smell of coffee shops and bakeries and cafes as we walk. Listen to the traffic. The beep beep of a green-man crossing. Watch as the gulls and feral pigeons dodge and dive. See how the colourful metal of passing cars glints in the sun? Their wheels sound sticky as they move over the heated tarmac of the road.

The pavements are full of tables and chairs outside eateries. People drink coffee, sip tea, suck smoothies through a straw. They smile behind shades and laugh easily. A baby in a bonnet cries to be let out of his pram. A dog sniffs around the foot of a table, its tail stiff in concentration. An old man in a flat cap drives a mobility scooter and looks grimly at the packed pavements and mutters to himself. He presses his thumb on the horn and lets it hoot abruptly.

As we walk we can see billboards advertising faster internet connections, alcohol, television programmes, loans, underwear. There is an overflowing bin next to a bench and empty cans of beer and cigarette butts on the ground. There is a smashed vodka bottle, and a few large shards have been kicked onto the road. A man in a shirt and tie and sunglasses is moving these larger shards closer to the kerb. A car honks as it drives past. The man replies with an irritated under-the-breath, 'Prick! I'm trying to help.'

A drunk man is swaggering towards us, can of *Special Brew* in hand. We look at him and already recoil at the expected scent that hasn't yet reached our nose, but will. Dirty skin, unwashed clothes, strong liquor, smoked ciga- rettes and ammonia. It is the smell of the homeless, the downtrodden, the lost. The invisible? We know the smell well, dear reader. Perhaps we even search for it in the air when we see a man like this approach. It is like the button that says 'do not press'. We don't want to smell this unpleasant smell and yet we want to be proven right. You look like you should smell like this, we say, and then sniff at the air like the dog around the foot of the table until – yes – there it is! And oh, it's bad! Jesus, why doesn't he just *wash*?

He is muttering something as we pass. 'Spare a little change?' But we should ignore him, shouldn't we? After all, we don't want to feed his habit – oh no! Whatever habit that is, for we all know he has one, right? Illicit drugs. Alcohol. Nicotine. Caffeine. Porn. Probably all of these and more. This man. He looks *full* of habits.

'Bless you,' he curses our retreating back.

Fuck you, we think. Why be so bitter? We all know you'll be able to pay for your next fix. We all know that beggars earn more than *we* do in a week. Call yourself 'homeless'? *Bullshit*, we think. There's no such thing. Not really. There are places for you to sleep. Night shelters and hostels. There are *Big Issue*s you can sell . . . right?

Whatever. I want to take you to the river, dear reader. Let's slip through the rolled-down window of this passing car filled with its group of youths, four girls, laughing and singing along to the radio. The music is loud. The girls are enjoying the spectacle they are making of themselves. The two in the back sing loudly and dance wildly. They know that pedestrians look up as they pass, but they don't care if they're frowned at – just flash them a V – what's their problem anyway? *IT'S SUMMER AND LOOK AT HOW MUCH FUN WE'RE HAVING!* And indeed, they *are* having fun. The small car is filled with happy, boisterous energy.

They are driving to what is known locally as 'The Bathing Pool' – a sandy alcove in the river on the outskirts of the city. It is where Marek and Max are winding their way to now and not far from where Billy set up camp. How convenient.

To the river, dear reader, to the river! Let's go and lie on its grassy banks and bathe in its symbolism, admire its metaphor, perhaps even strip down to our pants and run, dive-bomb, into its sweet, cool teachings of impermanence. Or maybe we should just do as many others are doing and lie back on the grassy bank and soak up the sun. Or join the younger children, the toddlers digging holes and making castles and mud pies in their buckets.

Ahead Marek's motorbike, a sportster, is parked on the grass. Marek is sitting only a short distance away. He has spread out a large throw to sit on and is rummaging through a saddlebag full of picnic goods. 'Come here, Lizzy.' His leather trousers and boots have been swapped for surfer shorts and sandals. His waistcoat has been taken off and folded neatly. 'Come here and put on this cream.'

Max is lying on her stomach on the very edge of the riverbank, staring down into the eddy of water and the whirlpools forming, disappearing, reappearing elsewhere.

She is watching the tiny fish darting through the clear water, all grouped together, until she stirs with her finger and startles them apart. But see how they always find each other again? They always regroup. 'Hello, fish,' she says. '*Jak się masz? Kocham cię!*'

'Lizzy, come over here,' she hears her father calling. 'Or do you want skin cancer instead of ice cream today?'

Max pricks her ears and turns her head. 'Are we getting ice cream?'

'On the condition you put on this lotion,' he says. 'Come on, quick, I can see your shoulders catching already and I'm not having you go back to your mother red and crispy.'

So Max gets to her feet. She joins her father on the throw and lets him rub lotion into her back and shoulders and underneath the straps of her brightly striped swimming costume. 'Here,' he hands her the bottle, 'you do the rest.' The bottle makes a sputtering sound as Max squeezes cream into her palm.

Marek watches his daughter. She is meticulous and silent as she rubs the cream into her legs and ankles and the tops of her feet, even in between her toes. She is careful to cover every patch of skin and makes sure to go just beneath the line of her swimming costume. Marek wonders where she learned to do that. From her mother? From her friends? Through experience? Had she been burned on previous years – a thin strip of painful red where the swimming costume stopped? Had she burned her feet before now? Marek often watches his daughter, her little quirks and developing traits, and sees her forming into her own person. She is becoming more and more *herself*. He wonders if Aggie can see it in the same way. Maybe not. After all, they live together, they spend a large part of every day in each other's company, so maybe Aggie can't see her growing in the same way he can.

'Are you hungry?' he asks his daughter. 'There's jammy pieces and crisps in the saddlebag. Some Scotch eggs. A pork pie. Well . . . the pork pie's mine.'

'OK,' she says.

He pulls out the goods and spreads them on the throw.

'What's that?' she asks, pointing to some unopened tupperware.

'Cheese and pickle,' he says.

'Urgh.'

'Have a sandwich,' he says. 'Have some crisps.' He pulls a carton of apple juice free from its plastic packaging. 'Here,' he says.

'Thanks,' she says.

Yes, he can still see in her his likeness, her eyes and nose and ears are his. And he can see Aggie, both physically and behaviourally. The way she scoops hair behind her ear despite it being cut short, a direct mirroring of her mother. The way she'll so often hold finger food with two hands like a squirrel eating nuts. That's Aggie. But more and more Marek has begun to notice the other things in Lizzy that do not come from him or her mother. From someone or somewhere she has picked up this derisive way of looking, as though she is staring over a pair of spectacles. Learned from a teacher, maybe? Or a television character? And she has an unusual crooked way of smiling, only one corner of the mouth raised. Perhaps a friend she admires?

But then there are other behaviourisms that seem so distinctly hers. Her boyishness. The way she walks, the way she runs, the way she throws and kicks balls. Despite her mother's best efforts to iron it out of her, Lizzy remains boyishly creased. Then there is her creativity, always playing and always talking to herself, always drawing pictures or writing stories. Neither he nor Aggie care for such things, nor were they like that as children. It belongs to Lizzy. As does her aloneness. So perfectly content away from others her own age. Not that she doesn't have friends, of course. She seems to have quite a circle of them. But she is clumsier in their presence. She becomes loud, extroverted, a joker. More like *him*, he thinks. But as soon as the attention is drawn away she finds her moment and skulks off to be alone again. Is it something to worry about? Is it normal?

Marek watches his daughter nibbling at a mini Scotch egg with two hands. *That's* not normal, he thinks. He hopes it's a habit she'll soon break. Maybe someone will tease her at school and she'll stop it. Or perhaps he should just tell her? Right now?

'Hey, Lizzy,' he says. She looks up, big bright eyes and keen ears, the half-nibbled Scotch egg still pinched between her fingers. He hesitates.

'What?' Max asks.

'Oh,' he says. 'Nothing.'

'No,' she says, 'what is it? A secret?'

'No secret.'

'So what is it?'

'Nothing,' he says.

'*Tell me.*'
He bites his bottom lip.
'That's not fair. You *have* to tell me!'
'OK, OK.' He pauses. 'I was just going to say . . .'
She quietly waits.
'I love you,' he says. 'You know that, don't you?'
'Is that it?' she says.

Not far from here, just beyond a small wooded stretch, is Billy's encampment. It has become a base of four tents now, though there are more people in number than could possibly sleep under canvas/polycotton/polyester/nylon. Teenage boys and girls lie on beach towels on the grass, others are swimming in the river or paddling in the shallow rocky rapids upstream. Music is playing. Rolled tobacco and the sweet smell of burning green hangs in the air. Litter is strewn all over the ground, beer cans and bottles, crisp packets, juice cartons, ice-cream wrappers, a cooked sausage, several blackened dead disposable barbecues. But there is a conscientious troop already at work picking up the mess and putting it into carriers. They are heckled by those who sit nearby. One boy – we have met him already, it's the boy nicknamed 'Goon' – calls out to one girl litter-picking, 'Hey, Sarah!' Goon finishes his beer and tosses the can at the girl's feet. 'You've missed a bit.' A few smart-assed guffaws ring out from Goon's most loyal friends; other voices say simply, 'You're such a prick, Goon.' Billy, however, does neither. He is sitting slightly away from the group staring sullenly at his phone.

We need to talk, Billy.
Let's meet later? x

It was the 'x' that confused him.

'Seriously, Billy,' Goon has turned his attention to his quiet friend, 'you've been staring at your phone all day. What's with you?'

'Piss off, Goon.'

'Why? What have I done?'

'Just piss off, I'm not in the mood.'

'Don't be like that,' he says. 'We're friends. Best buds. Homies.'

Billy is tearing at the grass around his feet.

'Is this about your bird, Bill, is that it?'

Someone else – it sounds like Ness – mutters at Goon to leave it.

'Bill,' Goon ignores the advice, 'you know what I think? I reckon you're better off without her. I mean how long have you been dating, man? And she still hasn't put out? Why not get rid of the fridge?' There is the sharp sound of a hand slapping skin. 'Hey! What was that for?'

'What was it *for*?' The slapping sound comes again.

'Jesus, Ness!'

'Well stop being such a prick, Goon. Lucy is my friend.'

'So what? She's not here, she can't hear us.'

Billy's eyes remain on the river. He watches as two boys climb up, dripping wet, onto the diving rock where the water runs deep. A circle of girls sitting further down the bank holler at them to do somersaults and back-flips.

Why would she sign off with a kiss if she was going to end it?

'Hey, Bill,' it's Goon again, 'you know what I reckon? I reckon she's a dyke. Like her mum. A drinker of the furry cup. A muff diver. Well what, Ness? They say it's hereditary, don't they?'

Billy turns to see that Ness has got to her feet. Goon is cowering slightly, his arm raised, anticipating a kick, but Ness is glaring at Billy, not Goon. 'So what,' she says, 'you're just going to sit there and let him badmouth your girlfriend?'

Billy frowns.

'It should be *you* sticking up for her, not me.'

'Fuck off, Ness.' The words are out before he has time to think about them. 'Maybe Goon is right. She's been keeping me cold for weeks. She ignores my texts. Cancels our dates. She's making a fool of me.' Billy can see Ness clench her fists. 'What?' he asks her. 'I've got a point, don't I? You can't call me a crap boyfriend when she's acting like a crap girlfriend.'

Goon is looking perfectly smug. 'You tell her, Bill.'

'Seriously, Goon, I'm going to kick you in the face if you don't shut up.'

The two boys at the diving rock are climbing up again. They are laughing. Their faces have caught the sun, cheeks streaked red. They begin to play-wrestle on the rock, grabbing at each other's elbows and wrists trying to push the other off.

Billy looks back down at his phone.

'Bill?'

He is getting to his feet.

'Bill, homie, best bud, where are you going? It's *summer*, man, come back!'

Let's follow Bill through this small cluster of trees, flat-foot picking his way carefully so as not to stub his toes on the twisted roots breaking up from the ground. When he is far enough into the shade and out of sight, he stops to brush the pine needles and dirt from the soles of his feet and slips on his trainers.

It is cooler underneath these boughs. The sunlight breaks through the branches above making bold shapes of squares and triangles on the path. Billy steps into a warm square of light. Above him a bird calls and flutters from one branch to another. Another bird sings in reply. Something moves in the gorse, a mouse maybe, it makes a rustling sound, and two white butterflies startle into the air, spiralling and dancing around each other. Billy both watches these things and doesn't watch. He sees them and hears them but nothing registers. He is thinking about Lucy. He is feeling hurt and confused and bitter. He has an urge to run or shout or lash out but instead stands in this small square of light with hands in his pockets. He stands very still. Despite the small block of sun, he shivers. His skin goosepimples against the cool air, the pale sun-bleached hair on his arms rises up. He shivers again. It is this shiver that moves him forward, through the trees and out into the bright summer sun and the busy bank of sunbathers and paddlers and children playing. If you were to ask him now, *Billy, where are you going?* he wouldn't be able to answer. He doesn't know himself. He is walking away from his friends, that's all. He wants to be alone to think.

A woman calls out to her sun-bonneted toddler, 'Don't go too far, Jinnie. Stay where I can see you,' and the toddler looks up, waves a spade at her mother. A group of older children play and dance around with a dog in the sand. The dog barks up at the ball being thrown high in the air. People swim and splash and fish with tiddler nets in the shallows. Billy winds his way through the groups of picnicking friends and sunbathing bodies. And yes, one such picnic belongs to Marek and Max.

Marek does not even see the blond boy as he passes. He is watching his daughter. She is lying on her stomach reading what seems to be, if he is not mistaken, a bible. Of course, it does not entirely surprise Marek to see his daughter with a bible in her hand – that is Aggie's influence. It is only natural that young Lizzy will carry the Book of God around with her, Aggie may even insist upon it. But it's quite another thing to see Lizzy actively and willingly poring over its pages in this way.

'Lizzy?'

'Mmm?'

'What are you reading?'

'The Bible,' she says.

'Aye, well yes, I can see that. But which bit?'

'I'm reading about how the Jews killed Jesus.'

'Oh,' the words sounded crude in Lizzy's young voice, 'well,' there was something not quite right about them, 'I think . . . maybe . . .' he struggles, 'well, maybe we shouldn't blame the death of Jesus entirely on . . . Jewish people.' It was the definite article he hadn't liked, he thinks. 'The Jews'. It sounded so 'other'.

'No, Dad, it was definitely the Jews.' His daughter seems unfazed.

'Well, I just think . . .' Marek raises his eyes to the blue of the sky, 'you should be careful. That's all. You can't go around saying things like that. You know, like "the Jews killed Jesus".'

'Why not?'

'Because, well, you just can't. It sounds bad. Like you're damning a whole race on the actions of one event in history. But every race has done bad things in the past.'

'Have the Polish done bad things?'

'*Every* race has done bad things.'

'But what have the Polish done?'

'Well, you know . . . war . . .' Marek knows his daughter feels a strong connection to the heavily diluted Polish blood in her, something he's never quite understood. 'Every race does bad things, Lizzy.' The truth is he knows nothing of Polish history. Why would he? The only really Polish thing about him is his name. 'It's just human nature,' he says. 'No matter where you're from, humans do bad things. I mean . . .' he begins to backtrack, he is being too negative, 'I mean, humans do bad things, they make a lot of bad decisions, but they do a lot of *good* things as well. You know, two sides to every coin and stuff like that.'

'Jesus did good things.'

'Well, I guess Jesus was one of the good guys.'

And they fall into silence.

It would be interesting to know, don't you agree, what these two individuals are quietly thinking as they sit there in the summer sun watching paddlers in the river and listening to the sound of laughter and dogs barking? Well, let me tell you that Marek is busy cursing his ex-wife and her damned Christianity for imposing such set-in-stone beliefs on their daughter. I mean, why is

236

she reading the Bible, for God's sake? She's ten years old. She should be reading Roald Dahl and Jacqueline Wilson and *Narnia*, not the cruel and bloody torment of a man nailed to a cross! And our Max? Finally she is thinking about the nameless man again. It was the talk on good and bad guys that brought him back to mind. It triggered the memory of that sunny afternoon in the park, interrogating the sad man sitting on the bench. Are you a paedophile? A murderer? A thief? as she tried to determine if he was safe to talk to. One of the 'good' guys.

'Dad?'

'Uh-huh?'

'I met a man the other day, in the park, who didn't know who he was.'

'What do you mean, Lizzy?'

'He didn't have a name.'

'Everyone has a name.'

'That's what *I* said,' Max replies. 'But the man told me he'd had lots of names in the past, but none of them were his.'

'Jesus, Lizzy, how old was this man?'

Max shrugs.

'Was he older than me?'

'Maybe,' she says. 'I don't know.'

'Now listen here, what have both me and your mother told you about talking to strangers?'

'It's OK, Dad, he was a good guy.'

'You don't *know* that.'

'I *do*,' she says. 'I checked.'

'Lizzy, trust me, good guys don't hang around parks

claiming not to know their name. That's not good, that's *weird*. Now what did he look like?'

'Sad,' Max says. 'He looked really sad. And a bit like Jesus.'

21

'So let me get this straight,' says the girl under Jacob's arm, 'you've spent the last ten years or so travelling from place to place, changing your name and living as different people?'

'Yes,' says Jacob.
'So . . .' says the girl,

'. . . how do I know you are who you say you are?'

A SERIES OF FRAMES
IN THE GALLERY OF A LIFE

FRAME ONE

Mounted on the artist's easel, a canvas framed with twisted wicker rods, pinned with small plastic flowers and woven with ivy vines. This picture is not a painting but a pencil drawing divided in two; one half is in colour, the other is in charcoal. A young boy is walking through the front gate of an overgrown garden. Cracked paving slabs with weeds pushing through the gaps, black slugs, an upturned bucket, a buckled wheel left twisted in the long grass. These things are all drawn in charcoal. The path is leading to the front door of a house that looks dark, blinds lowered, curtains drawn.

On the coloured side there is a neatly kept garden, the mowed bright green of a lawn, purples and pinks and yellows in the flowerbeds, and standing on the step of the red-brick house is a woman, heavily pregnant, hand resting on the swell of her belly, scooping the ends of her halo hair behind one ear as she basks in the warmth of the sun.

FRAME TWO

Oil on canvas and large gilded frame. Here is a painting of a busy nightclub. In the foreground there is a dance floor. Spinning lights and disco ball. Grinding bodies are throwing shapes. Drunk faces contort in fixed moments of laughter, conversation, oblivion. A glass collector weaves

240

his way through the crowd. A woman snorts coke from her handbag. Groups sit in booths or at open tables drinking cocktails full of props, sucking mixed liquor through a straw or swigging at brightly coloured alco-pops. See the wailing woman with mascara-smeared eyes? The dodgy dealer in the shadows? The bouncer standing to attention? The frantic, sweating bartenders pulling pints, mixing drinks and shaking cocktails? There are a few bored faces amidst all this cliche, staring glassy-eyed through the chaos, but mostly the participants participate in this obscene '*Where's Wally?*' for adults.

And yet there is an odd calm in the very centre of this painting. Our eyes are drawn towards it. Two people are sitting at the bar: a sad-looking young man and a blonde-haired woman. The young man is staring into his drink. The woman is staring at the man. And below, on an engraved plaque attached to the gilded frame, the title of the painting, *You Look Depressed*.

FRAME THREE
A living room that seems washed out and ghostly pale in colour, enhanced by the painted white of the wooden frame. There is a settee (faded floral); a coffee table (cream); a fireplace (ivory tiles) and on its mantelpiece a ticking French Champlevé enamel repeating carriage clock.

Perhaps it is the artist's clever use of light that gives the room its ghostly appearance? A brightness that gleams through the slits of a blinded window. Or perhaps it is the grey-looking woman sitting in the matching off-white and faded floral armchair by the window? She is sobbing. Her body is curled inwards, her hands cover her mouth, her cheeks are wet with tears. Yes, the artist has implemented clever techniques in this painting. The way this woman seems to melt back into her surroundings and become almost transparent. Passing this painting at a glance you might see only an empty room. It is only by stopping still and looking closely that the pale woman creeps out from the furniture and walls.

FRAME FOUR

A graffiti-covered wall filled with toilet poetry, obscenities and juvenile scribblings of cocks and fannies. It is lit by a lurid neon blue light; the sort of light used in public toilets to deter spotty youths from loitering and make it difficult to find a vein for jacking up. From somewhere comes a faint and yet penetrating high-pitched whistle, a nerve-twitching tinnitus ringing out from a hidden speaker. It smells of urine. Viewers walk past this installation piece mostly without stopping. Occasionally one might thrust a finger in their ear and say, 'Can you hear that whistling?' Others shake their heads and say, 'I hate modern art. Even *I* could produce this shit.'

FRAME FIVE

Here is a painting of a full-length mirror and in it the reflection of a woman with blonde wispy hair falling in long ringlets around her shoulders. She is nude. Her breasts plump and pert, pubic hair trimmed. You will recognise this mirror image. The blonde-haired woman is pointing to her left breast. She has slanting shoulders and squarish hips. She has large round eyes that are not looking at you but somewhere beyond you and slightly off to one side. It is Solace. The painting replicated in another painting. And yet standing before the mirror we see the back of a person mismatched to this reflection. A bare back with wide bony shoulders and sore swollen spots and a head of dark greasy floppy hair. The painting is entitled simply *Self Portrait*.

22

'I've brought you a gift,' the girl says. *'Pillows!'*

It had gone something like this:

He'd said, 'Wow, you look really . . .'

She'd said, 'Yeah, look, we need to talk.'

He'd said, 'I know, listen, about yesterday . . .'

She'd said, 'No.'

He'd said, 'But . . .'

She'd said, 'It's just not working, is it?'

He'd said, 'What's not working?'

She'd said, 'I think it's best if we become just friends.'

He'd said, 'Friends?'

She'd said, 'Yeah. Friends.'

And that had been that. Or almost. He'd fallen silent for a moment while his face slowly pickled into a bright red of humiliation and embarrassment before boiling into a vicious and resounding, 'Do you know what? *Fuck you!*' He'd turned to leave, but spun back when his brain bubbled up with spite, 'Oh no, wait, *that* would never happen, would it? You *frigid cow*!' and then he'd left.

A hugely unoriginal break-up by all accounts, but none-theless it hurt. And it was Lucy's first. She made sure she wept bitterly. Fierce, hot wet drippy tears of teenage distress. She even managed to wail, the sort of wide-mouth wailing where saliva webs from upper teeth to lower and snot runs freely from the nose. Her mother did her best to comfort her (despite the shock of seeing her daughter blonde). She made all the right shushing noises and said all essential time-tested platitudes, 'It's OK, Luce. I know it feels awful now, but time is a great healer. Plenty more

245

fish and all that stuff . . .' It wasn't until later, when Lucy
was lying in bed, her mother cradling her head on her lap
and stroking her bleached hair softly (*why on earth did
she do that?*), that Lucy suddenly couldn't understand why
it was she was crying. Wasn't this what she'd wanted? And
so she sniffed and pushed herself up into a pillowed sitting
position, breaking free from her mother's hold. 'Thanks,
Mum. I think I'm OK now.'

'Oh, Lucy.'

'No really, Mum. I think I'm fine. It's for the best.'

'Well,' her mother paused, 'you know, dear . . .' but she
stopped herself. She was going to say something along the
lines of '*you're still so young*' but decided against it. Instead
she said, 'I love you so much.'

'I love you too.' Lucy sniffed again. 'I think I just want
to read for a while.'

'I'll make you some hot chocolate,' said her mother.

Lucy stays sitting propped up with pluffed pillows and
glazed eyes staring ahead of her. Her face is tear-streaked
and drawn. She blinks. Sniffs once. She turns her head
towards the window. Where is Billy now? she wonders.
Back at the river surrounded by friends? She imagines the
growing camp that would be set up for the second night
of summer, groups squatting around disposable barbecues
and cooking up meat. She imagines them all having a really
great time. But it doesn't make her feel jealous, it makes
her feel . . .

far away.

It is Anya who returns with a mug of hot chocolate; she
knocks and peeks first the red tendrils of her hair round
the door and then her head. 'Hey,' she says, stepping in.

'Your mum told me . . .' she trails off. 'Boys can be *such* bitches,' she says.

And Lucy laughs through a sniff. 'Like you would know?'

'Mmm . . . good point.' Anya sets the mug of hot chocolate down. 'I should rephrase. Break-ups can be *such* bitches.'

'I'm over it,' says Lucy.

'Really?'

Lucy wipes at her eyes. 'It was me, Ani. I was the one who called it off.'

'Oh.'

'But he said such horrible things!'

Anya sits on the edge of the bed. She rests a hand over Lucy's foot.

'He called me a frigid cow. He's annoyed because I've never . . . you know . . .' Her eyes well up. 'I *hate* him,' she says. 'He's *horrible* and I hate him. All I said was I wanted to be friends.'

She is sobbing now into her sleeves. Anya moves up the bed and hugs her daughter close. She strokes her head. 'Hey,' she says, but doesn't know where the sentence is going. Inside she is thinking 'that little *shit*', but she doesn't say it. She closes her eyes. 'You remember that daft story I told you about the man with many heads?' she asks.

Lucy groans, 'How can I forget? It gave me nightmares.'

'Really? Oh. Sorry about that. I didn't mean . . .' She pauses. 'Anyway, what I was going to say is we *all* have these many heads, you know? We all get angry, we all get sad, we all get jealous. And it's whenever we feel this crazy emotion stuff most intensely that we say stupid and hurtful things.'

'Billy is *not* my prince.' Lucy's words are bitter.

'No, no, and I'm not for one minute saying he is. I'm just saying . . .' She stops. 'What am I saying?'

'That Billy's human and break-ups are hard?'

'That's it!'

'I know, Ani,' Lucy says. 'But that's not what you're supposed to say. You're supposed to say Billy's an asshole and I'm better off without him.'

'Ah,' Anya nods. 'I knew I was missing something out.'

Mr Benson is holding a biscuit. He is watching the pink-haired woman as she pulls the wrapper off a *KitKat* and runs a nail down the silver foil. He is thinking a thousand thoughts as she snaps the biscuit and pops a piece into her mouth. He is thinking of the weeping Olivia, of his angry wife, of the curious young Jacob all those years ago listening to his every word as they sat together in the ticking study. The young man had shown such enthusiasm. So eager to learn. It was how Mr Benson had imagined a son would be. 'It's a girl, Stan. Stan . . . can you believe it? We have a daughter.' And then again, three years later. Another girl. He thinks of the baby Thomas, his grandson, and wonders if he will ever have that same interest, the same eagerness to learn and listen to whatever his old granddad has to say?

'Are you all right, Mr Benson?'

The old man looks up. He can feel that his face has been set into a tight-lipped expression. He un-furrows his brow, loosens his jaw. He sets the biscuit down on the table. 'I'm sorry,' he says.

'Don't be. You seem like you have . . .' the pink-haired woman pauses, 'a lot on your mind.'

'Yes.' The old man turns his head towards the window. Outside he can see the young boy practising keepy-ups. He can hear him call out to his father. 'Dad, watch this, watch this. Are you keeping count?' The old man's eyes drop to his hands on the table. His fingers lace together in a prayer-like grasp. 'My wife doesn't know that I'm here,' he explains and massages one thumb with the other. 'If she found out she'd be . . . angry, to say the least.'

'Oh?'

'She didn't ever trust Olivia.'

'I see.'

'She believed that Olivia may have had . . . *feelings* for me.'

'Mr Benson, are you trying to tell me your wife thought you were having an affair?'

The old man squeezes his hands together.

'Were you?'

'No.' His response is quick. 'There was never any affair, let me make that *quite* clear. But as yet I've been unable to persuade my wife otherwise.'

'I see.'

'No,' says Mr Benson. 'No, I'm not sure you do.' And how could he even begin to explain to this cold, brash woman? The truth of the matter was Olivia Little *had* had feelings for Mr Benson. It had become increasingly clear the more Mr Benson had visited. Oh yes, of course, the friendship had begun innocently enough. He would pop round of an afternoon or early evening to comfort the desperate woman, to provide company and conversation. It was Mr Benson who had advised Olivia Little to contact the police. It was Mr Benson who had helped pin up posters around town of that strange thin sombre face. But mostly he would just sit on that soft broken-springed settee and let Olivia Little talk and talk and talk about the boy. It seemed to help the poor woman; and strangely he found himself wanting to listen. He was curious, you see. About Jacob. And the more he heard about him, the more curious he became.

'I'm so certain he was bullied at school, Mr Benson. But he would never tell me so. He'd come home and sit at the dining table or quietly take himself off to his room. He never watched television. He liked to read books. Occasionally he listened to the radio. He preferred to play board games on his own, you know, like chess and *Risk*. Such an unusual boy. I tried to be a good mother, Mr Benson, I tried to integrate him with other children his own age. I asked him once if he'd like to join the local scouts and he told me that he would rather die a victim of the plague.'

An impression of Jacob had begun to form in Mr Benson's head of a young boy, his thoughts and inner angst all bottled up, socially inept and yet academically bright, a no doubt gifted child whose gifts hadn't been recognised. Mr Benson felt himself strangely attached to the image of the young Jacob he'd created. He wanted to reach out to this boy from the past, pick him up and hold him. He wanted to sit with him on that cold concrete doorstep at 23 Gunney Drive and just watch what he might be watching. A silent companion. He wanted to challenge him at chess or paint toy soldiers or make model aeroplanes together. And the boy Jacob would look at him with that same enraptured expression as the young man he'd met in his study all those years ago.

Mr Benson had found himself visiting Olivia Little more regularly. He would say to his wife when she questioned him, 'What would you have me do? Leave the poor woman alone? She is in need of help, Ada.'

'It's not *right*, Stanley.'

'What's not right? To help someone in need of support? Come, come, Ada. Have a heart.'

It had been unfair of him, he knows that now. His wife had been hurting from the sudden shift in his behaviour and yet Mr Benson had blinkered himself, he had become unwilling to acknowledge his wife's feelings and his own guilt for fear it would mean letting go of this strange and special thing he'd discovered. Not Olivia Little. It had never been about Olivia Little. It had always been about the boy, Jacob.

And so he continued visiting the sad grey woman.

'He was such a sensitive soul, he had hidden depths. He had secrets, Mr Benson. I would often watch him sitting in the garden, writing in little green exercise books. Pages and pages he'd write. And when I'd ask him if he wanted me to check his homework he said it wasn't for school. It was for him. He called it his journal.'

Mr Benson would sit with her and drink his milky tea, listening to the strange woman talk, the ticking of the clock keeping time on the mantelpiece. He'd do odd jobs around the house, tightening a cupboard door hinge or putting up shelves; he'd help her in the garden, weeding out nettles and putting down pellets for slugs. But it had all been for Jacob. He began to piece together Olivia's memories as though they were his own.

'He burned them in the end, those journals. When he

was in his mid-teens. He'd found a barrel from someplace and rolled it into the garden. I came home and saw the smoke – such a filthy black it was – I thought the whole house was on fire. But it was Jacob in the back garden, hurling those little green exercise books into the barrel. And photographs. He'd taken my box of photographs and was pouring them into the fire. I tried to stop him, Mr Benson. I screamed at him to stop. And he screamed back at me: "*Why are you talking to me? You can't see me. I don't exist.*"'

A troubled soul, Mr Benson thought. But could it have been any different? Was it the nature of the boy or was it his nurture? And Mr Benson would look at Olivia Little, the meek grey weeping woman, and tell himself that yes, it could have been different. It *could* have been different. If only he'd known them then. If only Jacob had been *his* little boy.

Elizabeth Mary Duda, the boyish blonde-haired Max, is sitting in an American diner-styled cafe eating chips from a paper bag and biting into a hamburger. She is talking to her father with such a blasé tone of indifference, licking absentmindedly at her salty fingers, that the intent look on her father's face is almost comical. He is watching his daughter with frowning sincerity, confusion, disbelief, an expression mostly conveyed through his raised eyebrows and furrowed brow. His fingers squeeze together an overspilling burger, but he makes no move to lift the food to his mouth and bite. 'What on earth do you mean, Lizzy?' he asks when finally the girl stops to slurp at her Coke.

'What do you mean, "what do I mean?"' the ten-year-old asks. 'I want to change my name to Max. It suits me more than Elizabeth Mary.'

'No,' he says, 'I mean the bit about being a boy.'

'Oh,' Max says. 'That.' As though it was nothing. 'Well,' she says, 'I am, aren't I? Isn't it obvious?'

Big Sal, the *big* woman, proprietor of Pauper's Inn, stands large and alone in her empty pub. Large, alone and very still as she stares at the painting hung on the wall. It is of a lighthouse. A stormy sea. Waves lashing against rocks and the sea spray lifting high against the lighthouse wall, the shining beacon beaming out from its glass room through an angry sky of grey and black.

Big Sal stands and stares. In her right hand she holds three empty glasses collected from a table, the dregs of whatever drink still in their bottoms. Her breath is heavy with this muggy summer air and Big Sal's body sweats. She pulls free the handkerchief tucked into the elasticated waist of her leggings and mops at her forehead and neck. It is so. Uncomfortably. Hot. Big Sal cannot seem to draw in enough breath. She fans at her face with handkerchief and hand, breathing back what little she can of this self-made breeze.

Of course, if she wasn't so fat . . .

Big Sal, still with handkerchief in hand, reaches out to the corner of the painting's wooden frame and lifts it a little, an attempt to straighten it, but the walls and ceiling and doorframes of this old pub are no longer aligned; the painting will always hang at an odd angle.

Vicious seas and angry skies and the strong, proud

lighthouse standing tall and safe. A powerful image. But what Big Sal loves about this painting isn't what can be seen, but what remains unseen. The man inside, living lonely on his rock, working the lantern that lives depend on. The man inside those walls, listening out as the winds howl all around him and the rain and waves crash. He is there. Of course he is. The light proves it.

Big Sal turns from the painting and with a deep sigh moves back to her barstool and electric fan. She dumps the empties in the sink of soapy water and takes a clean tumbler from the shelf. She is thinking about Bev as she pours herself a large Scotch. She is trying to picture him wearing a hardhat and sleeveless high-vis tabard, bending over to adjust metal chains of crane-like machinery that reach from the rigs down into the choppy sea below. She is imagining him calling the all-clear to his co-workers, gesturing for them to go ahead. Although she has no idea what he is waving at them to do. No idea what the machinery is, whether these chains really need adjusting, or if indeed there *are* any chains. After all, she has made these images up. In reality, Big Sal has little clue as to what her man does on the rigs, she knows only that the rigs are there to drill for oil.

From the hallway she can hear the back door open and close with a click. 'Mr Little? Is that you?' Big Sal doesn't move from her perch on the barstool. 'You should join me for a dram,' she calls.

It is almost one o'clock in the morning. Big Sal takes another tumbler and pours out a second whisky.

'A wee nightcap,' she says. Already she is feeling better sitting in front of the large electric fan.

Jacob appears in the doorway. Tall and gaunt and wearing his long grey coat.

Big Sal turns. 'Well, well,' she says, 'just look at you! New haircut, is it? Very nice.' She waves at Jacob to take a seat at the other side of the bar. 'Very dapper,' she continues. 'And you've shaved too?' She pushes the whisky towards him. 'So who're you trying to impress? New employer? Or is it a woman you've got your eye on?'

Jacob picks up the tumbler. He seems to sway a little on the barstool. 'Perhaps,' the word slurs into the whisky, 'perhaps I'm trying to impress *you*,' he says.

Big Sal throws back her head and laughs at this. She playfully pushes the man's shoulder. 'Flatterer,' she says.

Jacob seems to smile as he drinks back the liquor.

'So Mr Little . . .' Big Sal is flirting now, 'how long have you been here? Two weeks, is it? And still I don't know the first thing about you.' Big Sal turns her face into the full cool breeze of the fan. Her thin wispy fringe lifts from her forehead and flutters. 'It's not right for a landlady not to know her lodger,' she says. 'Not when they live under the same roof.' Big Sal pours more whisky into both glasses. 'Tell me about yourself.'

But Jacob only sways and blinks at the whisky. 'I'm afraid,' he manages, 'I don't know what to say.' He hiccups.

'You're drunk, Mr Little.'

'That, madam, I am.'

'Then you'll join me and get a little drunker?'

'Indeed, madam, I will.'

Tucked behind the bar is an ashtray and a packet of cigarettes. Big Sal offers them to the lodger.

'*Camel*,' he says, taking one. 'The beast of burden.'

'I've never smoked anything else,' says Sal.

'Stage one,' says the lodger. 'Stage one. We are all camels to begin with . . .' he hiccups, 'we all blindly follow. We all let ourselves be led. We all carry . . .' another hiccup, 'the heavy knowledge imparted on us since birth. But where is the *true meaning*?'

'You really are very drunk, aren't you?' Big Sal extracts the lighter from the lodger's swaying hand and helps him light his cigarette.

'Stage two,' says the lodger. 'Stage two, we are *lions*. We start to question. We question the given truths. We stand apart from the crowd and say, "I *will*!"'

Big Sal lights her own cigarette. Smoke spirals into her eye, making it blink and water. She wipes it with the back of her hand.

'Stage three,' says the lodger, 'we must become children again. We must forget our knowledge. Forget our will. We are given a new beginning. Only then . . .' he takes a long drag on his cigarette, 'only then are we spontaneous and free.'

Big Sal smiles serenely. 'Oh, right.'

'You don't understand,' says Jacob.

'Not really, no. Maybe I need another drink?' She pours herself another. 'Honestly, though, if you want my opinion, ye need some *meat* on ye. You're wastin' away. It looks as though you've been nil by mouth these past few weeks.'

'I'm not a very hungry person,' Jacob says.

Big Sal opens a packet of crisps and a bag of pork scratchings. 'Well, that's where we differ.' She pours some salted mixed nuts into a finger bowl. 'Here,' she says. 'Eat.' Sal picks out a cashew and pops it into her mouth as though demonstrating.

Jacob carefully selects a hand-cooked potato chip and lifts it to his mouth. The slow movement makes him sway in his seat. In his other hand, the cigarette burns and drops ash.

Big Sal watches the drunk man *crunch, crunch, crunch*. She picks up another cashew and pops it into her mouth, sucking on her salty fingers. 'Always been a big girl, me,' she says. 'Look at any baby photo, you'll see. I was born with the weight on me.' Perhaps it is in a bid to loosen the man's tongue that Big Sal has begun to talk like this. 'Healthy appetite,' she says. 'That's what my mother called it.'

'Was she fat too?' slurs the lodger.

The bluntness of this question strikes Sal with force, yet she is quick to compose herself. She picks up the whisky and pours Jacob another. 'Aye,' she says, 'my mother was fat and so was my father. And I'm no' so shy I won't say it.' She sucks on a pork scratching. 'But at least I *own* it,' she says. 'I'm *fat*. Always have been, always will be. It's part of who I am. They wouldn't call me Big Sal if it was any other way.'

The lodger sucks on his lower lip. His eyes droop heavily. '. . . K,' he says. 'So I have a question . . .' The cigarette has burned now right down to the butt. 'What is it,' he says, 'you see when you look in the mirror?'

Big Sal too is beginning to feel the effects of alcohol. She repeats the question. 'What do I see . . . ?' Then laughs at its ludicrousness. 'Is it a trick question?' she asks.

'No tricks,' says Jacob.

'It *sounds* like a trick question.'

'No tricks,' Jacob repeats.

Big Sal crunches on a crisp. 'OK, I'll bite,' she says. 'I see me.'

'*Right*,' says Jacob.

'Right,' says Sal.

The electric fan hums beside them.

'Is that it?' asks Sal.

'Apparently,' says Jacob.

The pink-haired woman is standing by the open bedroom window. She is watching as the old man, Mr Benson, gets into his car and sits. He sits very still, not doing anything, for quite a long time. The pink-haired woman watches him from the upstairs bedroom window, only slightly hidden behind a curtain. When finally the old man turns the key in the ignition, and the putting revs of his brown Saab can be heard coughing up to her, she picks out another cigarette from her packet of twenty and lights it. She watches as the Saab bumps down from the kerb and drives up the residential road lined with its parked cars neat in driveways and those slim baby trees in cages.

'Hey?'

She hadn't heard the squeak of the staircase or the foot-steps coming from the hall.

'You're smoking,' the man in the doorway says. The pink-haired woman turns and looks at the man. He has a hand resting on the doorframe, he is slightly out of breath from taking the steps two at a time. 'Are you OK?'

'Sure,' she says, 'why wouldn't I be?' She flicks the tip of her cigarette and a fleck of ash breaks off and drifts into the open air. 'That was Mr Benson,' she says before he can ask. 'Did you recognise him?'

'Our old landlord?'

'Yep,' and the cigarette is again at her lips, the smoke is drawn into her mouth and lungs and out again. 'He's looking for Jacob.'

'That little prick?'

She shrugs. The Saab has driven out of view but still the pink-haired woman looks on after it. 'I don't think he'll be coming back any time soon, B. You needn't worry.' And once more she flicks out her ash.

THE END

There it is.

Broken. Britain. Another example of. SCANDAL. And though everyone knows it is morbid and wrong, they all want to see him fall. Even Lucy watches the jump and thump, the dust from the skip billowing up into the sky. She listens as the sound of Jacob's voice moans out in agony.

Even Max, who no longer calls herself Max, but is back to plain Lizzy, now thirteen years old, an altar girl, even she watches the man step out, his foot hovering for that split second before his body falls forward. Like a plank, she thinks. He didn't 'jump' at all, he moved like a plank that had been stood up on its end and then left to fall forward. 'Why do they say he jumped?' she demands when the word is used on the news. 'He didn't *jump*, did he? He fell. He stepped off. He *dropped*.'

And the girl filming whispers, 'Fuck me.'

And the footage goes blank.

Mr Benson stares at the computer screen in front of him. His youngest daughter, Abigail, turns and looks up into his face. 'Do you want to see it again, Dad?'

'No, Abbie, no.' He feels as though the ground is moving beneath him. He holds onto the backrest of his daughter's swivelling office chair. 'That's it now,' he says, 'I've seen it.'

The story goes something like this: On 18 April 2014, two teenage girls had been sitting in the yard of the derelict Office Shop warehouse in Bristol. It was nine o'clock in the morning, grey and overcast. The girls were said to have been waiting for a friend. In the police statement they made later that evening they described how 'a Caucasian man, about 5 ft 11, with dark cropped hair, wearing a long grey coat that reached just past his knees, appeared on the roof, stood for a minute, maybe two, before slowly stepping out with his right foot and falling down, four storeys, into the skip below.

'What I don't understand,' says Lucy's mother, 'is how they could *film* it. I mean God, what is wrong with young people today? You see a man about to jump off a roof and your first thought is "I know, let's *film* it." It's just awful, isn't it, Lucy? It's sick. Just *sick*.' She pauses. 'Are you still there?'

'Yeah, Mum,' Lucy leans her head back against the wall and closes her eyes. She presses her mobile more firmly against her ear as a group of students bustle by, laughing. 'I'm still here.'

'That poor man,' her mum continues. 'And now it's splashed all over every newspaper, every radio station, every news programme.'

But, dear reader, *but* . . . in fact it is not our Jacob Little who is in the limelight. Oh no! What a bleak and dismal future Britain has, people are saying, if *these* are the mothers of the next generation. Those who seem eager to watch a man choose between life and death. How have the morals of our children become so distorted? So corrupted? And everywhere there are the pixelated faces of those two young girls. It is Trudy Attworth and Denise Boon who are the stars of this show. Jacob Little, at first, is simply a man who jumps.

'But he *didn't* jump!' Lizzy exclaims. 'He sways. He swoops. He swishes.'

And the ground beneath Mr Benson's feet moves, it treadmills backwards, and Mr Benson, the old man, falls forwards. 'Dad! Jesus, shit, *Dad*!'

But we are not there yet. Not *quite* yet. Though we are not so far off either. First we must finish up these developing stories, don't you think? Big Sal, Lucy Westbry, Max and Mr Benson, our loose threads flapping in the breeze. We should return to 2011, to Pauper's Inn, where Jacob is still residing in the shabby little upstairs room.

It is late. Big Sal is sitting alone on the stool behind the bar, face full of the blowing breeze from the electric fan. She is drinking.

From the hallway she hears the back door open and close.

'Mr Little?' she calls. 'Is that you?' She listens. 'You should join me for a dram. A wee nightcap.'

And there in the doorway appears the strange thin man wearing the long grey coat.

Not far from here, Lucy Westbry lies in her bed, both hands under cover and legs spread as she forces the rounded tip of the deodorant bottle up and into her. The experiment is uncomfortable and unpleasant. Her vagina is both tight and dry. She moves the bottle back and forth, back and forth, her face fixed in concentration as she focuses her mind on each sensation. Nothing enjoyable. Nothing 'orgasmic'. Is she doing something wrong? She pulls out the bottle and presses her fingers into her genitals, testing for blood.

Max is awake. She shouldn't be, but she is. For some reason she has woken up and is now staring up at the ceiling where the luminous green glow of sticky stars and planets break up the deep black of the bedroom.

> *Starlight, star bright,*
> *first star I see tonight,*
> *I wish I may, I wish I might,*
> *have the wish I wish tonight.*

Max closes her eyes and wishes for a giant tube of *Smarties* as somewhere in the southwest of England a kitchen light is switched on.

'Stan?'

Mr Benson is sitting at the table. He closes his eyes against the sudden bright of the spotlight. 'Please, Ada,' he says and motions for her to switch the light back off. With a soft *click* the darkness returns, filling the room with the deep bluish-white of the moon from the garden. Ada takes the seat opposite her husband.

'You can't sleep,' she says. 'Would you like some of my pills?'

'No,' he replies. 'I'm fine as I am.'

And so they sit, two silent silhouettes, in the dark at the kitchen table.

23

'Do you still love her?' the girl asks. 'I mean, is that why you're still looking for her?'

Sunday. Another bright day. A church bell is clanging out and there sits Jacob, watching the tolling bell from the opposite side of the road. A car pulls into the church car park and a smartly dressed couple step out carrying tupperware boxes and a tray covered in tinfoil that glints in the sun. Other smartly dressed churchgoers file in through the doors. They smile at one another and pat hands and say 'nice to see you'. The *clang clang* of the bell continues.

A woman passes by with a small Jack Russell on a lead. 'Come on, Charlie,' she says when the dog stops to sniff at the leg of the bench.

Jacob looks at the woman. He stretches his thin lips into a smile of sorts.

The woman smiles back as the dog lifts his leg to pee.

'Sorry about that,' she says.

'When nature calls,' Jacob replies.

The woman laughs politely and walks on.

No, no, that's not what happens. The woman doesn't walk on, she remains standing. She says, 'I've seen you around, haven't I? Yes, you do look familiar. I think we've bumped into each other a couple of times. Are you new in town?'

And Jacob says, 'I'm here for a short while.'

'Business or pleasure?' asks the woman.

'I'm not sure,' comes the reply. 'I'm looking for someone. An old friend. She used to live here.' And that's how the conversation starts.

Her name is Solace, he says, and he begins to tell her how they met. It was thirteen years ago in a nightclub called Synergy. Her opening line was, '*You look depressed,*' *and* she had to shout to be heard over the music. People turned their heads. People looked at him. At first when she told him her name he misheard her. He thought she'd said *Soul-less*. They drank together. They got drunk together. They exchanged a few words. Mostly they just sat and looked at their hands and into their drinks. After leaving the club, they fucked in an alleyway next to some dirty-looking skips. That's how it started, he says. She followed him home and for the next two years she was there. Always *there*. They ate together. They bathed together. They slept together. He hadn't noticed at first how she'd slithered into his life until it was too late. She'd cemented herself firmly inside of him. A central fixture that ever since then he had spun around. Like *Swing Ball*, he says. You know the game where you a bat a ball on a string around a pole? You know the game? It didn't matter where he went any more, it didn't matter who he became, his mind would always bat back to Solace and the memories of those two years. 'What do you make of that?' he says. 'Do you think I love her? Is that what love is? I *need* to find her. I need to tell her . . .' There is no one else more beautiful, no one else with the same smooth milky-skinned breasts and swollen pinkish nipple teats. No one with a mouth like her that could hold the whole of him, tongue thrusting, wet-mouthed massaging; the slow creamy fuck that bucks and writhes bodies, rubbing sweat and skin. No one like Solace. 'She knows who I am,' he says. 'She's the only person who knows who I am.'

But none of this is actually said because the woman didn't actually stop. She laughed politely and walked on, remember? Her small curious dog scurrying behind her. 'Come on, Charlie. There's a good boy.' And Jacob was left sitting in silence.

'*Soul-less*,' he says out loud, to no one. 'I thought her name was *Soul-less*.'

A different year, a different, time, a different place. A sunny September evening in 2006, some city in the east of England. A hippyish young woman (beaded dreadlocks and dungarees) is storming gracelessly through a busy street, stomping Doc-Martened feet, with a fierce look on her face that threatens elbows to anyone who stands in her way. She turns up an alleyway and stops outside a door. Her face is flushed. Her lips are tight shut. She holds the wall in an attempt to compose herself.

. . . and then buzzes Flat 3.

'Keith?'

With an electric belch the door unlocks and the angry hippy girl is in with a slam, *stomp stomp stomp* up the echoing stairwell, past the door of Flat 1, Flat 2 and then *boom* through the door of Flat 3.

'You nasty piece of lying, cheating, fucking *shit*! Keith, is it? Is *that* your name? Cunting asshole of a man . . .' and a flailing Doc-Martened foot has found a stool to kick over and those hippy hands are flinging cushions. 'Keith, is it? Or should I call you *Simeon Lear*? Or wait . . . maybe I should call you *Wilhelm the homeless fucking street artist*?'

'Ah,' and Jacob – our Jacob, who has been sitting in the middle of the living-room floor with a stack of library-borrowed archaeology books piled next to him – attempts to get to his feet. 'I see what's happened here,' he says as the angry hippy continues to attack both him and the flat. She pulls a lamp from its socket. She smashes a framed photograph against the edge of the coffee table (the photograph was of them, the hippy girl and Jacob, her arms clasped around his stomach, both their faces smeared with happy healthy dirt and dust from the dig site).

'Don't even *try* to wiggle your way out of this one,' and from her pocket the hippy pulls out a newspaper clipping. She thrusts it at Jacob. '*Help Our Homeless Help Themselves*', she cites the newspaper headline.

We've all undoubtedly seen him sitting in the street accompanied by his scruffy dog, Dodger, and his colourful paintings leaning against the walls beside him. 'I am a homeless artist', one large canvas reads in big bold lettering. 'All money donated goes on food, paint and art supplies.'

He signs his name simply 'Wilhelm' on the bottom right-hand corner of each painting. When we meet in the park I take the opportunity to question his identity further. 'So who **are** you?' I ask. 'You showed up out of nowhere some months ago and now you're the talk of the town. Where did you come from? What's your name?' The bedraggled man simply shrugs. 'What does it matter?' he asks. 'I am only as you see me now.'

We talk about his art for a while and what inspires him. 'I suppose you could say my style is quite abstract. I work with yellows and reds and black. I like spiralling movement. A spiral to me is the shape of life, continuous and circling, until the end entirely vanishes. Where to? We don't know.' He quietly reflects on this for a moment. 'I sound like a hippy, but I'm **not** a hippy.' He really stresses the 'not'. 'I'm just a homeless man who likes to paint, you know? I'm just a homeless man who happens to really love art.'

Perhaps tactlessly I ask Wilhelm about money, if he makes a good living selling his work. 'I don't sell my art. My art is free. But I accept donations,' he says. 'Through donations I have enough to feed myself and my dog, Dodger, and enough to buy the materials for the next batch of work. What more do I need?'

'But where do you sleep?' I ask and Wilhelm simply shrugs as though such things do not matter.

We move on to other topics, about homelessness and how he's treated on the streets. Again Wilhelm shrugs at my questions. 'People are good to me. I guess they like the fact they can see where the money goes. Not on drugs or alcohol. Although my art **is** an addiction of sorts. It's an obsession. I wouldn't be Wilhelm without it.'

'Ah,' Jacob says again. He is staring at the photograph of himself, long hair and wiry beard, holding a canvas in his hands of a swirling red and yellow mess. 'Yes, I see what's happened here.' He taps at the newspaper with his finger. 'Yes,' he says as the hippy girl stands and seethes.

'Is that it?' she says. 'Is that all you're going to do? Stand and point and nod your head like a gormless fucking idiot?'

'You don't think that's an appropriate response?'

'*Who the hell are you?* That's what I want to know.'

And Jacob sighs. He looks defeated. 'What difference does it make?' he asks. 'I am only as you see me now.'

*

Sitting on the bench opposite the church, Jacob shifts uncomfortably in the heat. He pulls his shirt collar away from his neck and opens out his long grey coat. His eyes follow a swooping gull. He blinks into the sun.

The church bell starts to ring again, the final call before service, and from somewhere further down the road comes another sound. The high-pitched wailing of a young voice in tantrum. Jacob turns to see a woman striding along the pavement, her stern face a mismatch with her bright floating summery dress. Her hand is gripping the wrist of a young girl struggling fiercely against her. 'Let *go*, let *go*, let *go* of *meeee*!' The young girl's face is bright red as she squirms in her mother's grip. 'You can't make me go. I don't want to go in *this*!' The girl is wearing a pale yellow dress with a pretty flower-print design and ribbons tied in delicate bows on the short ruffled sleeves. With her one free hand she tears at the ribbons with frantic fingers. 'I *hate* it,' she cries. 'I *hate* it!'

Elizabeth Mary Duda, the wonderfully vibrant Max, is kicking and pulling and wriggling as her mother drags her onwards. 'Now you'll stop this at once, Elizabeth. Do you hear? This is no way to behave. I'm losing my patience.' And mother hauls daughter to a standstill by her side. 'I'm very cross,' she says and slaps the girl's hands away from the ribbons. 'Leave it be, Elizabeth. Do you want a smack?'

'I'm *not* a baby.'

And Jacob just stares. He has recognised the girl as the young cheeky face from the park. The boy with cropped blond hair and grass stains on his knees. 'You look depressed,' the boy had said. Jacob cocks his head as he realises his mistake.

'For goodness' sake, *stop* playing with those ribbons.'

'But I *hate* it,' she says.

'You'll wear it, Elizabeth. I'll hear no more of this nonsense.'

As her mother reties the bow on her sleeve, Max looks across the road to where Jacob is sitting. Her eyes meet the man's stare. The sight of the strange, sad man on the bench stuns the girl into stillness. 'Now will you *please* leave these ribbons alone, Elizabeth?' But, dear reader, you need two hands to tie a ribbon; and now that Max's wrist is free from the cuff of her mother's tight grip . . .

she is off.

The hot blush and mortification of the moment has turned her heels and sent them into a sprint, polished leather buckle shoes slapping flat-footed on the pavement. *SLAP SLAP SLAP SLAP.* She's torn away from her mother so fiercely the ribbon has ripped from its pretty ruffled sleeve. '*Elizabeth!*' But she is gone. She is down the road, around the corner, out of sight before her mother can draw her next breath.

Let's follow her, dear reader, as Max shoves open the front door of her house and collapses through, wailing and kicking her feet at the walls and stairs. She takes herself to the bathroom and slams across its bolt. 'I *hate* yooooou!' The tears continue. Large lungful gasps between outraged sobs of indignation, followed by a fearsome belly-scream of protest. Max is in the throes of her humiliation, tearing the dress from her body, pulling off its buttons and ribbons and the lace sewn around the hem. Soon she is in nothing but her knickers, white socks and buckle shoes as she attacks the flower-print material with her mother's sharp little nail scissors. She stabs and rips and cuts the fabric. Such uncontrolled anger is a frightening thing to watch in someone so young. She herself has not even noticed in her fury that she has cut her left hand. A small wound near the thumb. The red of her blood stains the tattered dress with a garish speckled horror. She does not *care* how much trouble she will be in when her mother discovers the dress in ruins. She can no longer *think*, she can only *feel* the bitter upset, torment, regret at not only being forced to wear what she did not want to wear, but at being *seen* by the sad man, her secret discovered.

In future years she will laugh at this moment among friends. She will tell them the story in full, about how one evening she had confessed to her father her thoughts on being a boy, not realising the cataclysmic domino-toppling of events that would follow: her father informing her mother, her mother going ballistic, the baying and naysaying and backbiting and buck-passing between adults arguing over who was to blame. 'It's *you*, Marek, this is all *your* doing. You started her wearing those boyish clothes. You took her to play football.'

'Me? How is it *my* fault? I only get to see the girl every second weekend!'

'Well, perhaps that's too much!'

And on. Like that. And on and on. 'So help me God, Marek, if this *perversion* continues . . .' Until it draws to an end the following morning with the enforcement of the dress; and later still, the dress's demise.

She will not tell her friends, however, about the sad man sitting on the bench. It will seem too personal somehow.

Especially after that grey day in April 2014 when the man with no name had taken himself up to the roof of that derelict Office Shop warehouse and jumped.

'He did *not* jump,' she will always find herself saying. 'Everybody has *seen* the footage. Why do people say he jumped?'

Max is now drowning the dress in the bathtub, adding yet another dimension to its destruction. She has spotted the wound on her hand and is sucking and nursing it with her mouth. At least she has stopped crying. The water roars from the taps and puddles around the torn fabric until it's swimming in all the wet. Numbness gives way to the slow reveal of thoughts. Max is aware now of the trouble she is going to be in when her mother returns from church. She is uncannily aware also of her own situation, the sensation she experiences of mismatched body and mind. There is a prickly unease, a distaste, but it comes from outside of her. It comes from other people. If you asked the ten-year-old now to put these feelings into words she would not be able to. She would look at you and shrug. But the feelings are there even if they remain yet unnamed. It is not 'non-acceptance' but of something being fundamentally 'wrong'; and that wrong thing is a part of her.

Dear reader, we are not just witnessing here the destruction of a dress.

Max . . . no, *not* Max, we should call her Lizzy, shuts off the taps and sits on the edge of the bathtub. She shivers and clasps her goosepimpled arms around her bare chest. *Hide the dress* . . . she begins to think . . . *hide the dress, hide the dress* . . . And so she scoops the sodden mess into her arms and runs with it dripping out of the bathroom, into the hallway, throws open the back door and stumbles into the small square of garden where the wheelie bins are kept. She dumps the dress. She slams shut the lid of the bin. She breathes.

24

'I want to know about your family,' the girl curled under Jacob's arm says. 'You know, like what do your parents do for a living? What are their names? Do you have any brothers or sisters? Tell me *everything*. I want to know everything there is to know about Jacob Little.'

Love. What *is* love? On Sunday morning, during breakfast, as the Westbry Family Trio sit eating their soft-boiled eggs together at the table, Lucy notes the unusual feeling inside of her. There is the aching in her genitalia, of course, from the night before (Lucy's rendezvous with the deodorant bottle) – not sore as such, just bruised and stretched, a little tender 'down there' – but there was something else happening as well. A fizz in her guts. It had started small that morning after she imagined visiting Jacob again and slowly it started to grow, an excited unrest. What is it? This *feeling*. It was ballooning out. It made her want to burst into a sprint or beat her chest or shout at the sky.

Her parents are talking about the possibility of switching their electricity provider, 'to something more green', says Anya. 'But it costs more,' says her mother. 'Ah, but it costs so much less for the planet,' says Anya. 'And is the planet going to start paying our wages?' asks her mother. Lucy listens as she pushes the long thin soldiers into the orangey yolk. It isn't an argument. Not really. This is just one of the many roles her parents act out together, Anya always striving for more organic, more eco friendly, more Fairtrade and her mother always saying calmly, 'It's not that I don't *want* these things, but we're stretched as it is.'

Quietly Lucy interrupts them. 'What is love?' she asks.

Her mother slows her eating. Anya stops mid-sentence, 'But think of the polar bears—'

'I mean,' says Lucy, 'we talk about it all the time like we know what it is, and apparently we all *need* it and search for it. But what is it?'

Her mother frowns a little. 'Well,' she says, while Anya sets her mug of tea down and closes her eyes.

'Let me tell you what love isn't . . .' she says. 'Love isn't excitement. It isn't a fluttering in the chest. It isn't a churning in the stomach. It isn't being constantly caught in a daydream.' It was as though Anya had looked inside Lucy's body and pulled out everything she was feeling. 'It isn't walking on air or flying in a bubble. It isn't thinking about a certain person every moment of every day. It isn't obsession. It isn't being needy and dependent. It isn't happiness.'

'It *isn't* happiness?'

'No.'

'So what is it?'

'It's a *source*,' Anya says, 'not an emotion or state of mind. You can spend a lifetime seeking it. Some never find it. Some find it then leave it. Some find it then camp by the wayside. Some find it then tap their whole soul into it so nothing but love pours out.'

Lucy is quiet. The description doesn't seem right somehow.

Now Lucy is sitting outside Piccalitos cafe, drinking hot chocolate with whipped cream and marshmallows. She is here at this cafe for no other reason than it is close to Pauper's Inn and it is something to do. Of course, she could go to the pub. She could sit with Big Sal and drink hot chocolate free of charge in her kitchen, but she wants to be alone. She wants to think.

About . . . ?

In truth she is not thinking about anything, she is *feeling*. It is the intensity that comes with unknowing, the nervous excitement, the anticipation that curdles the stomach. Her guts twist. *But this isn't love?* Already she has been to the toilet to suffer through a sudden and brief bout of diarrhoea. If it's not love then what is it? She doesn't know.

As Lucy spoons at the thick cream and the pink and yellow marshmallow blobs she returns again and again to the moment she saw Jacob for the first time. The sunlight slanting through his bedroom window, cutting over the surface of the table, the green jotters and papers and the lit cigarette smoking in the ashtray. She remembers it now as though it were a scene from an old-fashioned film. He had stepped into the warm golden glow of the light. She had gasped.

'Hello,' he'd said.

'Hi,' she'd replied.

He is not a *handsome* man, Lucy allows herself to admit, not in the *traditional* sense of the word. She takes a long slurp of chocolate through the cream and wipes her mouth with her wrist. But there is definitely something about him. Something mysterious. Something compelling. Something . . . dangerous? Enticing? Taboo? The age gap between them excites Lucy; the thought that someone older, a real *man*, might be interested in her. Sweet sixteen and never been . . . Kissed quite a lot actually. Even fumbled at and groped a bit during early teens and with Billy. But never had sex. And almost certainly never been *loved*.

'You know, I don't think I know what love *is*,' her mother had said as they'd cleared the breakfast table, 'but I know what love *does*. It changes the world, Lucy. In loving Anya and loving you I've changed the world. Even if it's just a tiny bit. And that's how I know I love.'

It is time for things to happen, dear reader. It's time to pick up the pace. We all know that this teenage girl is soon to embark on a tumultuous 'love' affair with our protagonist Jacob Little, so why not hurry it up a bit? Here, take this copper penny and roll it along the pavement. Roll it so it strikes the metal leg of her table and *clings* to a stop. Or better yet, flick it towards her feet so that it lands nearby and makes that alluring sound of money dropping, a sound that pricks ears and turns heads. There. See? She is looking underneath her table. She spots the copper penny. She is picking it up. Watch, dear reader, watch as she turns the penny with her fingers. 'See a penny . . . see a penny . . .' She glances over towards Pauper's Inn. 'See a penny, pick it up . . .' She is remembering the rickety wardrobe covered in copper luck.

Lucy is not looking for a *source*. She is not looking to change the world, even if it's just a tiny bit. It is a wild, windswept love affair she dreams of, the Cathy and Heathcliff kind of love that consumes all thoughts and haunts the soul, it is the love that taps at your window at night when you're lying alone in bed. *Surely you and every body have a notion that there is, or should be, an existence of yours beyond you.* Lucy has pushed back her chair, metal legs scraping against pavement. She is on her feet, fingers still turning the penny in her hand. Her eyes move up to the sash window above the sign of Pauper's Inn. We can see him, dear reader. We can distinguish the outline of his lanky figure and movement as the man fumbles with the latch. *If all else perished, and he remained, I should still continue to be; and if all else remained, and he were annihilated, the Universe would turn to a mighty stranger.* It is a shared obsession Lucy is dreaming of as the loose sash window slides open and Jacob, our Jacob, leans out. He is looking our way. He is looking at Lucy. *My great thought in living is himself.* She is crossing the road. A car slows and beeps its horn. The penny is in her hand. *What were the use of my creation if I were entirely contained here?* The pub is busy with regulars and students, football commentary blaring on the small television above the bar. Big Sal is pulling pints and bantering with the punters; she doesn't see Lucy walk straight past, into the hallway, up the stairs. Outside Jacob's open door, Lucy pauses. There he is. Standing at the window. He is facing her.

'Hello,' he says.

'Hi,' she replies. She steps into the room. She holds up the penny. 'I saw this and thought of you.'

He looks at the penny. In three long strides he is across the room and taking the small copper piece into his hand and with it *her* hands. He says these words:

> *I whispered, 'I am too young,'*
> *And then, 'I am old enough';*
> *Wherefore I threw a penny*
> *To find out if I might love.*
> *'Go and love, go and love, young man,*
> *If the lady be young and fair.'*
> *Ah, penny, brown penny, brown penny,*
> *I am looped in the loops of her hair.*
> *O love is the crooked thing,*

There is nobody wise enough
To find out all that is in it,
For he would be thinking of love
Till the stars had run away
And the shadows eaten the moon.
Ah, penny, brown penny, brown penny,
One cannot begin it too soon.

And there follows the first skin-trembling kiss, warm tobacco lips and chocolate marshmallow breath. Lucy is so nervous she is shaking. Jacob's arm is around her, his hand in the small of her back. She opens her mouth to his. 'I *am* Jacob Little,' she thinks, 'he is always, always in my mind . . .'

25

'I sometimes wish,' Jacob says to the girl, 'that your breasts were just a little bit bigger. Then I could put my cock in your cleavage. I mean, I suppose we could try it, couldn't we? If you press your breasts together . . . would you mind? It's just I really like the idea of coming all over your chest.'

The lights dim. The heads of the audience turn into dark outlines and silhouettes. Mouths hush for silence amidst the final rustle of pre-play sweetie wrappers and the shuffling feet of latecomers finding seats. A sound can be heard through the speakers around the hall.

tickety-tickety-tickety-bok-bok-click-click-click-dong-clicketyticketytocktock-tick tock-tick-tock-tick-tock.

BENSON: I suppose you could say I'm a bit of an amateur horologist.

The curtains part to reveal a study, its walls covered with clocks, shelves lined with shoeboxes, books piled on the floor. The old man Benson is sitting at a desk, loupe over his eye, replacing the intricate pieces of a watch movement. In an armchair is a young man in a long grey coat. Jacob. He is leaning forward in his armchair, absorbed by what the old man is saying.

BENSON: *(continuing with his watch repair)* Time has always fascinated me. Time as a dimension and time as a measure. Most people are only aware of the operational definition of time. Nothing more than a counting activity that allows us to value time in terms of seconds, minutes, hours . . . days, weeks, years. This is the time that seems to us to 'flow'. It only ever increases. It moves forward in a straight line. It is the time that seems to make us grow old and die. *(pause)* Then there is spacetime. Space exists in three dimensions. Time is the fourth. Space and time are combined into a single continuum. It has shape. It curves. Our concept of time ticking and moving forward in a uniform Newtonian way is an illusion. It does not tick, tick, tick, like the ticking of this watch, but is relative to the conditions of our own personal experience. It depends on how fast we are moving through space and how close we are to a gravitational pull, that is what Einstein taught us. *(pause)* Then there is imaginary time, which runs perpendicular to real time. Now, when I say the word 'real' and the word 'imaginary' I do not mean that one is true and one is not. Imaginary time allows us to navigate time as a dimension. Just as we can move forwards, backwards, up and down in space, we can move forwards, backwards, up and down in time. Forwards and backwards is real time using real numbers. Up and down is imaginary time and uses imaginary numbers. *(looks over at Jacob)* I know what you are thinking, we are in the realms of Doctor Who and his TARDIS now. If we can move backwards and forwards and up and down in space-time, is time travel possible? Could we go back to the past or forward to the future? It is an interesting question.

JACOB: *(leaning forward)* And? Is it possible?

BENSON: *(laughs)* Well, in theory, we are *already* travelling into the future.

JACOB: But what about the past? Could we travel back to the past?

BENSON: Ah. Yes. *(pause)* Backwards is regrettably much more complicated. *(looks up at the ceiling and takes a deep breath)* But I have a theory. My own old watchmaker theory . . .

26

The girl curled under Jacob's arm strokes his chest and circles his nipples with the tip of her index finger. 'Sometimes,' she says, 'I wish I could open up your head and look inside your brain. I want to *know* what you're thinking. I wish I could crawl inside and sit there with all your thoughts swirling around me, bubbling about, like a great big mind-jacuzzi. I wish I could immerse myself in your thoughts. Drink your ideas. Bathe myself in your dreams.

'Jacob,' the girl says, 'I think I love you.'

Elizabeth Mary Duda is sitting on her bed, her arms hugging her knees. From downstairs she can hear the key in the front door turn and the sound of the handle being pushed down. The young girl closes her eyes and tightens the grip on her legs. She waits for the explosion. She is expecting her mother's fury. She anticipates shouting and stomping and to be hauled off the bed and struck around the legs and buttocks by stinging hands, but the bang doesn't come. She listens closer to the sounds reaching up from the hallway. There is the jangle of keys, the squeak of leather trousers and two heavy biker boots on lino.

'Lizzy?' her father calls to her softly.

'Dad!'

And she is up and out of the room in an instant, hurtling down the stairway and into the arms of her father. 'Mum is going to be so angry with me!' she is wailing into the leather scent of his jacket. 'The dress . . .' she says. 'She made me wear . . .' she can barely get the words out through her tears. Her father crouches down and is shushing her into his arms. 'Hey,' he's saying, 'it's OK.'

'But it's not OK,' she sniffs. 'I've torn the dress.'

'Never mind the dress, Lizzy, it's all right. You can get a new one.'

'But I don't *want* a new one!'

'No, OK, I didn't mean . . . all right, shush now . . .' and he's stroking her hair. 'Listen,' he says, 'I'm not here to tell you off. I don't know about any dress. I'm here because your mother called me.' He rocks his daughter and holds

289

her head. 'Your gran has had to go into hospital,' he tells her. 'She's had another stroke.'

'Another one?'

'I'm sorry, Lizzy.'

There is no time to lose, dear reader. Life is short and time is swift. Time and tide wait for no man. Lizzy knows that her granny is going to die. She knows by the way her father speaks to her using soft tones and by the way he touches her shoulder and looks into her eyes. 'Go and pack your bag, Lizzy, you're staying with me for a few days.' So Lizzy packs her bible, her teddy bear, two of her favourite GI Joe men and the Evidence Box, while her father counts out seven pairs of underwear, two T-shirts and a pair of shorts.

Yes, Lizzy knows that her granny is going to die because her father instructs her how to get on the back of the motorbike and how to sit, even though she's done it a thousand times before. 'And don't wriggle,' he says without humour, 'you mustn't wriggle, it makes me unsteady, we don't want to come off, do we?' No, she thinks. We don't want to come off and die, do we? Death is something we don't want. Death is something we try to avoid.

But Granny is old. She is old and weak and crooked in her wheelchair. She never fully recovered from the first stroke. Then there was the second stroke. And now this, the third. Things come in threes, her mother so often said. Like the Trinity; Father, Son and Holy Ghost. Peter betrayed Jesus three times. Christ rose again after three days. Christ is crucified. Christ is risen. Christ will come again.

Lizzy knows that her granny is going to die because her father cooks her favourite meal, turkey drumsticks and chips, even though he says there's nothing good in them. He, however, doesn't eat. He's not hungry. He sits at the kitchen table and watches her as she dips her chips into tomato ketchup. He asks about what happened at church that morning.

'It doesn't matter,' Lizzy says. Because nothing does, does it, when someone is going to die?

Getting ready for bed that evening, her father comes to tuck her in. He never usually does this. Perhaps Granny is already dead? Lizzy wonders. Why else would her father seem so sad? He even tucks the teddy bear in beside her and presses down on its stuffed little snout. 'I remember when me and your mother got you that,' he says. 'We were pushing you in your buggy around a store, marvelling at how quiet you were being. It was only when we were leaving and the attendant stopped us at the doors that we realised why. You had somehow snatched that little bear from its shelf and were holding tightly onto his ears.' He smiles. 'We felt we had to buy it for you then, if it kept you *that* quiet.'

Death makes people nostalgic.

Lizzy reaches out and touches her father on the arm. 'It's OK, Dad,' she says. 'Don't be sad. Granny is going to die, but she'll be with God. She'll be in heaven.'

And her father stares at her. He is silent.

'We all have to die,' she says. 'It's part of life.' She pats him on the arm. 'Jesus died. If he can do it, so can we.'

27

'I want to know about your family,' says the girl curled under Jacob's arm. 'Why won't you tell me anything? Is your past such a secret?'

'You don't understand,' Jacob says. 'I wasn't born. I'm not alive. I've never really existed. I don't have a family. There is just me.'

When the young Lucy Westbry has long been an adult, once she has finished her first degree, her Master's, her PhD, once she has become Dr Lucy Westbry, professor of philosophy, with an impressive résumé of published articles and essays and her own book on the subject of Self and Identity, *The 'I' in the Mirror*, affording her some notoriety in the academic world, only then does she seem able to look back at her scandalous Jacob Little love affair with any clarity. And how is that? she will wonder. Is it the passing of time and the growing haze of memory that affords her some objectivity on the matter? Or is it the impact of other life experiences, other love affairs, that allows her to compare one obsession with another, constantly re-evaluating her relationship with Jacob Little until the intensity of all emotions fades to . . . what? Indifference? Is that what she becomes?

'He shall never know how much I love him'. It is a quote from *Wuthering Heights*, 'and that, not because he's handsome, Nelly, but because he's more myself than I am.' That's the type of love Lucy had wanted to experience, a sweeping, gushing, ever-expanding love that seemed not just to fill every part of her but go *beyond*, to fill the room, the house, the whole street; she wanted her fingers to feel the energy in everything she touched, she wanted her aura to twist and intertwine with the aura of those around her, like some kind of ethereal love tango. She wanted to feel *electric*. She wanted to feel *alive*. And that's what she felt during that one week – yes, only one week – with Jacob

Little. 'Whatever our souls are made of, his and mine are the same.'

But they weren't, were they? It would seem to Dr Lucy Westbry, when she finally achieved the clarity to revisit the memories of that eventful week, that in fact her soul and Jacob's were as different 'as a moonbeam from lightning, or frost from fire', as Emily Brontë had written. Her soul, she would come to think, had always flown like a river, whereas Jacob's sunk like a rock. Her soul was made of spirit, uncatchable wisps of wind, whereas Jacob's seemed like a sluggish viscous liquid that stuck to the people it came into contact with. It had certainly clung to her, she would think. The stains would always be visible.

It didn't hurt, the sex. Not really. It was uncomfortable, but . . . Lucy will always be amazed that even though she had no idea what to do, her body did. When he touched her breasts her nipples became erect, her skin became clammy, her vagina became wet. No, more than just wet, her vagina *throbbed*. That first time, although she felt clumsy and awkward and even afraid, her body didn't. Her body craved. When Jacob brushed the tip of his penis against her clitoris, it had been Lucy who had said the words, 'I'm ready' – not that Jacob had asked. Jacob just trembled and breathed heavily. When he pushed himself inside her he said only, 'Oh God, that's good . . . oh God, you're tight,' and she gripped hold of his shoulders as that first sharp push took her breath away.

He hadn't even known her name. She'd never told him. 'I don't want to know your name,' he'd said. 'Not your *real* name. And shhh,' he'd held a finger over her lips, 'don't tell me one true thing about you. See, you can be anyone with me. Anyone at all. Just make it up. Names can be so binding, don't you think? So limiting. But with me, see, you are limitless.' And Lucy had felt as though she was melting as he pulled her close, their skin sleek with sweat. 'Come here,' he'd said. 'I want to hold you. We should do this again sometime. Tell me you'll come again?'

She had fallen so very deeply in love – or so she believed. *Love.* Not quite the kind her parents had talked of. It was more intense, less subtle. It might not have changed the world, she thought, but it changed *her* entirely. She had been snared. She played along with Jacob's limitless game and told him on their second occasion together that her name was Freyja, the Norse goddess of love, and Jacob had become aroused by it. 'Are you Freyja?' he'd asked, 'or are you the shapeshifting Loki, wrapped in Freyja's feather cloak? Or the great god Thor, dressed in Freyja's bridal gown?' He had told her then that once upon a time, perhaps eight obsessions ago, he had been known to a city as Graymalkin, the street preacher. 'A preacher not of religion,' he'd said, 'but of mythology.' He told her how he would stand on a beer crate in a park every Saturday morning and tell a gathering crowd the greatest stories of old; of warring gods and goddesses, of love and betrayal, of murder and mystery and intrigue.

'What do you mean you were known as Graymalkin?' Lucy had asked. 'What do you mean, "eight obsessions ago"?'

And Jacob had tried to explain. 'Obsessions preoccupy the brain,' he'd said. 'Obsessions give a life meaning, albeit a manmade one. Without obsessions we, as humans, are empty, worthless. For a time my chosen obsession was mythology; and I gave that obsession a name, an identity. It was Graymalkin, the street preacher.'

During that one week together, Lucy learned of Kenny Berk, the bike mechanic and opera enthusiast, Isaac Featherstone, the gardener, Lindsay Ray the penny-whistle-playing litter-picker. Merton, Otto, Gifford, Lear. 'I don't understand,' she would say. 'Having interests and obsessions is one thing, but why change your name? Why move from town to town?' Wilhelm and Archie and Lambert and Keith. 'I mean, it's deception, isn't it?' she would challenge. 'You're basically lying to people about who you really are.'

And Jacob replied, 'Really, am I such a cad? Have I been acting so very differently from everyone else? We are only actors after all; playing out the role of the individual we're each deceiving ourselves into being.' And Jacob had fallen at once upon Big Sal as an example. 'Let's look at our fat friend from behind the bar,' he'd said, 'she who wears her weight like a gold medal. She's deceiving herself. Her husband works on the rigs; she says, "It's hard having your husband work away. A woman's not right without her man around." I could probably guess what's closer to the truth. Bev is a cumbersome oaf, all meat and no brain, who married because isn't that what people are supposed to do? And perhaps Big Sal may have loved him once, but surely not now, she only wishes she did, growing ever more whimsical as she remembers those early years. *Oh, where has it gone?* I can picture her now, picking up that framed photograph gathering dust in the hallway, staring down into the face of her happy self and the face of her husband who used to make her smile so! Perhaps it's still there? The love? Perhaps it hasn't all gone?

'Yes, I can see it all so clearly now,' Jacob continued, 'Big Sal heaving herself around in a fat woman's rush as she prepares everything nicely on the day Bev is due home. Cooking him his favourite dinner, meat and potato pie. Candles. Incense. Why not? She'll tell herself he's worth the effort. They need a bit of the old romance. Big Sal will wash and soap herself thoroughly in anticipation (a nightmarish thought, that big body cramped in the tiny bathtub, lifting those heavy wings of fat around her waist to scrub properly underneath). Perfume, make-up, clean bed sheets. Of course the love is still there! How could she ever think otherwise? Until the moment he walks through that door and the bubble bursts and the truth comes pouring back in.

'Where is that wagging finger now that points and says "liar!"? Big Sal, who hides behind her jovial name as though it were armour. 'I'm *fat*,' she says, 'but at least I *own* it.' Telling strangers she loves her husband, a good man, and how she misses him terribly. Is self-deception so much better than deceiving others?'

'Surely,' Lucy had replied, 'neither is good.' Her short, simple sentence after such a tirade had plummeted them both into silence.

Trevor Bolter, believe it or not, was Jacob's attempt at being a fitness fanatic. He went to the gym every day, he lifted weights, he jogged, he swam, he attended mixed martial arts classes and wrestled and sparred with other men and women on padded mats. He bounced about on a giant inflatable ball to improve his core strength, he lunged and he squatted. There were spinning classes, cardio-tennis, circuit training, assault courses, aerobics. Never had Jacob sweated so much and slept so well! But the exercise was making him cough up more black than usual from his lungs, and so he stopped.

'I tried Buddhism for a time too. The philosophy of "non-self" appealed to me. I went by the name of Teza and shaved my head and walked around in robes. Do you know what was strange? People would so often come up to me in the park or sit beside me on the bus and start pouring their hearts out to me; and I'd sit with my hands clasped in my lap and smile as I listened. People would tear out their tormented souls and lay them out for me to see; and I'd nod and smile and look sincere.'

'People trusted you,' Lucy said to him.

'People see what they want to see,' Jacob replied.

As Teddy Two-Fingers, Jacob had not just tried his hand at stand-up comedy, expounding tongue in cheek upon the science of laughter in dimly lit and sparsely populated bars; he'd also whiled away hours learning how to fold paper into swans, butterflies, hopping frogs, a praying mantis. He'd earned his money 'busking origami' on street corners.

'I even tried to believe in God for a while. I called myself Lambert and threw myself into Christianity. I went to church every day. I prayed. I meditated. I shook hands with everyone in the congregation and smiled and nodded. I used all the right words, ticked all the right boxes. I was a living sacrifice. A disciple of God. A follower of Jesus. I ate of his flesh and drank of his blood. I feasted on the body of Christ on the cross like a vulture picking at the poor man's bones. Forgive me my sins; I am not worthy; glory to God in the highest and peace to his people on earth. But nothing happened. Where was the magic? Where was the miracle? I knocked and nobody answered.'

'You were in it for all the wrong reasons,' Lucy said to him.

'Ha! You sound like Solace,' he replied.

Was it wrong that on hearing this Lucy was pleased?

Love. Was it love? Dr Lucy Westbry will so often wonder. Or had it simply been lust? Was it the young virgin naivety of any teenager? Or was it abuse? Jacob had somehow captured her in that small shabby room above Pauper's Inn; and on top of that grossly stained single mattress, bare of bedclothes, she had become besotted with her captor.

'So let me get this straight,' Lucy would eventually ask, 'you've spent the last ten years or so travelling from place to place, changing your name and living as different people?' She paused. Thinking. 'So, how do I even know you are who you say you are? How do I know you are in fact "Jacob Little"?'

'You don't,' he would answer. 'So why ask such a thing? I am only as you see me now.'

Indifferent? No, Dr Lucy Westbry would never become indifferent. If anything she would become more and more fixated over the years; not with the man, but with the myth of the man. For that's what Jacob Little becomes, a *myth*. One which Dr Lucy Westbry will build her life around. Though unlike Graymalkin the street preacher, balancing precariously on his beer crate, she will stand firmly behind her lectern and teach to a theatre full of university students lectures on Self and Identity. Those were *her* myths.

'Jacob,' she had said, 'I think I love you.'

28

'You don't love me,' he says. 'That's just the oxytocin talking.'

Jacob Little jumps.

There it is.

And his jump causes a seismic social event, it creates ripples and reverberations, people can feel it nationwide, setting all tongues wagging. Thanks, of course, in no small part to those two girls who filmed the fall. But their small ripples soon become waves as Jacob's mystery is uncovered. The man who jumped didn't exist, the police announced. No identification records could be found, no family could be traced. It was important, the police said, that anyone who knew the jumping man should get in contact, as they were 'eager to piece together his story'.

Wilhelm and Merton and Trevor and Ken. Slowly people began to come forward. A man from Spennymoor knew him as Isaac, a woman from Norwich said he was Keith. Lambert and Teza and Simeon Lear. More people stepped forward. More names were given. A man from North Uist claimed he was Otto. An old lady from Kent said he was Ray. 'Lindsay Ray. He was a litter-picker around these parts, always playing his penny whistle.' One newspaper joked the jumping man was everyone except Spartacus. Another dubbed him 'Westwood', the man with all names. It was soon uncertain whether the jumping man had truly portrayed himself as all these different identities, or whether the general public had become swept up by mass hysteria. Stephen and Ali and Boris and Joe? An online forum appeared, whoisjumpingman.com, where people could post their experiences of him, names and dates and places and times.

Mr Benson stares at the computer screen as his youngest daughter reads these posts out to him: 'I know this man very well. His name is Gifford Baintree and he lived in the block of flats across the road from me. A science enthusiast who mostly kept himself to himself. He had a nervous disposition, spoke with a lisp and walked with a limp.'

'It doesn't sound anything like him,' Mr Benson says.

'Or listen to this one: "The man is called Teddy Two-Fingers, he was a terrible comedian who hung around Edinburgh during the Fringe Festival in 2007."' She laughs. 'Teddy Two-Fingers, now *that's* funny.'

Mr Benson isn't smiling.

'Oh, Dad, this has really upset you, hasn't it?' She turns in the swivel chair and takes hold of her father's arm. 'Why don't you go forward? I mean, if you know something about this guy—'

'I don't,' Mr Benson interrupts. 'I don't know anything about him.'

Mr Benson returns to his study and slumps in the chair at his desk. He sighs. From the drawer of his desk he pulls out a shoebox, rests it on the table and lifts the lid.

There it is.

The French Champlevé enamel repeating carriage clock. Late nineteenth century. Greek-key shaped handle. Moulded brass cornicing. Bevelled glass panelling. And with it the note. *Stanley. It just stopped ticking.* 'What then is time?' says the old man out loud. 'If no one asks me, I know: if I wish to explain it to one that asketh, I know not.' It is a quote from Saint Augustine. Mr Benson is thinking back to the afternoon three years before that he spent with the pink-haired woman. Solace.

'Solace?' she had said, on hearing the name. She laughed. 'Oh God, Mr Benson, I haven't had someone call me that in years.' And she told him about the night she met Jacob in a club called *Synergy*. He'd been drinking alone at the bar when she approached. Her opening line had been this: 'You look depressed.'

'And you know what he did?' she said with a smile. 'He took his finger and held it over my lips and slurred, "Shhh! I don't want to know your name. Not your *real* name. And please, don't tell me one true thing about you. See, you can be anyone with me. Anyone at all. Just make it up. Names can be so binding, don't you think? So limiting. But with me, see, you are limitless." And so I told him my name was Solace.' She laughed. 'It was the name of the cocktail I was drinking. Scotch Solace.'

Mr Benson remembers how their conversation had been interrupted at that point by the young boy playing outside. He had run up to the kitchen window and pummelled his fists against the pane to get the attention of his mother. 'Mum! Mum! Twenty-three keepy-ups!' And his mother had smiled and waved. 'Twenty-five and I'll let you have a beer with your dad tonight.' It seemed to Mr Benson a strange reward, but the boy had seemed excited by it. It spurred him on. As he turned to run back onto the lawn, his eyes locked onto Mr Benson's and he paused, ever so briefly, curious at seeing an old man sitting at the kitchen table opposite his mother. And then he had gone. 'Dad! Pass!'

'He seems like a bright kid,' Mr Benson had said, and the woman had humoured him with a smile. 'How old is he?'

'Ten,' she said.

'Ten?' The number seemed significant. 'Ten, of course he is,' and Mr Benson's hand had reached into the inside pocket of his tweed jacket to retrieve the photograph of a young woman, a blonde, wispy-haired woman, holding a baby in her arms. 'This,' he'd said, showing her the photo, 'this was in the box that Olivia Little left to me. It's you, isn't it? And the boy?' The pink-haired woman took the photo and stared at it long and hard. 'On the back,' Mr Benson continued, 'you wrote your address.' The woman was looking more uncomfortable now, or at least Mr Benson thought so. She placed the photograph on the kitchen table and picked up her packet of cigarettes. 'You must have wanted to be found by Jacob at some point,' Mr Benson said.

'Of course,' she replied, pushing the words past the cigarette she had placed in between her lips. 'I loved him, Mr Benson. Of course I wanted to be found by him.'

'And the boy?' Mr Benson had said. 'Is Jacob the father?'

The woman had sucked on her lower lip as the smoke from the cigarette curled.

'Yet you don't want to be found by him any more?' Mr Benson could feel the indignation rising in him. 'But what about the boy? Doesn't he have a right to know who his father is? Doesn't Jacob have a right to know he has a *son*?'

'Calm down, Mr Benson.'

'*Calm down?*' Mr Benson had clenched his fists. 'A piece of information like this is enough to turn a man's life around. You said yourself how troubled Jacob has always been. What if this could help fix things? And the boy . . .'

'Don't bring my son into this.' The pink-haired woman glared. 'Don't tell me what is best for my son.'

'But let me tell you—'

'No, Mr Benson, let me tell *you* something.' The woman was flushed with maternal anger. 'I was swept up for a time with Olivia Little, much like you were. She was the closest thing I had to Jacob, so I went to her, I tried to help her, for a while I even *lived* with her, hoping that he would come back. But that woman was *mad*. I saw it first hand. And that madness manifested itself around my son.' Her hand had been shaking, Mr Benson remembers it well, when she flicked her cigarette at the ashtray. 'She began to believe that *she* was his mother. She even began to call my baby boy Jacob.'

'That's preposterous!'

'Is it?' The pink-haired woman looked fierce. 'Then you are unlikely to believe the rest! Jacob Little doesn't exist, Mr Benson. Whatever idea you have of him, it's a fiction, it's a story he's told you, or perhaps that mad woman he called Mother has told you, but it's a story nonetheless. Jacob Little is a *lie*, do you understand? And that lie is worse than any lie I tell my son regarding who his father is.'

Thinking back to that conversation now, sitting quietly in his study, Mr Benson wonders what it was exactly he had been going to 'tell' the pink-haired woman. 'But let me tell you . . .' What? Had he been going to tell her how he had so very much longed for a son all his life and how Jacob had somehow filled that space within him? How much more good it might do for a man to hear that in fact he *had* a son? Or had he simply been going to tell her that he didn't much care for her tone? Or her attitude?

Mr Benson sighs. He supposes it doesn't matter any more what it was he had been going to say back then, three years ago. But he remembers perfectly well the clear clipped tones of the pink-haired woman as she said the words, 'Jacob Little is dead, Mr Benson. The *real* Jacob Little, I mean. He died at the age of fifteen the day after a school teacher was hit by a car and killed.'

Nobody really knew if the two incidents were related, but it was assumed they were. Perhaps the death of the teacher triggered something deep within the young Jacob. He had always been a quiet and pensive teenager. His behaviour had worsened after the death of his father a few years before. It was thought he may have been bullied, but nobody knew for sure. Nobody really knew anything for sure. Apart from this: Jacob Little had left school that day and spent his lunch money on a train ticket to Bristol. He'd taken himself to the Clifton Suspension Bridge, where – who knows – he may have held out his arms like a bird in flight and felt the soft breeze against his palms, ruffling the sleeves of his school sweater. And then . . .

'He didn't *jump*,' says Lizzy, bursting into the room. 'Why do people keep saying he jumped?'

'Lizzy, for goodness' sake, this isn't the time.' Her mother is sitting at the kitchen table, pouring tea from a teapot into two china cups. Reverend Francis averts his eyes with a smile and clasps his hands on his lap. 'As you can see, we have guests.'

'I can see we have *a* guest,' says Lizzy and she turns to the reverend in her fury. 'Reverend Francis,' she says, 'I couldn't help but overhear your conversation. You were talking about the man in the news.'

'Yes, Lizzy,' the reverend says. 'We were talking about how terribly sad it is for someone to feel so hopeless that they should want to take their life.'

'Yes, but you keep saying he *jumped*. He didn't jump!'

'Well,' Reverend Francis glances over at Lizzy's mother, who sits blushing into her tea, 'I suppose I see where you're coming from, Lizzy. It's a question of semantics. "Jumping" in this context does not mean he actually bent his knees and sprang from the roof . . .' He laughs awkwardly and sips his tea. He glances again at Lizzy's mother and then back at the girl with cropped hair standing clumsily in the doorway. She has changed, dear reader; she looks quite different three years on from the young Max who tore up the dress on that sunny Sunday. She has grown tall, there is more weight around her face and puppy-fat on her belly, her shoulders hunch inwards to hide her developing breasts. 'I can see that the story has upset you somewhat,' says the reverend. 'What is it that upsets you most?'

The question seems to knock poor Lizzy off guard. She covers her ears. 'That maybe,' she says, 'I could have stopped him. If only I'd got there sooner . . .' and she cries up at the ceiling, shocking both her mother and the reverend, 'His name is Jacob Little! His name is Jacob Little! His name is Jacob Little!'

It had been the week her grandma had died that she'd discovered the name. It had been hiding in the kitchen drawer at her father's house all along. A crumpled picture of a blonde-haired woman in the nude, pointing at herself. Lizzy had been looking for elastic bands when she found the picture (her father was going to show her how to make a slingshot). 'What's this?' she'd asked, pulling out the card.

'Oh . . .' her father had said. 'That.' He seemed unsettled. 'It's nothing, Lizzy, put it away. Better yet, throw it in the bin.'

'But why do you have it?'

'A man gave it to me.'

'A man?' Lizzy turned the card over.

'Lizzy, did you hear me? I said throw it away.'

But she was transfixed by what was written on the back.

SOLACE.

'Was it a skinny, sad-looking man?' she asked.

'Lizzy, for goodness' sake!' and the card was snatched from her hands.

'No, wait!'

It was torn into two.

'No, stop!'

It was thrown in the bin.

'Now listen here,' her father had grabbed her wrist and shook it, 'you're not to go telling your mother I have pictures of naked women lying about the place, do you understand?'

His outburst had frightened Lizzy. She flinched from his angry face and struggled against the hold on her wrist. 'You're hurting me,' she said.

Immediately her father softened. He let go of her arm and took a step back. He smoothed his handlebar moustache with finger and thumb. 'Lizzy,' he said and then stopped. 'I didn't mean,' she was rubbing her wrist, 'I didn't mean to hurt you.' He covered his face with his hands. 'Oh God, Lizzy, I'm sorry.'

She had never seen her father like that. She had never known him angry or sad, she had never seen him cry before. She soon forgot about the pain in her wrist when she saw her father pressing his fingers into his eye sockets. 'I know you don't really understand what's been going on,' he said. 'I know this all must be so confusing for you. But I'm afraid, can't you see? I'm afraid of losing you.'

And she had comforted him, in a way only a young person can. 'Dad, it'll be OK. Dad, don't cry, I'm not going anywhere. I love you.'

Later. Brushing aside the remains of their dinner in the dead of night, Lizzy was in the kitchen retrieving the card. She pieced the two halves together. SOLACE, it said. And underneath it was written 'Jacob Little, Pauper's Inn'.

'My dear girl,' Reverend Francis is sitting at the kitchen table, holding Lizzy's shoulders gently. 'This isn't your fault. You can't blame yourself for this.'

'No,' Lizzy says, 'you don't understand, he didn't know who he was. That's why he was so sad. That's why he did what he did.'

'Then perhaps it's our duty to inform the police.' The reverend looks over at Lizzy's mother. 'Then when this poor soul meets the Lord he'll at least have his name.'

'Adam Garret.' The pink-haired woman gets to her feet with a sigh. 'That's his real name, Mr Benson. Adam Garret.' She picks up the ashtray and empties it into the

310

bin. 'He is Jacob Little's half-brother. You are already familiar with his story. Now, if you'll excuse me, I feel quite worn out by our meeting and wonder if we might draw it to a close?'

29

'You're still looking for her,' the girl says. 'But I don't understand. Do you still want to find her? I mean, as much as you did before?'

If it had not been for her grandma dying, Lizzy would have gone sooner. But her gran's death came the morning after she retrieved the case-closing clue, the nude woman called Solace and the name Jacob Little. She would have gone sooner, but her gran's death came as a surprise to her. Not that she wasn't expecting it to happen – she had been – but she wasn't expecting to feel her parents' emotions as keenly as if they were her own. Her mother's grief. Her father's anxiety. She bore the weight of them as both parents clung to her hand as they walked through hospital corridors or sat in the funeral-home waiting room.

It was not until the end of that week that Lizzy found an opportunity to break away and sneak out, to make her way through those winding alleyways and past the playground where she had met the nameless man. Out onto the street with its cafes and estate agents, past Piccalitos, crossing the road to where the short, two-storied pub stands crooked, gold lettering on a black background. PAUPER'S INN. Let's join her in real time, dear reader, as young Lizzy cups her hands and stares in through one of the grimy bay windows. The old-fashioned sign above her squeaks on its iron bracket as the painted red-faced fool sways in the wind and raises his tumbler to the sky.

Lizzy enters the old lopsided pub decked out with all things sea and sailor. Lighthouse paintings, nautical maps, ship's wheels and compasses. Fishing nets drape down from the ceiling. Two oars are nailed to the wood-panelled bar.

It is dimly lit in here and completely empty apart from a man standing behind the bar, polishing pint glasses. A *big* man who isn't smiling. He has a meaty, bald head, fleshy jowls and a flattened nose. He looks serious and gruff. Beverley. He is eating something. Lizzy can hear the *crunch, crunch, crunch* of his teeth grinding. He grunts when he sees Lizzy. 'We're closed,' he says.

Lizzy is clutching the picture in her hand. 'I'm here for Jacob,' she says.

Beverley grunts again. 'What, you?' He sets the pint glass down on the bar with a bang and leans forward to peer at Lizzy more closely. 'He said he'd send someone along. Didn't think they'd be so damn young.' Lizzy can see the remnants of nuts on the man's tongue and protruding lower lip as he speaks. 'Go on up,' he says and jerks his head towards the door that leads into the hallway. 'Up the stairs. First door on your left. Be quick about it. And kid . . .' Lizzy stops at the doorway, 'you can tell that little shit from me that he's lucky to be alive.'

And that is how the young Elizabeth Mary Duda finds herself standing alone in a small, dirty room above Pauper's Inn, a room that has been ransacked. A table upturned, a chair on a mattress, an ashtray smashed leaving a greyish-black stain on the wall, the carpet littered with cigarette ends. There are clothes strewn over the floor, some books scattered and endless green jotters flung, their pages flapping from the breeze that comes in through the open sash window. Lizzy looks about her, like a detective surveying the scene. And what's that on the wall? Red spots of blood? And on the carpet too.

She plucks a green jotter from the floor at random and begins to read one of its pages:

Foolishly stumbling have I been, from one town to the next, acting as though I knew something, that somehow a wisdom was bestowed upon me, a key, a truth, that I could see the world and human nature as it really was. A farce. A lie. An act. So I lived my farce. I lied and acted out my irony with a theatrical flamboyant flourish! But perhaps it is so, that while I pranced and pirouetted and brandished those made-up names, those histories built of nothing, the onlookers around me simply looked through, they didn't even reward me with so much as a glance. And while, there I was, taking my leave of each city with an overeager bow, no curtain call, no encore please, let's not wait for the applause, move on, move up, move out – actually, in truth, most of my inattentive audience hadn't even realised I'd been there, let alone left.

Lizzy drops the jotter back onto the floor. Too many big words. It does not interest her as much as the rickety wardrobe covered in copper pennies. She approaches the wardrobe and touches it curiously. She opens its door and peers inside to find . . .

a box.

An unopened box.

She pulls it out and stares at it.

Of course, we know what is going to happen, don't we, dear reader? Why else is the box there if not to be opened? Lizzy does not even close the door. Within moments she is pulling the cardboard flaps open.

Clothes.

Lizzy begins to rummage. No, wait, not *just* clothes. She picks up something grey and furry and holds it up to inspect it. A fake beard? She lays it to one side. And what's this? A pair of glasses. A set of teeth. Some rubber ears. This isn't a box of everyday clothes, this is a *dressing-up* box. It is a box of disguises! How could she resist, dear reader? How could any ten-year-old resist such temptation to *play*? Lizzy in her excitement and youthful curiosity begins pulling on clothes and affixing accessories so that before our very eyes her appearance begins to change and grow into a melange of Jacob identities. Wilhelm and Merton and Lambert and Otto. They appear in flashes and slices and then disappear as Lizzy tugs on another pair of trousers, another waistcoat, another wig. Teddy and Isaac and Kenny Berk. There's Benny Silverside with his brightly coloured ties. There's Gifford Baintree with his jutting-out teeth. Lizzy blows on a penny whistle. PEEP, PEEP, PEEP! And to the lapel of her jacket she pins an origami rose. Archie and Eric and Simeon Lear. We even, on occasion, seem to see a moment of someone else we've met – a hint of Marek, perhaps, or a splash of Billy. Those unruly eyebrows are reminiscent of old Mr Benson and that thinning grey bob could belong to Olivia. The box seems to be bottomless and Lizzy keeps pulling on clothes, layer after layer. 'Although we are many,' Lizzy says out loud, 'we are one body.' She slips her feet into some wedges to increase her height. She tugs off the grey bob to become a long-haired brunette. Oh, how much fun Lizzy is having! She opens the wardrobe door wide to view herself in its mirror. Wow, she thinks, I am LARGE!

'Sal?'

Standing at the door is a blonde-haired woman, a young

woman who Lizzy believes looks just like the painting of the nude.

'Solace?'

30

The girl picks up a book that has been set next to the bed and fans through its pages. 'A dictionary of names?' she says. 'Are you trying to work out who you want to be next, Jacob? Does that mean you'll be leaving soon?'

'What do you mean, he's gone?' Lucy says. 'He can't be gone! Where's Big Sal? And who is *this*?' She points to Lizzy who is sitting quietly at a corner table, legs swinging from the height of her stool. She is in her own clothes now, wigless and sipping Coke through a straw, glancing warily from the angry blonde to the big man behind the bar.

'Leave the kid alone.' Beverley is still polishing pint glasses. 'He ain't done nothing wrong in my book.'

'But what is he doing here?'

'Beats me, blondie,' and Bev smirks. 'I thought your Jacob Little friend sent him.'

'You know,' Lizzy pipes up from the corner, 'you really *do* look like the picture . . .'

'Oh God, yes I know, you keep saying!'

'No, but really . . .'

'I *know*. The spitting image. You said already.'

'Hey, Lucy,' Bev leers, 'how come you dyed your hair anyway? Is it true what they say? Do blondes have more fun?' He snorts at his own jibe and spits into the sink. 'If you want Sal, she's in the bedroom, though I doubt she's up to having guests.' He taps his head. 'Got a bit of a headache.'

Big Sal is lying in the dark. The only light coming into this small untidy room is a thin strip of sun breaking through a gap in the curtains. We can see the bulk of her body heaped on the bed. We can hear her groan as a sharp tapping comes from the door. 'Sal?' *Tap tap tap.* 'You in there?'

Sal's voice is muffled by the pillow. 'No light, please. No light . . .'

But Lucy has already opened the door; her finger is on the switch. 'Sal, what's going on? Where's Jacob?' and the room is filled with the brutal electric bright of the bare bulb hanging from the ceiling.

'I said no light . . .' Sal is lying on the bed, covering her face with both hands. 'Please . . .' She is wearing only a short nightdress. 'I'm not dressed,' and her toes curl in protest. She lies flat on her back, her big body spreading over half the mattress. Swollen ankles, thickset legs, excess flesh around the knees. The nightdress is pulled a little too high and Lucy can see Sal's fat thighs mottled with cellulite, the skin on the inside rubbed raw. Her massive breasts beneath the nightdress droop to each side of her like heavy sacks. 'Please . . .' she repeats. She does not remove her hands from her face.

Lucy steps forward, then stops. She has noticed the blood on Sal's nightdress, spots of dark red smeared onto its thin faded fabric. 'Sal?'

'Oh God, *please,* just leave me be . . .' and Sal tries to twist her body away from the girl standing by the door. 'I don't want you to see me like this,' she says. She attempts to pull down the hem of her nightdress, freeing one hand from her face. Lucy can see now that her lower lip is purple and puffed out, blood congealing liver-black in the split of the skin.

'Jesus, Sal, what happened?' Lucy moves forward. 'Did Bev do this to you?'

'And what of it?' Beverley has followed Lucy through. He is standing large in the doorway. 'Hey, Sal, don't be shy.

Why not show our Lucy your beautiful bloodshot eye? I always thought red was your colour.'

'You did this?'

Bev looks ready to spit again, but doesn't.

'You're *vile*,' Lucy steps back. 'How could you do this to her? She's your wife!'

'How could *I* do this to *her*?' he snorts, nostrils flaring. 'Did you hear that, Sal? Lucy wants to know how it was I lost my temper. Do you want to tell her or shall I?'

'Leave it, Bev.'

'Leave it?' he says. 'Well of course you would say that, wouldn't you, Sal? You're the one with something to hide.' And he strides over to Lucy then; fierce, fast steps that cause Lucy to cry out. She flinches and shrinks back against the wall. 'But I want our good friend Lucy to know the truth,' he says, so close Lucy can smell the peanuts on his breath. 'After all, Lucy is pretty much family . . .' He lifts strands of her bleached hair with his meaty fingers. 'Who would have thought,' he breathes in a whisper, 'that I would come home late last night to surprise my beautiful wife, only to find those pretty lips of hers wrapped around the cock of that skinny little shit of a lodger. Now, what do you make of that for a coming home present?'

It is too much for Lucy: the stench of Beverley's bad gums, his warm breath on her face and those words. She lashes out, slapping him first on the throat, then on his chest. As he recoils she slithers past him and slips into the hallway. The back door slams.

Beverley grunts. 'Was it something I said?'

And Sal from the bed sighs. 'Leave her be, Beverley. You can do what you like to me, but don't frighten the girl.'

'How very nice of you, Sal,' Bev says. He stands like a giant with hands on hips. The violence has aroused him. His penis bulges against the trouser material around his crotch. 'And I *will* do what I like to you, you're right. Did you think a black eye was all you'd get? I'm going to ruin you this time, do you hear me, Sal? I'm going to sell Pauper's and leave you once and for all.' He spits as though to mark his statement with a piece of himself. 'Did you hear that, Sal? It's over now.' And he would have left the room at this point, leaving his wife to sob alone on the bed, only as he walks towards the bedroom door, still gloating with so much self-perceived power, the muffled sounds coming from Big Sal suddenly seem to him less like sobbing and more like . . .

laughter.

Big Sal is laughing.

'Oh, Bev,' she calls out to her husband, her face puckered against the pain of her swollen-lip smile. 'Bullshit!'

31

'I've seen it written,' Jacob says, 'that man is part creature, part creator; and that it is the creator in us that tortures and re-forms the creature we assume ourselves to be. But this assumption is surely an illusion? If it were a truth then it can only be one of many truths in that I exist equally as a creature in the creator-mind of Others. How can an Other's illusion of who I am be any more or any less true than my own? They are all true. And they are all untrue. I am fact and fiction in equal measures. I cancel myself out. I don't exist.'

Jacob Little jumps.

There it is.

'And his body was shattered on the jagged cliffs and found broken on the muddied embankment below,' the pink-haired woman said.

As for the jumping man, nobody knew who he was.

'I think you'll find,' said one very well-to-do gentleman interviewed, 'that his name is Eric Germain Huber, he lived in the apartment above my own on Bonnington Road and always seemed to me an excellent fellow, incredibly polite, very astute, remarkably intelligent. A philosophy post-graduate with very fine credentials. He informed me he had studied at Oxford Magdalen. Well, why wouldn't I believe him?'

'OK, everyone, OK, settle down.' Dr Lucy Westbry claps her hands for attention, her amplified voice booms around the auditorium. 'Thank you and welcome to Perspectives on Self and Identity. My name is Dr Lucy Westbry and I am a professor here of Philosophy, specialising in the works of Jacob Little. For those of you who have not familiarised yourself with the course outline, it is Jacob Little's work we will begin our module by studying.'

The young Lucy Westbry had returned, of course, to Pauper's Inn. She had returned the following day (hair dyed back to black) to tell Big Sal that she quit, there was no way she could work for her any more. Big Sal blamed Beverley: 'You frightened the girl off.' But then Big Sal knew nothing of Lucy's own affair with Jacob.

'Listen, Lucy,' Sal had tried to reason with her, 'Bev will be gone again in two weeks. Why not just work here when he's away?'

'I can't.' Lucy could barely bring herself to look into the bruised face in front of her. 'I just can't, Sal.'

How could it be, she would later wonder, that someone could feel such contempt for another and yet pity them at the same time? Bitterness and compassion. Lucy allowed Big Sal to think it was Beverley that had frightened her off, not the thought of Sal's own affair with the lodger. Lucy had been sickened by the mental image. Those pretty lips wrapped around the cock of the lodger! Lucy had felt *pain*. It was real, physical pain that burned like coals in her belly and chest. It hurt so much she had screamed when she was alone in her bedroom. She had screamed and wept and flung her teddy bears and pillows around the room. In the end it was her own reflection that had disturbed her the most, the blonde hair and wide-eyed gaze – almost the spitting image, don't you think? The more she stared the more she could no longer see herself in the reflection, but Solace staring back.

'Is it true, miss,' a brassy young male in the auditorium pipes up, 'that you had an affair with this guy?'

Dr Lucy Westbry smiles. 'A scandal in itself. He was a thirty-three-year-old man and I a mere sixteen-year-old girl. But if it hadn't been for that affair I would not be standing here in front of you all today. Without question, it was Jacob Little's influence on me that inspired my decision to study philosophy. And it is the journals he left behind that have allowed me my career.'

That was the real reason Lucy had gone back to Pauper's Inn the following day, to collect those journals. If you had

325

asked her at the time why she wanted them, she may not have been able to answer. Was it because she hoped she might see Jacob again and return them to him? Was it because she was curious? Did she hope they might contain some sort of explanation? Perhaps Jacob had written about her like he had written about Solace? *Love is tainted. Love is imperfect. Love is not good enough for you.*

Big Sal hadn't seemed to care what the reason was, or what Lucy was going to do with Jacob's belongings. 'He won't be back,' she said. 'Bev made sure of that. You can burn 'em for all I care, Lucy.'

And so it was that Lucy found herself packing away those boxes that only weeks before she had carried up the stairs for the new lodger. She even packed them onto the green cart, one wheel broken, and heaved it away from Pauper's Inn.

'And it's *you* in the novel, isn't it, miss?' the same bold student asks. 'He's used the same name and everything.'

'Does that make it me?' Dr Westbry replies.

Yes, there had been a novel. Unfinished. Lucy had found it in amongst Jacob's possessions. Pointless, relentless, full of encounters too insignificant to remember and completely irrelevant characters. A novel full of empty conversation and even emptier events. Unrelated. Fleeting. Riddled with cliches and laden with stereotypes. It was thoroughly anticlimactic.

After Jacob jumped . . . 'He *didn't* jump!' . . . Lucy had taken what there was of the manuscript to Anya. She had knocked quietly on the door of the Writer's Block and opened it to see her Other Mother sitting, smiling up at her, hands poised over keys. 'Lu,' she'd said. 'I'd say come in,

326

but there simply isn't much room.' Lucy had given her the manuscript.

Later in life, Dr Westbry will wonder if in fact it was through working on the novel with Anya that she truly began to know and love Jacob. She committed much of the contents of those journals to memory as she scoured them for details to include in the book. His thoughts and philosophies began to shape her own, so much so that she would often assume her own ideas to be his, believing she had read them in one of those little green jotters. So much did Jacob become a part of her that years later, whenever she called to mind that wicked footage, it was *herself* she saw standing up there on the roof, foot slowly stepping out, hovering for that split second, and then . . .

'Only a few years will pass before I go on the journey of no return.' Elizabeth Mary Duda is staring at the passage from the Bible. Job 16:22. It is the line at the very end of the chapter with the word 'solace' in it. *Only a few years will pass* . . . The clues were all there, Lizzy tells herself. Why didn't she look that little bit more closely? She might have predicted everything. She might somehow have stopped him if only she'd known.

It was his face that unnerved Lizzy the most, in those moments before he stepped out; he looked empty and exhausted. Lizzy had taken a still from the recording and zoomed in. The image was pixelated and of poor quality, but the emptiness in the sad man was there. It was in the way he held out his arms, elbows bent, as though too weak to straighten them. It was in the way he stared ahead of him and not below, his head weighted a little to one side.

He was *tired*, thought Lizzy. He had spent the whole night wrestling his demons and wrestling with God, just like the Jacob in the Bible. Lizzy even fancied he stood a little awkwardly with the weight all on one foot, as though suffering a hip injury. She fancied he had a black eye and some swelling on his left cheek. But maybe it was all shadows and light?

'I'll tell you what happened,' she says to no one, 'let me tell you what happened . . .' Jacob was up on that roof all alone when a man appeared beside him. A man he didn't know. They began to fight. They wrestled all night long until the breaking of the day. Jacob fought fiercely. Even the man, who was as strong as a lion, could not master him. So much like a lion was this man with his long mane of yellow hair and large hands like heavy paws that Jacob began to think it *was* a lion he was up against. The two struggled on all night until the sun began to rise, and it was on seeing the sun that the stranger touched the hollow of Jacob's thigh and dislocated his hip. One touch! That's all it took. But Jacob held on in his agony until at last the lion-man demanded, 'Let me go, for the day is breaking.'

'I'll not let you go,' came Jacob's reply. 'Not unless you bless me.'

'Very well,' the other said. 'What is your name?'

'My name?' replied Jacob. 'My name?' He fell to his knees, his hands gripping the elbows of the strong man. 'Who is it that you say I am?' Jacob wept. 'If *you* do not know, then who does?' And as the sun rose the birds began to sing and there grew a great whirring and flapping of wings as countless gulls and pigeons flew from the rooftops up into the sky. They filled the air around the two men on the roof. The wind from their wings beat down over the men's tired, trembling skin. And as Jacob wept the lion-man bent low and licked the tears from his cheeks.

'I am lost,' Jacob wailed.

'But I have found you,' said a female voice.

And there she is, dear reader, with the triumphant sounding of trumpets and horns and all the angels and archangels and the whole accompaniment of heaven singing her praise and glory. Solace. She is standing before him, her long blonde hair falling in thin wispy ringlets, her rose lips parting slightly into a gentle pout. It is *her* arms Jacob is clutching. She bends down again, low, to kiss his cheeks softly. 'I have found you,' she says.

Lucy Westbry fans through the book she is holding in her hand, *Thus Spoke Zarathustra*. It is the copy she had found with Jacob's journals. The spine is creased, some of the pages are loose. She runs her fingers over the pencilled notes in the margin, all in that careful back-slanting hand. On one side a name stands out in bold, **MR BENSON**, and underneath it are the words: *Can a consciousness travel back in time?*

Once upon a time there was an old watchmaker
who believed he could make the cleverest clock.
A clock that proved that time doesn't exist at all.
A clock that both ticked
             and didn't tick.

'I have a theory,' Mr Benson says, 'my own old watch-maker theory, that travelling back in time would always be impossible *bodily* because our bodies are too big. Everything *big* ages and dies according to physical law, do you under-stand?' He sits with his back hunched as he bends over his desk, piecing together the intricate parts of a watch move-ment. 'It is impossible for a body to go back in time because it would still be ageing, you see? Thus it would also be going forward in time, which doesn't make sense. So bodies can only ever move forward in time, they can only ever age. Are you with me?'

The young man watches him with such quiet intensity. His teeth biting down so hard on his bottom lip they leave marks.

'But travelling back in time on a quantum level *could* be possible. There's no way our big clumsy ever-ageing bodies could be transported back, but perhaps elements of our consciousness could. To my mind, thoughts are physical, like sound and light, creating waves in spacetime. And who knows? Perhaps in the future we will find a way of separating mind from body so that a complete conscious-ness can be transported back to a moment in time. Though of course without a body, I suppose there is little that mind could do.'

'So it is impossible?' the young man asks.

'Well, now, myself, I like to wonder if perhaps a returned consciousness could somehow influence the minds of others, if you get my meaning. Implanting thoughts or guiding ideas. Perhaps it already does. We say that if time travel *is* possible then why aren't there more sophisticated people from the future popping up all over the place? But we assume that the only way to time travel is to return *bodily*. Who is to say that elements of consciousness from people in the future aren't already influencing us? Perhaps that is the real catalyst behind mankind's speedy progression and evolution?'

Mr Benson will too often torment himself with the memory of this conversation. If only he had refused to show Jacob the clock collection, if only Jacob hadn't seemed so fascinated. It had been the beginning of Mr Benson's obsession with the young man who hadn't really been there at all, the young man who hadn't really existed.

A student sitting in the lecture theatre thrusts up her hand. Dr Lucy Westbry nods in her direction. 'But he *did* exist, didn't he?' the girl says. 'Jacob Little *had* been all these people. I mean, he was still the same man even if he did change his name. So he *did* exist.'

Dr Westbry smiles. 'I don't think Jacob Little could ever have been so preoccupied with existing if he didn't exist.' She picks up her notes and taps them on the lectern. 'There were seventy-seven journals in total,' she continues with the lecture. 'These journals reveal most of what we know about Jacob's life and philosophies as he changes from one identity to the next. There were seventeen dominant identities, each identity having its own dominant obsession. For example, Wilhelm was obsessed with art, Lambert was obsessed with Christianity, Gifford science, Merton literature and so on. Jacob Little believed that due to life not having any meaning beyond survival, it is man's duty (if he desires contentment) to create his own meaning. "Obsessions preoccupy the brain. Obsessions give a life meaning, albeit a manmade one."'

Is that what Jacob Little became? Dr Westbry will wonder. Her very own obsession? Or was that all he ever was? Something that preoccupied her brain and gave her life meaning.

'Throughout his early journals Jacob is primarily occupied with this continuing discussion of his "Theory of Obsession". As soon as Jacob begins to experiment more frequently with name-change, however, his philosophy takes a dramatic leap in a new direction. The "Self", Jacob claims, is an illusion. It's entirely concocted in a person's brain. Jacob tells us that we go through life collecting and discarding characteristics that we feel describe what kind of person we are. "Good", "caring", "funny". We can only do this, however, by observing and interacting with "Others". Without Others a Self cannot exist.'

She teaches this now, year in, year out. She writes papers. She presents at conferences. She is invited onto discussion panels and debates. Without Jacob, would she exist? Certainly not as she is now. So who would she have become? What would her life look like?

'Perhaps it frightened him,' Lucy tells the class, 'that lack of control. The question no longer being "who am I?" but about the conditions of our environment and who else is there. Changing identities and obsessions was his way of regaining control. Eventually, however, this became the thorn in Jacob's own philosophy that snagged him every time. He often writes in his later journals that he no longer exists or that he no longer knows who he is. And it seems that this is the reason he began his search for Solace.'

Dr Westbry had met her once. Solace. It had been seven years after Jacob's death, shortly after her book, *The I in the Mirror* had been published. Dr Westbry had been speaking at the Edinburgh Book Festival and Solace had been sitting in the small crowd, listening, even asking questions. A tall, slim, fair-haired woman with streaks of pink in her hair and a glittering stud in her nose.

After the event she had been standing outside on the roped walkway, waiting. 'So you're the one,' she had said when Dr Westbry slowed down. 'You're the one who resurrected Jacob Little from the dead.'

What struck Dr Westbry most, after the woman had introduced herself properly, was how remarkably *unlike* the painting Solace was.

'Don't believe a word I say, will you, Dr Westbry? I mean we were lovers, Jacob and I.' The fair-haired woman scoops at the froth of her cappuccino. 'If I'm honest, I've never loved a man in the same way since, as though . . . you know . . .' She stops. She presses her lips together and raises her eyes to somewhere above Dr Westbry's head. 'He was a part of me,' she says. 'It's a cliche, I know, but that's how it is. It wasn't *true love*, it just . . . *was*. He lived in me. He was in my bones and my every breath. He was in my hair and my skin. We were the same person.' Her eyes move back onto Dr Westbry's face. 'I still love him,' she says to her. 'With the same indulgence and obsession and with the same indifference and disregard as I love myself. It's a dangerous sort of love, don't you think? One not to be trusted. It's the sort of love that isn't really *real*, wouldn't you agree, Dr Westbry? Because you never see the person as they really are, only as you imagine them to be, as part of you. And for that reason I beg you, don't believe a word I tell you with regard to Jacob Little. Because together we make a fiction. Solace is his creation. And Jacob is mine.'

*

'CUT,' says a voice somewhere offscreen. 'That was great, guys, really great. Really squeezed my heartstrings, you know? OK, let's take five. Has anyone seen my Big Sal? Where's Big Sal?

Is she still in the fat suit?'

It had been a terrible film, dear reader, but that final scene, despite its hideous Hollywood mawkishness, stayed with Dr Lucy Westbry. It reminded her of the love in *Wuthering Heights,* the love she had so desperately wanted to experience. 'My great miseries in this world have been Jacob's miseries, and I watched and felt each from the beginning.' Of course, the conversation between these two adult women had been nothing like this in real life.

'I'm not here to steal your glory,' the woman had said. 'Jacob is officially all yours, Dr Westbry. I just thought you might like to hear my story. Perhaps you could make it your own.'

In the days that followed Jacob's jump, Mr Benson had not been himself. That was the phrase his wife used to describe his restless and pensive behaviour. 'For goodness' sake, Stan, what is wrong with you? You've just not been yourself these last few days.'

'Not been myself?' Mr Benson had stopped in his tracks. 'My dear woman, then who on earth have I been?'

It was becoming too much for Mrs Benson. Her husband seemed to her so very far away. When she reached out to touch him, he would too often flinch. 'Stan,' she pleaded, 'talk to me, Stan.' But he would say nothing.

'It's like he's grieving,' she told her two daughters. 'But what a foolish thing to say. This man was our tenant, not our son!' And perhaps against her better judgement, she found herself telling her daughters everything. About the day Jacob had lost his key and stayed for hours talking with their father in the study, about when Jacob went missing, about how Mr Benson had gone round to Olivia Little's house to collect rent due but then kept going back . . . time and time again . . . he kept going back. 'I would watch him in the morning, getting into his car and driving off. "I'm just popping out," he'd say, and I *knew* he would be going to see that woman.' She told her daughters about the day she confronted him. 'You're having an affair, Stan. Do you take me for a fool? And while I'm certain this Olivia Little appreciates all your time spent "straightening her cupboard doors" and "weeding her garden", *I* do not. And *I* am your wife.' Yes, she had given him an ultimatum. 'I am not asking you to leave me,' she'd said, 'I promised to be true to you in good times and in bad, in sickness and in health. I promised to love and honour you all the days of my life. Do you remember? But I will not have you lie next to me each night and then go to that woman each morning. So choose your bed, Stanley Benson, and then lie in it.'

It is a strangely brutal moment when a child's image of their parents as stronghold and fortress comes tumbling down. Mrs Benson, on seeing the horror in her two daughters' eyes, immediately regretted confiding in them. Her two beautiful daughters, who held their father in such high esteem! He was their unmovable rock in a fast-flowing stream, and she the calm, resting in the eddy. Their relationship had become to her children an ideal to aspire to. How could she destroy that?

'Dad had an affair?'

Mrs Benson had found herself quickly shaking her head. 'I thought myself so sure,' she said, 'but your father always, always denied it. And he did as I asked. He stopped going round there.'

But this is where Mrs Benson ends the story. She doesn't tell them about how Olivia Little later hanged herself. Or tell them it was their father who found the body. She couldn't bring herself to explain the grief she had witnessed in her husband then and the guilt she had felt, but kept hidden.

'If Dad denies it,' her youngest had said, 'then we *have* to believe him, otherwise there's no trust any more.'

Mr Benson is sitting on the bench in the garden, eyes closed. He is breathing in the honeysuckle scent of the yellow blossom climbing and winding its way through the wooden arch above him. From somewhere a bee hums.

He opens his eyes on hearing the sound of the back door. His youngest daughter, Abigail, is making her way towards him. Kind, gentle, wise Abigail. She says nothing, but sits in the space next to him. Together they listen to the bee humming and the soft whisper of wind in the grass and bushes. The stillness between father and daughter seems to ground Mr Benson somehow; he feels a little more able to take root with her by his side.

It is the weight of carrying the name that is wearing him down, he thinks. As the rest of the world continues to gossip and banter and bicker over who the jumping man is, Mr Benson carries the name on his shoulders like Atlas carrying the world. Adam Garret. What is it that upsets him so? Is it the deception? He had after all been deceived, had he not? By both the young man and his stepmother. *Adam Garret. His name is Adam Garret.* He says this to himself every time he hears a news report or interview with someone claiming to know who the jumping man is.

But why doesn't anyone come forward? Someone who knew the Littles when they lived at 23 Gunney Drive? Someone who knew that a certain Mr Garret had died and this boy, Adam, had gone to live with the strange weeping woman with the heart-shaped face and her quiet, introverted son? Teachers? Neighbours? Family? Friends? Where were they? Why had nobody mentioned anything about the young Jacob Little's suicide?

Abigail places her hand over his.

'I looked on the forum like you asked me, Dad.' She squeezes his fingers gently. 'There's no mention of anyone called Adam Garret. There's no mention even of just "Adam".'

'What about a half-brother?'

'No, nothing.'

'And the father? Is there mention of his death?'

'Several,' she says. 'And all of them different.'

Mr Benson closes his eyes. 'But that can't be right,' he whispers. 'Has anyone mentioned anything about a boy called Jacob Little who jumped from a bridge at the age of fifteen?'

Abigail hesitates before quietly saying, 'No. And I think if that happened it would have been reported by now, don't you?' She lifts her head to look at him. 'Dad, I don't understand, you *knew* Olivia Little.' Mr Benson is surprised by the hot flush that creeps into his cheeks on hearing these words. He looks away.

'I don't know anything,' he says. He clears his throat and reddens all the more. 'I'm convinced now that Olivia Little was perfectly mad all along. I no longer know what to think.' When he glances at Abigail, she too is blushing.

'The thing is, Dad,' she says, 'the police have all but officially announced that the man is Jacob Little. You also knew him as Jacob Little. Not only that, but you knew his mother, Olivia Little. I don't understand,' she shakes her head, 'why are you trying to turn him into someone else?'

Mr Benson raises his eyebrows and looks at his youngest.

'Do you know what, Dad, I'm not even sure it matters. Whatever his name, you've got to feel sorry for him, right? I mean, he must've been pretty messed up.' Her face is still flushed bright red. She closes her eyes and clasps her hands. She would look prayerful, Mr Benson thinks, if it weren't for her jaw, clenching and unclenching.

The bee hums.

When finally Abigail opens her eyes again, she looks straight at him. 'I love you, Dad,' she says. 'And I'm going to help. But all this stuff about Jacob Little, Adam Garret and some pink-haired woman called Solace . . .' She stops with a sigh. 'Let it go.' Her eyes are glassy as she looks at him. 'Listen, I have to pick up Tommy.' She tries to smile. 'Hey, Dad, maybe you can tell him that terrible story about the world's cleverest clock later?'

There's a time and a place for everything, dear reader. Time hangs heavy. Time works wonders. The third time's the charm. There is a time to go, a time to run, a time to call it a day. You can spend time, serve time, buy time, make time. You can take time, steal time, give time, waste time.

'Mr Benson,' the curious young man had said all those years before, 'if your old watchmaker theory on time travel is correct, than it gives me some hope.'

'Hope?' Benson had replied.

'Well, don't you agree? Our ability to mould for ourselves a desirable life would no longer be directed just at our future, but at the possibility of changing our past.'

Mr Benson remembers his face. He had seemed so keen, so enthusiastic; he'd hung on his every word, but for what purpose? False hope? To temper his regrets? 'I've always wanted to go back in time,' he'd told the old man. 'There are so many things I would change.' And Mr Benson had quietly watched as the strange young man got to his feet and turned back the hands of a ticking wall clock to four and thirty.

Now the old man sighs as he sits on his garden chair. He smells the honeysuckle. He hears the soft wind in the grass and in the fruit trees, he can feel the breeze against his thin skin. A butterfly, white, touches down on his knee and in the next moment flutters off again. 'Oh, Abbie,' he says, even though his daughter no longer sits with him. He bows his head. 'I am an old fool of a man.' From somewhere a lawnmower engine revs and *put-put-puts* into action. There is the clinking of cups and the boil of the kettle from the kitchen. See, now he is quietly getting to his feet, back stiff from sitting too long. He stretches with a groan, muscles aching, bones creaking. He is moving stiffly towards the house, opening the door. He is in the kitchen where his wife and two daughters are preparing a pot of tea.

'Dad? Will you join us?'

'Not now, Abbie, there is something I need to do.' He pauses. 'But I will,' he says. 'Later. I promise.' Down the hallway he goes and into his ticking, ticking study, where he sits at his desk and places the loupe over his eye. He begins to prepare his tools. 'I'll tell you what happened,' he says to no one, 'let me tell you what happened . . .'

He was standing up there on the roof of that building, palms reaching out for the cool of the breeze. Trouser legs ruffling. The hem of his trench coat flapping like a cape. And then. His foot. Slowly stepping out. Hovering for that split second.

There it is.

He drops.

Arms flailing.

Thumps

into the skip below.

Fuck me.

Now, reader, watch closely as we turn the arrow of time.

First the dust from the skip that billows up into the air is sucked back in. The *thump* pushes Jacob upwards, back-paddling arms and kicking his feet. His body contorts into wild shapes, twisting as he levitates up, up, up until his toe touches the edge of the roof and he swings upwards to a standstill, hovering foot back to firm footing.

'He didn't jump,' Lizzy says, 'he *flew*.'

God speed.

Across fields, across forests, over mountains, through gorges.

Don't linger.
Don't lag.
Over rivers, through valleys.
Feel the gust, the thrust, the rush of wind.
Grip tight and ride, glide, swoop and slide.

Ha!

Mr Benson picks up the French Champlevé enamel repeating carriage clock, with its twin barrel movement, bimetallic balance and silvered lever platform escapement, which *would* strike and repeat on a coiled steel gong, if only it wasn't broken. If only. It wasn't. Broken.

ACKNOWLEDGEMENTS

My thanks to all family and friends who managed to delicately approach (avoid) the topic of 'Book 2' in conversation these past four years. Same big thanks to my editor, Carole Welch, and agent, Will Francis, who both patiently took a step back while still feeding me reassurance and positivity. Thanks to Claire Gatzen and all at Sceptre who worked on the book! Tess Farlow, Kelly Dyer, thankee for talking to me about my writing and reading the sketchy first draft in its entirety. To Del Prosser and all the staff at The Arc Cafe (in the undercroft of St Mary Redcliffe, Bristol), thank you for allowing me to linger for hours writing, rewriting and editing the final draft. You looked after me when I was hungry for toast, thirsty for coffee and in need of a laugh. Revd Dr Hester Jones, thank you for your insights, encouragement and prayer. And Amy Cook, thank you for the love and support you showed me throughout the writing of it all.